SUGAR HOUSE

A NOVEL

ALLISON MUIR

HIGH FREQUENCY PRESS

Cover: "Tentacle" (2025) 17" x 9", Watercolor, ink and digital collage
"Family tree" (2025) 12" x 9", Watercolor, ink and digital collage (front matter)
"Bouquet" (2017) 9" x 12", Watercolor, ink and digital collage (Book One)
"Charred" (2017 9" x 12", Watercolor, ink and digital collage (Book Two)
"Succulent" (2017) 9" x 12", Watercolor, ink and digital collage (Book Three)

Published by High Frequency Press
www.highfrequencypress.com

Postal mail may be sent to:
High Frequency Press
PO Box 472
Brunswick, ME 04011

ISBN: 978-1-962931-32-8
LCCN: 2025905905

Printed in the United States of America

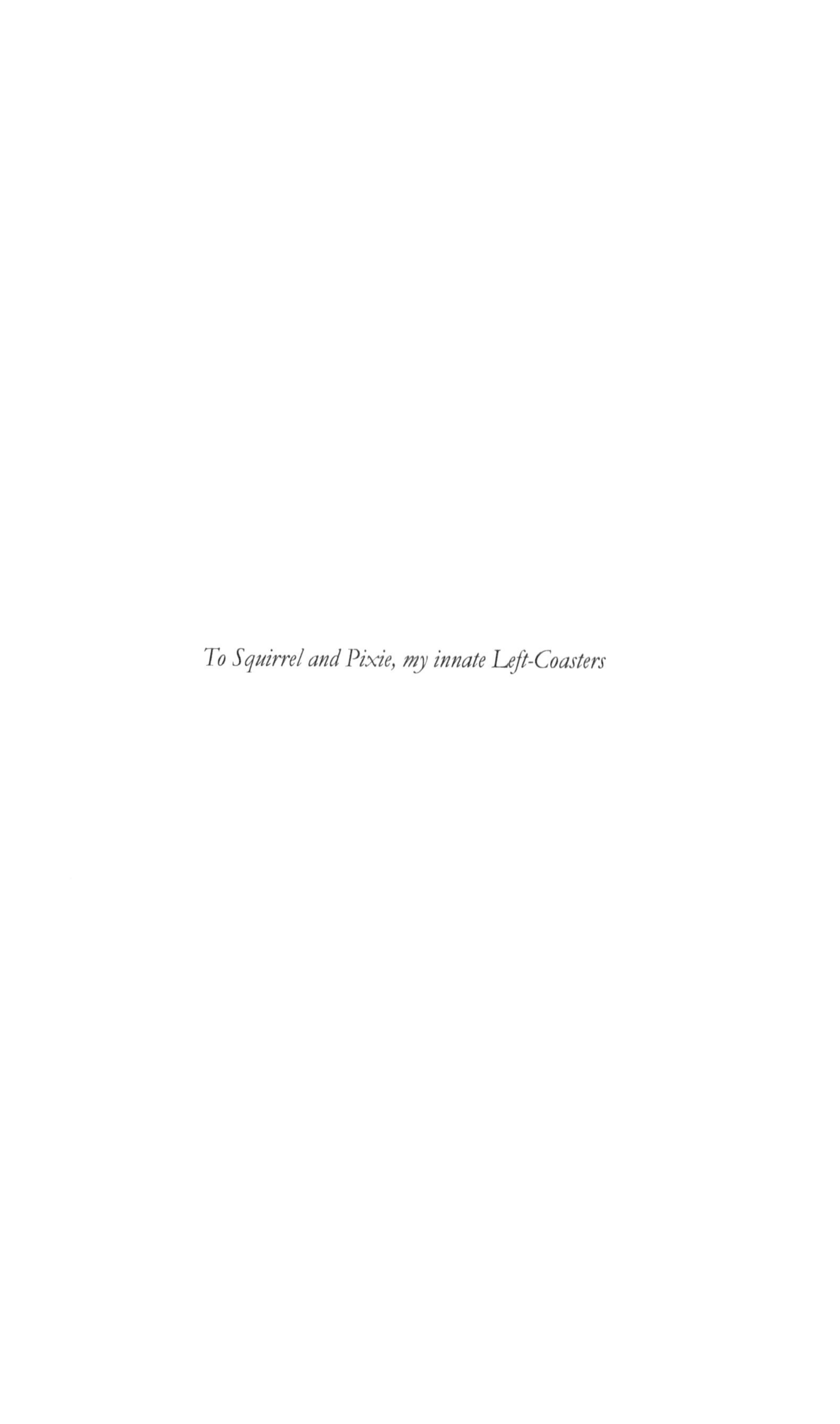

To Squirrel and Pixie, my innate Left-Coasters

This old earthquake's gonna leave me in the poorhouse.
It seems like this whole town's insane.
—The Flying Burrito Brothers, 1969

THE SWEENEYS
Shirley-Dwayne
Gary Franklin Delano
THE CARLYLES
Vertiline-Gunnison - Harriet Delby Smimes
Adelaide Emmet Floyd -Vernice Blenheim
Dolores Pearson-Douglas Arthur Marie
Judy Douglas Jr. -Phoebe Remillard
Jonah Phillip Nina
THE LUNDGRENS
Daen-Lucinda
Fenella Ina

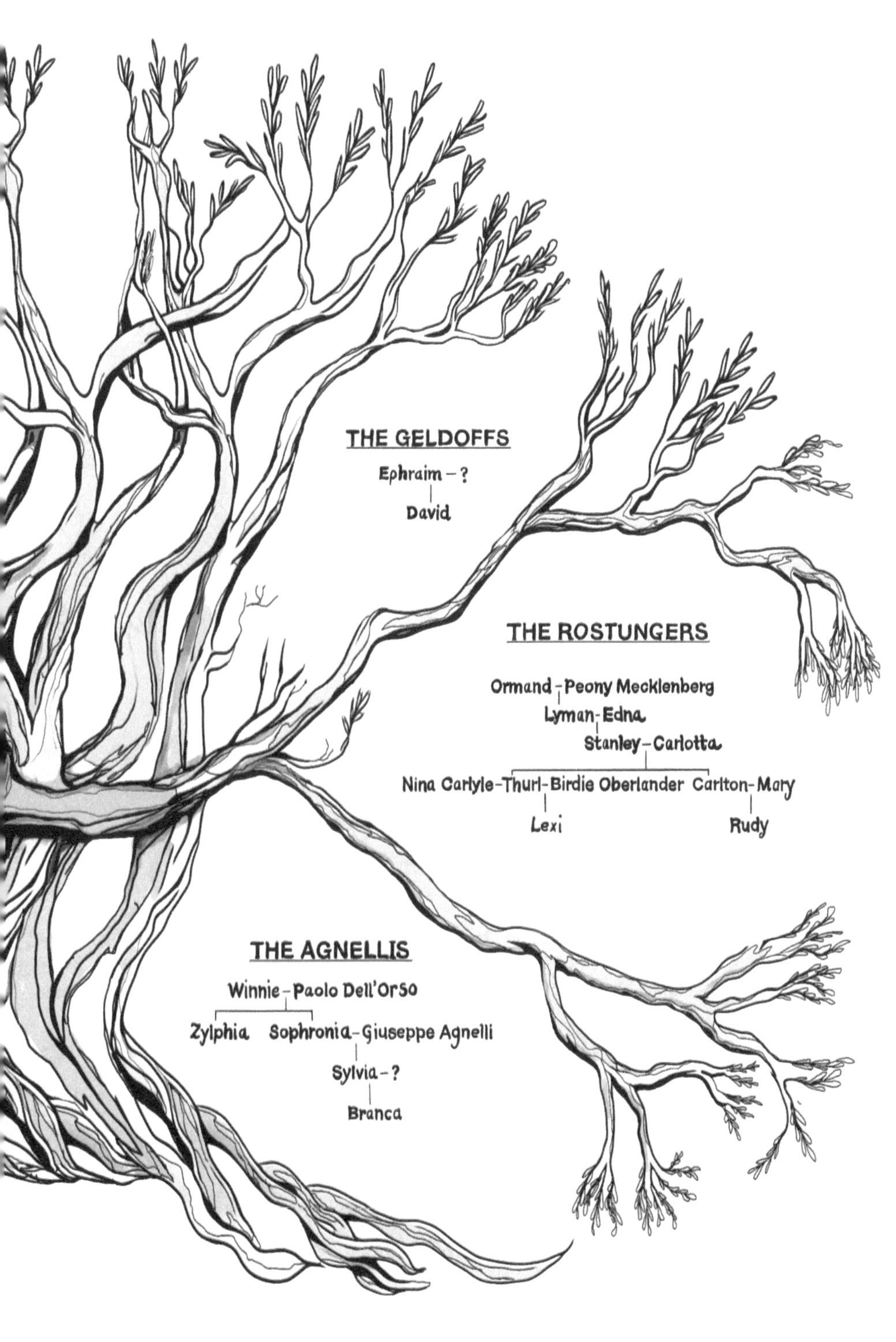
THE GELDOFFS
Ephraim – ?
David
THE ROSTUNGERS
Ormand – Peony Mecklenberg
Lyman – Edna
Stanley – Carlotta
Nina Carlyle – Thurl – Birdie Oberlander
Carlton – Mary
Lexi
Rudy
THE AGNELLIS
Winnie – Paolo Dell'Orso
Zylphia
Sophronia – Giuseppe Agnelli
Sylvia – ?
Branca

BOOK ONE

Perdita Library Lecture Series

Perdita History: Pirate Shores through Periwinkle Palace

Presented by: Branca Agnelli

—*April 15th*—

Local historian Branca Agnelli has compiled journals, university archives, ephemera, and video footage to construct this in-depth lecture and slideshow featuring highlights from Perdita's storied history. Admission: ten dollars.

Sponsored by Friends of the Perdita Library

—*Black and White Photograph*—

A young boy stands in front of a fireplace. The flames dwarf him. The boy appears to be seven or eight. He is bare-chested. In the high-contrast light, it appears as though he is wearing some sort of rough-hewn skirt or loincloth. Flanking the boy are two small creatures; petite horned animals with antelope eyes that reach mid-chest to the child. Their eyelashes are demur and their noses pointed, revealing shy grins and delicate breasts. Tiny horns the size of inverted sugar cones bow slightly in deference to the boy who is holding a watering can. On the floor and closer to the camera lens are a pile of McGuffey's Readers and collection of dull pencils.

The boy looks content, proud, as if he has been elected the president of a secret club or has learned a new trick on a yo-yo. His slight chest puffs behind the watering can.

MANY PEOPLE WHO HAD NEVER BEEN TO FENELLA'S part of the world believed it to be a warm, tropical place. In fact, Fenella's earliest memories were of the cold. She remembered walking with her mother Lucinda to a neighbor's house inside a fog so thick that she could only see four or five feet of the road in front of her. People in Barnby Dun called a fog like that a Pogonip. When the wind on the road began to lash, Fenella would crouch down every few steps to cover her legs with her dress, if for only a moment or two, before her mother Lucinda yanked her forward by the hand.

"It looks like Nonna's house has been shoved off the end of the world," Fenella would say as they pushed through the mist.

When the kids were young, Lucinda worked at the mushroom packing plant on the southern outskirts of Perdita, the seaside town visible from high above their home in Barnby Dun, an old mill town. Fenella's father, Daen Lundgren, ran a small auto repair shop out of a converted barn in Barnby Dun that was nestled into one of the larger peaks of the Pobre Clarita Mountains on the central west coast of New Concepción. When the packing plant closed during Fenella's middle school years, Nonna Agnelli taught Lucinda to make stained glass. Then Daen and Lucinda opened a roadside stand on a pine needled turnout on the highway running past their wood-shingled house. They sold Lucinda's stained glass and the redwood bears Daen carved from fallen logs with his chainsaw.

They made most of their money in the summer months, when tourists bypassed the main highway from the sea to head over the mountains for leisurely drives up the winding roads that took them past the shop. The glass and bear stand was aptly situated. It was far enough from Perdita, such that the turnout was a natural place to stop for leg stretching and it was high enough in the mountains for both a picturesque view of the Picaroon inlet down below and the old Turbinado Sugar Factory sign. When it was hot, Lucinda sold lemonade, and in the fall she heated apple cider made from the apples that grew between their lot and the Sweeney's.

The couples and families who stopped at the stand gathered around the largest bear carving that peered down at them from a totem-esque height of fourteen feet. The bear held a wooden sign in his mammoth paws that read "Klassy Kaniforms," the business name that Lucinda had insisted on. Daen was at a loss to explain it. He was less of an explainer and more of a shrugger.

Tourists who stopped took photos of the large bear, perhaps with a child or two pointing up to the sign. Often, they'd take another photo of their hats and sunglasses on the head and face of one of the smaller surrounding bears. Some of the tourists would inevitably get to chatting with Lucinda, telling her how much they'd love to take a bear home to the City, but that their car was just too small.

"We do offer delivery . . . " Lucinda would suggest, pointing towards Daen's Ford, partially concealed by the redwood trees and twirling rainbow makers.

Once every two weeks or so, provided the Lundgrens had made sales, Daen would load the pickup with bears. His most popular models included a "Welcome Bear" that held a sign proclaiming "Howdy Folks!," as well as a "Gone Fishin' Bear" with pole slung over his shoulder that was popular with newly divorced men. Daen would drive over the mountains and into the City where he'd double park, heft a bear down from the bed of the pickup onto a dolly, then wheel it into a building's elevator. The bear's purchasers would open their doors, often with a phone held to their ear by a shoulder, give a double thumbs up, then motion Daen to put the bear on the balcony or next to a large screen TV.

"It really IS big, isn't it," they'd say, and tip Daen a twenty.

Most often, when the spring came, the bears would appear overnight by the curb, where they'd become rustic sentries, growling silently at the air until someone with a large enough vehicle and a measure of brawn came to take them somewhere else.

—Video Diary—

A lumbering man's torso walks into frame. The lighting is dark, illuminated by a single Edison bulb from a table lamp on a leather-topped desk to the left. The man's body positions itself in front of a chair. The man places both hands on the armrests and lowers his body into the seat slowly, rigidly. He squints as his face appears in the lens. His wiry eyebrows obscure deep-set eyes that rest over wrinkles and bags that extend to his jowls. He takes a sip of water from a glass placed on the desk off-screen. He clears his throat.

"Hormones, pheromones, molecules and jewels," he enunciates. He rubs the bottom of his nose with his forefinger, extends his neck forward and stares into the lens, then wipes the lens with a shirtsleeve edge and a thumb. He resettles into the chair and pulls out a small notebook and begins to read.

> mi neme Vaclav. I praktiz vriting. Vuman sho mi in kold pleys. I puhts de vateh on de asperguhs. I give pleAnths to Dusan en Kasimir. I give de chee to de Loocreeza en maks de fihyeh. Hera see me.

—Post on New Calafia Kevin's List—

HOUSEHOLD ASSISTANT

Needed imediately! (Picaroon River area)

Creative and organized individual needed as assistant for high energy household—Young, intelligent (preferably female) person desired for position as an executive assistant to married couple involved in philanthropy, filmmaking, and conservation. High pay and possible travel. Some light filing required. Serious applicants with strong references only as I am very busy and don't have a lot of spare time!!!!

Reply to n.r.@rostunger.com

THE OLD TURBINADO SUGAR FACTORY, ON THE BANKS OF the Picaroon River, was surrounded by a chain-link fence topped with razor wire. Two fuzzy and wind-burned topiaries, in the shape of dolphins, shuddered anemically on either side of the front gate, which was merely another section of chain-link on wheels. A small guard house stood just behind the gate. Beyond it, a broken asphalt road led to the megalithic temple to sucrose that spread along the riverfront in odd brick and steel offshoots and formidable concrete additions. Two smokestacks abruptly punctuated the architecture.

Fenella approached the gate. She had gangly knees and hair that only curled at the nape and a pleather purse that shed threads like hangnails. A young man stepped out of the guard house. He rubbed his hands together and released a trail of vapor into the air with his sigh.

"Oh, hello . . . I . . . I have an appointment with Nina Rostunger?" said Fenella.

"Just a sec."

The man stepped back into the guardhouse and picked up a telephone handset.

Fenella pulled her coat closer to her neck as wind from the river stung her cheekbones. A hum sounded, and the chain-link gate rolled open.

"Through here," said the man. When he spoke, Fenella noticed his silver teeth.

She walked her bike into the gravel courtyard. Above, perched on the Factory's roof, was a peeling billboard featuring a red neon light-up crown. The crown announced in filigree script, "Turbinado! The Sugar on Top!" During Fenella's childhood in Barnby Dun, she could see the red lights from the crown when it lit up at night. She'd stand on her tiptoes and look at the sign during the sliver of time when Perdita was visible in the dark night before the fog moved in.

A rusty groan came from within the Factory. A mammoth commercial steel rolling door rolled open. A small woman struggled behind it, pulling the door's chain hand over hand. Fenella's nose began to run in the gelid shadow of the building.

"Raúl, recoge la entrega en la parte de atrás!" yelled the woman.

The man sighed again, then headed off in another direction. Fenella stopped for a moment. The woman fixed the chain to a stop on the wall, and motioned to Fenella.

"Hello! Here, here!" she called.

Fenella walked the expanse of pavement between them, then extended her hand at the threshold of the rolling metal door.

"Fenella Lundgren," she said.

The woman looked bewildered, then wiped her hand on her pant leg and met Fenella's.

"Catalina," she said. "Come this way, okay?"

They walked to the far end of what Fenella surmised had been a loading area at some point. From behind Fenella, leaves scuttled through the open door, scraping along the concrete floor until they pasted themselves against cardboard boxes that lined the walls. Catalina twisted a doorknob and pushed her shoulder into a heavy door that led to a windowless brick corridor. At the far end of the hallway, they passed under a dim pendant light towards a utilitarian staircase. Fenella felt a pinch on her heel from her good shoes after the first two steps. When they turned to climb the next flight, she peered down the staircase shaft to the darkened levels below that echoed her footsteps.

A green oversized stenciled number five appeared on the wall some flights up, and Catalina opened another fire door, again with her shoulder. Natural light appeared through doorway. Directly across the hall was yet another set of doors, though these were paned with opaque glass. Catalina straightened her shirt front, then pushed through to an enormous light filled room. Fenella's good shoes tapped beneath a domed glass ceiling. As she attempted to gauge her distance from it, she felt something on her forehead. She made a quick sidestep and batted at a tendril from one of the potted elephant ferns that sat by either side of the door. The tendril swished.

The floor was a sea of white marble, separated by continents of Turkish rugs. Smaller seating areas near the edges of the room were furnished with high-backed carved wooden chairs detailed in golden flourishes of Javanese tracery. Moorish-style tables were set with leaping-tongued cymbidium orchids. In the center of the room, a bronze Japanese Buddha sat in lotus position, heavy eyelids cast downward. Wooden tables with drake-footed legs were arranged around his girth. A grey cat sprawled on the nearest table and undulated its tail lazily as it tracked Fenella across the room.

"Have a seat, okay?" said Catalina as she motioned with a slightly raised hand towards one of the heavy chairs.

Fenella seated herself uneasily and placed her hands awkwardly on the scrolled armrests, then put them in her lap. Catalina padded across the Conservatory and then was obscured by the palms. Fenella's eyes met the cat's; then she craned her neck to take in the expansive ceiling. She pulled her skirt down. She scanned her coat for hairs, lint.

A door slammed from the far side of the room, and Fenella's throat tightened as she stood. A woman, fortyish, with thin, small legs, pushed aside a frond with a swipe of her hand. She was an attractive woman, with a long, aquiline nose and wavy auburn hair. She stopped for a moment to place a teacup into the waist-high soil of a nearby potted palm then continued to saunter towards Fenella without making eye contact as Catalina stooped to pick up the cup.

"Nina Rostunger. Lovely to meet you," she said with a casual shake.

"Fenella. Nice to meet you as well."

"Why don't you come back to my office. It's filthy, you'll see, and it smells like smoke, which is something I do when I'm very, very stressed."

Nina turned abruptly on the balls of her bare feet and Fenella followed her. There was a slight tinkling sound and the grey cat darted in front of them, scooting under a potted datura tree that set the yellow trumpets swaying.

"The cat's name is Lokum," said Nina, without turning.

"Oh, nice," said Fenella.

Nina pushed open a set of French doors, and they were in another dim industrial hallway, with exposed plumbing running overhead and concrete floors. They passed under several cones of dim fluorescence until Nina opened a final door on the left, and once again Fenella squinted at the abrupt illumination.

Nina's office was decidedly feminine at first. The view of the river was framed by high floral curtains, tied back in oversized swags. The predominate state of the room however, was appalling disorder. Teetering paperwork piles lay a foot thick over the entire floor, save for a narrow walkway between two chairs. A mahogany desk was partially visible under receipt wads, band-aid wrappers, fingernail clippers, up-ended clutches, cat toys, and half empty glasses of different colored liquids holding floating cigarette butts.

"You'll have to excuse the mess," said Nina. "I never allow Catalina in here while I'm in the middle of working. It's a creative process."

"Of course. I completely understand," said Fenella.

"Toss that stuff to the side and have a seat. Sooooooo," sighed Nina, as she fell into a Herman Miller. Fenella pushed a stack of papers and moved a scarf. She found a corner of Nina's desk for her hip. "So, basically, I mean the job is really sort of a personal assistant type of thing. I'm deeply involved in many charities, so I need event coordination help. Plus some organization, obviously."

"I did a lot of event planning in art school. I helped put up a lot of the group shows."

"Wonderful," said Nina. Lokum entered the office, jumped on the wide mahogany desk, and did a dive roll onto her back. She began pawing at the air, shifting her oily weight back and forth upon a stack of magazines. "And Thurl. My husband. He saw the art thing on your résumé. I think he needs some help too, with some art projects of his own. He's doing some film and he's doing marine life preservation."

"Sounds great. Exactly what I'm looking for. I'd like some experience. You saw on my résumé that I only graduated… "

"As I said, there will also be some light filing. Help in getting the right stuff to the accountant. But I have a number of different interests, so there's lots of opportunity to advance, really make this a career for yourself."

"Oh, great. That's part of what attracted me to the ad."

"Well. I'm supposing you're free regular hours? Nine to five?"

"I am," said Fenella. Her eyes were beginning to itch, most likely from the cat.

"Every once in a while, there will be an evening event. You can stay later?"

"No problem."

"And I pay very well. No health benefits, but, in this economy… Shit." Nina leaned forward abruptly. "Ah shit! The cat's chewed the power cord to my answering machine again. It's kaput. Ugh. There were new messages too. Well . . . If you start, add that to your list. A new answering machine. And get a cord protector. And, like I was saying, the job pays very well in this environment." Fenella struggled to get a notepad out of her purse.

Nina opened a drawer in her desk, pulled out a band-aid, pushed her sleeve up, pulled off another band-aid and applied the new band-aid. Fenella tried not to let her eyes relax on the highlighted dust motes from the column of riverside sunshine that had fallen between them.

"Cat scratch . . . so I'll check your references. Give you a call by the end of the week?"

"Sounds good. Nice to meet you, Nina."

"You, too."

The back of Fenella's neck was wet with sweat. She left the room and turned left down the corridor although she was not exactly sure that was the correct way to go. She wandered the halls until she found an elevator and took it down to the first floor. She was let into a windowless room with stainless steel walls and an acoustic drop ceiling and a concrete floor. She pushed through another door and found herself in the river-adjacent courtyard with the wind-burned topiaries and the guardhouse. Homeless men shouted from over the fence.

ꕥꕥꕥ

—Sign On Island House Refrigerator—

THE RULES

Help Make Bed in Morning

Ask Before Leaving House

Finish Your Meal

No Picking Flowers From the Onishi's Yard

No Going Outside Naked

ꕥꕥꕥ

Perdita Historical Society Quarterly Newsletter

Dedicated to Preserving the History and Heritage of Perdita and its People

Branca Agnelli (President)

The Perdita Pier, An Early History

By Branca Agnelli

The Perdita Pier and Amusements were built by entrepreneur Quentin Rokeby on the seashore, south of the inlet to the Picaroon River whose source lay above in the Pobre Clarita Mountains. The Picaroon was integral to early industry in Perdita as it had been used to float redwood trees down from mountain logging camps, such as Barnby Dun. Transport steamers could dock on the other side of the Picaroon Jam, where the logs would be loaded on board and carried up the coast to a mill outside Perdita. The booming skyline of the City to the north had been largely constructed from the felled trunks of

Perdita's Brobdingnagian conifers. Grand saloons and private parlors and tea houses alike displayed the reddish grain of the Pobre Claritas.

Perdita's lumber barons, after some years of establishment, lobbied the government for a railroad in the name of national infrastructure, seeking to secure a more economical transportation route for their product. Once completed, the rail line brought timber along the eighty-mile stretch to the City. A few years later, day trippers began to make the return trip back down to Perdita where they frolicked in the dunes and beaches that for so long had been inhabited solely by brown pelicans, barefooted Liwa fisherman, and the Hiberian ranching families. Quentin Rokeby, the City's notoriously opprobrious gambler and rogue, was among the early riders of the line's newly-added passenger car to Perdita.

Rokeby is alternately referenced in the annals of the coastal area as "The Genteel Jayhawker" and "The Sheik of Shenanigans". Misdeeds attributed to his person include the formation of a secret "Golden Circle Society" known for its Copperhead sympathies, the establishment of a cadre comprised of "Celestial rounders" who operated a backroom hustle at high profit to Rokeby alone, and the shooting of bandit Pio Bigote. One fact without controversy is that Rokeby purchased twenty acres of Perdita Seashore with funds from a streak of Rouge et Noir winnings, acquired at the iniquitous Four in Hand Club, a den of vice and prostitution aboard a run-aground ship in the City's dockyard.

The *SS Minerva*, whose route extended to the Far Coast, and the National Railroad brought an ever-increasing number of new inhabitants to the City, and sightseeing trips to Perdita's seaside increased prodigiously. Within a year of his land purchase, Rokeby had a pier constructed within walking distance from Perdita's main railway stop, upon which he'd built a series of interconnected dance halls. The Pier and its cupolaed nighteries soon proved popular with sailors who were able to take the train from the City to Perdita for rum-permeated nights that alleviated judgement and pocketbook alike.

Rokeby successfully managed the Pier's operations from an office in the City as he preferred being near to the Four in Hand Club, taking the train down to Perdita by railway once a week to meet with his managers. Ten years later, Rokeby decided to expand his enterprise and hired a French inventor by the name of Gustave du Jardin who had made a name for himself on the Continent devising various attractions of whimsy.

Mssr. du Jardin arrived at the Perdita Rail station on Seahorse Road, which ran parallel to Rokeby's property. Immediately inspired by local lumberjacks who rode down from the Pobre Claritas on the log flumes, Gustave went to work, utilizing the Picaroon River outlet on Rokeby's land to create an inclined boat ride. He also convinced Rokeby of the financial wisdom in creating a series of façades to house sideshows and games of chance. But it was a gravity railroad, a train car on wooden rails let loose through a series of switchbacks down the beach cliffs, that transformed Perdita into a true destination.

To oversee the construction of the "Drumlin Pleasure Way", Rokeby conceded that it was time to relocate to Perdita, and he had a house quickly built for himself on Beach Hill. As construction of the Pleasure Way neared completion, Rokeby placed ads throughout New Concepción advertising his attraction.

The inaugural day of the Pleasure Way became a town-wide affair. A parade was led through the streets by the Perdita Marine Auxiliary Band, famous for its rousing marches and dueling hélicon and flügelhorn sections. The procession crossed Seahorse Road, where it concluded at the Pier's Periwinkle Grande Pavilion with a bumptious oration by Mayor Wicksteed Horseley that brimmed with the type of mellifluous demagoguery that had made Horseley a populist legend in his own time. Following the mayor's speech, the honorariums to the new roller coaster continued with a hymn sung by the Perdita First Christian Church choir, and following this, the delegate of the Perdita Mendicity Suppression Society, a slight ginger-headed debutante by the name of Adelaide Carlyle, stepped forward.

Adelaide had been nominated by the Society to christen the roller coaster's initial public ride by breaking a bottle of champagne on the lead car in order to convey the mayor and his wife, the Perdita First Christian choir, Rokeby, and du Jardin. After several unsuccessful attempts by Adelaide to actually smash the bottle against the car, Rokeby was compelled by the attendant press to assist in the matter. *The Perdita Village Bugle's* archives still holds a daguerreotype featuring the louche and mustachioed Quentin Rokeby, with broad-cuffed wrist and gloved hand grasping the neck of the bottle above the demurring paws of Adelaide Carlyle.

Adelaide was the only child of Vertiline Carlyle, who had died of consumption during Adelaide's infancy, and the timber baron Gunnison E. Carlyle. Carlyle was a socially unrelenting man who was quick to discourage the noted interest that Rokeby began to display towards his nineteen-year-old daughter in the weeks following the roller coaster ceremonies and described Rokeby to his associates as "a rapscallion of the first order." Mr. Carlyle, however, was easily distracted as he was in the process of building a labyrinthine second residence above Perdita, which he referred to as Madeira House, due to his ardent love affair with fortified wine.

Madeira House had been intentionally positioned on the uppermost part of Ice Cream Hill affording him a downward-cast view of the estate belonging to the Geldoffs, a rival timber family. Gunnison Carlyle was so absorbed by the timber business, rice futures, his home construction and the ongoing tug-of-war with the Geldoffs that he failed to notice the marked uptick in Adelaide's Mendicity Suppression Society Embroidery Committee meeting attendance.

Rokeby and Adelaide made regular rendezvous to the Picaroon Lodge, a tranquil, mountainside inn, tree-cloaked from a back road, with a lobby and dining room built over an exposed Picaroon tributary. Guests reached the front desk of the hotel by crossing a small bridge and fell asleep in their beds with the sounds of rushing water below. Long held lore by Picaroon Lodge staff maintains that Rokeby loosened a rock in the retaining wall behind the Lodge. Though the rock cache is thought to have been repaired by an unsuspecting handyman long ago, it was there that Rokeby would allegedly place the key in the Persephone Suite, which was to become the couple's habitual hideaway. The Picaroon Lodge staff filled Rokeby's regular order, supplying the suite with great quantities of shad-roe, diamond terrapin gelée and flights of champagne.

For the next few years, the Drumlin Pleasure Way provided Rokeby's coffers with such quantities of lucre that he was able to expand the Perdita Pier and Amusements further. He added an indoor saltwater pool to further attract the sailors who streamed in from the rail station across Seahorse Road. The Animal Menagerie was added to the north of the pool building, and housed foxes, bears, raccoons, peacocks, eagles, several spider monkeys, rock hyraxes and a lone Bengal tiger.

A natural ad-man, Rokeby devised several stunts calculated to infuse the Perdita area with mystery. Letters reveal that upon Rokeby's request, du Jardin fashioned a floating assemblage of barrels covered with amorphous heaps of imported rubber—resulting in various sightings along Perdita's coast of a great "Amphibious Abnormality".

Rumors of Perdita's monster fomented widespread interest in the town, far past the purview of the City, and brought new throngs of patrons to the Attractions.

Rokeby's success continued when he filled in a marshy section of his property and built "Adelaide's Quay," a beer garden featuring a sculpture of Adalaide-as-Mermaid named "The Siren," a clamshell-shaped dance floor, and an actual "band shell", a building-sized conch, housing an invisible yet live band for the guests. The Adelaide's Quay Orchestra would be remembered years after for popularizing the short-lived but sultry dance number, "The Mazurka de Mer". Dancers promenaded to the triple-time beat as the sea foam from the clamoring West climbed the Quay's redwood-hued pilings.

In the end, Adelaide and Rokeby's happiness was to be short-lived. Upon the completion of the East Wing of Madeira House, Gunnison Carlyle coerced Adelaide into accepting an engagement to the much more appropriate Pickett Snellgrove, of Snellgrove's Dry Goods and Mercantile in the City, by threatening to withhold her inheritance. At first, Adelaide protested her father's plans vehemently. She began, however, to have second thoughts after several incidents in which Rokeby exhibited a somewhat capricious and unreliable character.

Rokeby often played faro or grand hazard in Perdita's Palais Royale card room until he lost his cufflinks. In another famous instance, Rokeby challenged famed lawn tennis champion Cyril Legume to a match, then arrived at the court with an iron skillet he insisted on using as a racket. Then there were multiple occurrences when he was pulled from the sea by Gustave du Jardin after simply walking into the ocean.

In actuality, Rokeby had begun to go mad as a result of syphilis that he had surely contracted from the Four in Hand. He disintegrated into increasing bouts of syphilitic dementia. Adelaide's letters reveal that she had little choice but to acquiesce to her father's wishes.

One afternoon, plagued with debt, heartbroken over the news of Adelaide's engagement and delirious with fever, Rokeby climbed to the top of the diving platform above his saltwater pool. Unbeknownst to Rokeby, an angry creditor known by the epithet "Coarse Edgar", followed him up the ladder to the platform, where he stabbed Rokeby several times between the ribs with a Bowie knife.

As fortune would have it, at the very same time, the 3:45 p.m. train through Perdita derailed, crashing at an oblique angle through the glass front of the pool building. While the engine car narrowly missed falling into the water, the following two transport cars carrying loads of muriatic acid and ax heads to the lumber yards in Barnby Dun did not. Perdita was uniform in their opinion that Quentin Rokeby suffered a wildly gruesome death.

Gustave du Jardin took charge of Rokeby's interment arrangements. His funeral was a sparsely attended closed-casket affair. The mortician was instructed to place a handkerchief on top of the remains, which was said to have been lavishly embroidered with the initial "A", surrounded by silken rosettes and needlepoint garnets.

Shortly after Rokeby's death, Adelaide was married to Pickett Snellgrove and moved to the City. Four months later, she wrote in her diary that a doctor had diagnosed her with syphilis as well. Rumors about Adelaide's condition spread throughout the City, and Pickett Snellgrove himself was often mentioned as the source. When Pickett escorted another woman to the City's Opera opening, Gunnison Carlyle, ever the defender of his daughter's honor, challenged Snellgrove to a duel.

Armed with a pistol on a spring dawn near the Rosicrucian Society Hall in the City, Carlyle fired upon Snellgrove, killing him instantly. A key supporter of Mayor Horseley, Carlyle was enabled by the politician's connections to neutralize the jury in the trial that followed. After several donations to Horseley's reelection campaign, Gunnison E. Carlyle was rewarded with a favorable verdict.

Adelaide returned to Perdita with her father and moved into the East Wing of the as-yet-unfinished Madeira House. The diary of Ephraim Geldoff recalls that during this period, wailing was heard nightly from the top of Ice Cream Hill. In the summer, Adelaide succumbed syphilitic amblyopia and paralysis and was laid to rest that autumn.

❧❧

JOURNAL OF CLINICAL SLEEP MED, 15;4(8):588-90
Department of Neurosciences, University of Perdita
Dr. Pierce Asclepius

Abstract

Pontine demyelination as a result of rapid correction of hyponatremia: Cause of Negative EEG Activity?

The case study is presented of a fifty-three-year-old man complaining of akinesia and hypersialorrhea after waking. IR images showed possible Hyponatremia. Lesions on MR were best viewed as areas of hyperintensity on T_2-weighted images in the central pons with sparing of the pontine tegmentum and ventrolateral pons. Possible Cholinergic Syndrome was treated unsuccessfully with atropine. EEG testing while patient was wakeful did not indicate epilepsy, tumor, stroke or other brain disorder. Psychiatric examinations were unremarkable. Polysomnography during multiple sleep tests were normal until mean sleep latency of eight minutes (with no REM periods), at which point EEG activity ceased. Motor function, blood pressure, heart rate and organ functions were somehow maintained. Patient showed no response to evoked potentials or any REM periods during sleep tests.

❧❧

IT WAS OF LITTLE SHOCK TO FENELLA THAT THE ROSTungers lived in a Factory. She was from Barnby Dun where the gossip of Blatchington Hills and their ilk rarely penetrated, it was true. But having almost no experience with the very wealthy, Fenella assumed that money naturally primed those that had it for being eccentric. She'd lived in an industrial space while in college herself and had once written a paper entitled, "Challenging Domesticity: Residential Spaces in Post-Industrial Landscapes".

Fenella had received an email from Nina the day before with the simple statement, "Let's try it! 80K?" And so, after having a celebratory cocktail, she spent the night before her first day of work clipping hangnails and flossing, checking her nose for hairs, and getting a good night's sleep.

In the morning she put on extra deodorant, making sure not to get any on her dress, and put some tissues and a brush in her backpack. She thought about putting on perfume, but wondered if Nina was allergic, or if her perfume smelled as inexpensive as it was, and so she opted not to. She pedaled slowly to work in the April fog, leaving the sounds of the gulls at the shore behind her. She was careful not to let the bike chain rip or put a grease mark on her tights, or to work up a sweat that would make her seem disheveled.

At the front gate, beyond the homeless camp, she formally introduced herself to the young man with the silver teeth as he let her through.

"Raúl," he said in return and he told her to park her bike along the chain-link as he patted the shoulders of his jacket against the cold. The endless hallways of the Factory posed a challenge, but after making a few wrong turns and trying a few locked doors, Fenella eventually found her way into the glass-domed Conservatory, and sat in a carved wooden chair beneath two ten-foot stone griffons with opened beaks and talons and paws that were poised to rip apart the marble floors beneath them. Her watch read 9:01. On time, just as Nina had instructed in her email.

Fifteen minutes went by. Fenella wondered if there was some confusion. Was she supposed to go to Nina's office? She thought about going back down to talk to Raúl. Maybe ask if he could call somewhere? She thought better of it. Nina could come in at any minute.

Fenella had called Dr. Charles and Branca the night before to thank them for being her references, and to tell them she had gotten the job. No one had contacted them, they'd said.

Another five minutes passed. She watched the room change from bright white to shadowed, and back again as the clouds rushed past the glass dome overhead. She observed the birds outside the window over the Picaroon. They were bigger than the gulls near her apartment, most of them. She thought about songs that matched the rhythm of the flashing bulbs in the Turbinado Sugar sign on the billboard. She studied the woodworked scrolls on her chair. Checked her watch again.

And then, when Fenella had almost given up and was about to go looking for Raúl, the sound of the door made her jump and Nina entered the Conservatory, barefoot, looking dry and thin like the leaves caught on the Factory walls. Nina sighed as she dropped herself into a chair near Fenella. She didn't meet Fenella's face, but began scratching at her cuticles.

"So, great . . . " said Nina. "I had a little chat with Thurl this morning. I'll use you Mondays, Wednesdays, and Fridays on this side, and then you can help him on Tuesdays and Thursdays over there," she said as she waved her hand to the far left.

Fenella was unsure of what "over there" meant, but didn't want to seem unwilling or overly quizzical, and so she nodded her head enthusiastically.

"Perfect." said Nina. She raised her feet and sat cross-legged in the chair. "So, if you could start by sorting my office, that would…"

There was a deep thud, and a high chinking splash, followed by the sound of wind mixed with mechanical shrieks, and a scattered noise, like hail hitting the inside of an empty metal pail. Fenella squinted and covered her head instinctively.

"AgggGGGH! Fuck!!! Goddamn birds!!!" yelled Nina, raising her arms. Fenella watched as a shard of glass drop from the domed ceiling, then crash onto the head of the bronze Buddha.

Nacreous feathers of a cormorant hovered above the marble floor. Down floated lazily onto the tops of the orchids and palms. Fenella was dazed. She remained still, constricted. Drops of blood spread from the bird's beak and from under its under wing. Its black eyes swirled as its body thrashed. Then it shuddered and lay still.

"Raúl!!! Raúl!!!" shouted Nina. "Oh Goddammit." Nina walked to the side of the room and picked up a handset that was wired to the wall. "Raúl! Listen, come here to the Conservatory. The fucking birds again. Bring a broom."

She thrust the phone back into the wall, then brushed off her thighs and ran her fingers through her hair.

"Unbelievable. Second time this has happened, actually," she said, regaining composure. "Really. We had this whole dome built just four months ago. The first time the birds flew into it … well it hasn't been fixed for more than a month, I can tell you that much. I've had to move all the fundraisers and the bridge days downstairs."

"Oh my god, how awful. Wow . . . I'm sorry . . . um, yeah, sorry . . . "

Fenella averted her gaze from the cormorant. "Oh, look at the dome up there. That's terrible."

"Stupid architect. He never told us that this could happen you know. And we spent a pile. I actually cut myself on the glass last time. Here, look, you can see where I had to get stitches . . . right here, near my ring finger . . . Well, listen, why don't you have Catalina take you downstairs for a cup of tea or something. She can give you a tour of the place. Then maybe you can start by getting my office in order . . . you remember where it is?" Nina seemed suddenly more tired, as if her eyes had receded a bit farther into her skull.

"I think I can find it. No problem," said Fenella.

Footsteps thudded outside as Catalina and Raúl entered with brooms.

"Well, Catalina can show you. Listen, I'm a bit overwhelmed here as I'm sure you can see. Such a relief having you here to take care of things like this." She made a casual circular motion with her hand. "I'm going to lay down for a bit. And maybe you can help Catalina call the glass people."

"Of course. Yes, relax," said Fenella.

"And you're not cut or anything?" asked Nina.

"No. No, I think I'm fine. A little surprised is all." Nina gave Fenella a tight smile.

"And have Catalina introduce you to Lexi."

"Will do," said Fenella. She felt self-conscious, ungainly, as if she could feel a piece of food on her front tooth.

Nina got out of her chair and began to cross the room.

"Oh God! Your foot! Your foot!" exclaimed Fenella. Nina looked baffled for a moment.

"Oh shit."

She lifted a dirty sole and examined it, holding it in both hands while balancing, then picked out a significant piece of glass. Blood seeped from the arch.

"Do you need me to get you a towel? Some shoes?"

"No. I'll do it. See what I mean about this place? Chaos. So fucking unbelievable." Then she left the room, casually avoiding another pile of glass, leaving blood streaks on the marble.

Catalina now returned with a black garbage bag, and Raúl came in with a push broom.

"Can I help?" asked Fenella, "I feel so bad . . . "

"No, no it's okay," said Catalina.

Another loose piece of glass from the dome fell and crashed onto the floor. Fenella opened one eye before removing her forearms from above her head.

"Raúl! Oye, he's gonna take you to the kitchen right now, okay?" said Catalina.

"You'll be alright in here alone? It seems pretty dangerous. And I mean, sorry, but do you remember the name of the people you used last time to fix the glass, because I can call them, or whatever."

"Sure, yes. I'll find you in the kitchen, okay...Raúl." said Catalina as she swept, pointing with her elbow.

Fenella followed Raúl out of the Conservatory, through yet another set of doors. They walked down another dimly lit industrial hallway, painted on one side with primer, and passed a stack of wallpaper rolls. At the end of the hallway Raúl pressed a button to the side of a large metal door and an elevator car roared and chugged in the shaft beneath them, then stopped with a deep clang. Raúl bent down, turned the latch and pushed the door up over their heads. Sunlight from the top of the shaft hit Fenella's shins, chest, then cheeks as the door opened. Raúl rolled back the wooden gate and Fenella squinted and stepped uneasily into the freight elevator. The car lurched down, and Fenella turned her face toward Raúl's and looked at his teeth and his sweaty upper lip.

"Well, that was pretty crazy," she said smiling. "I was not really expecting something like that to happen on my first day," and she laughed a little, but Raúl did not join her.

"Stuff like this goes on, like, all the time," he said.

Fenella looked into the yellow light at the top of the shaft until they stopped. They exited the car and walked down yet another long hallway, naturally lit by a set of windows at the far end. When they reached the windows, Fenella looked onto the ground floor of an interior courtyard that had raised beds of hollyhocks and vines climbing up the many-storied brick walls towards the open sky.

Raúl pushed open a swinging door across from the windows and led her into a steamy kitchen decorated in country yellows that had a view of the Picaroon. An Asian man stood peering over a table, with his hands on his aproned hips. Raúl wiped his upper lip with the back of his hand.

"Fenella, hi, nice to meet you," she said quickly, extending her hand. The man turned around, and wiped his hand on his apron while walking towards her.

"Oh, hi. I'm Peter. I'm the cook here," he said.

"I'm going to be helping Nina, and I guess Thurl? Thurl is his name, right?" Fenella shifted her weight. "Helping both of them. Around here."

There was a pause as Peter looked over Fenella's shoulder towards Raúl. "Oh yeah? Well. Welcome. Sorry . . . , I don't mean to be rude or anything, but just I found this." He gestured to the marble table. There were thick gashes of red spray paint across the top.

Raúl sighed. "Lexi."

"Yeah," said Peter. "That's what I'm going with. I don't know. Maybe you could get a sander and buff it out?"

"Who's Lexi again?" asked Fenella.

"Thurl's daughter."

"Oh."

"Well, anyway Fen . . . Fenella? Like I said, welcome. Uh, would you like something to drink?"

"Sure. That would be great."

"Tea?"

Fenella nodded and Raúl left the door to the hallway swinging on its hinges as he left. Peter flicked the gas on under the kettle.

"So, Catalina's supposed to come down here, show me around," said Fenella. "But, I don't know if you heard. Birds crashed into the glass upstairs in that big room."

"What? Again? Ah, I'm telling you . . . Hey, hang on a sec."

Peter went to a back pantry and brought out a metal platter piled high with white asparagus and set it on the counter. Then he went back and returned with a baguette on top of a large bucket filled with live crabs.

"Whoa, big dinner tonight?" asked Fenella.

"It's what Thurl always wants. Earl Grey? Darjeeling?" asked Peter.

"Darjeeling, thanks. So, hey what's up with Lexi?"

"Well, I mean. I shouldn't be telling you this…" He leaned in closer. "You'll find it all out anyway. Here's a tip; when she travels make a list of what she's what she's packing when she's packing it so when she comes back you have proof it hasn't been lifted." He moved back to piling white asparagus. "I haven't even really seen Lexi's mom since we moved into this place, so I don't know if the kid has seen her either. I guess she wants attention. I don't know about you, but my dad would have smacked me in the face if I did something to a table like that. I dunno, I hear Thurl's busy setting up his new Aquarium."

"Huh. I'm supposed to be helping him. Two days a week, that's what Nina said."

"Oh yeah? Well, if you see him, ask him if he needs me to bring him anything else. I don't even know if he's eating this stuff or what. I just put crabs and club sandwiches and asparagus every night by the door on his side of the house, or whatever this place is. Maybe he's eating something else. Catalina and Raúl let workmen and delivery guys in over there pretty regularly. Jesus, these are nice Dungeness. They're probably fish food. Expensive fish food, huh?"

"Yeah . . . Hey thanks for the tea and everything."

"You're welcome. Look I'm gonna go deliver this stuff before starting the regular dinner."

"Okay. Well, nice talking to you. Uh, I don't know when Catalina's going to be done cleaning the glass up over there. I mean, it looks like kind of an intense job, but I'm supposed to start organizing Nina's office. I hate to sit around drinking tea on my first day with the ceiling falling in and stuff. Can you tell me how to get back to Nina's office? This place is kinda confusing."

"Oh man. Look. I'll draw you a map." He grabbed a paper towel and took a pen from a kitchen drawer and scribbled for a minute or so. "Hope you get there," he said.

Fenella oriented the paper towel so that Peter's black star and line matched up with the kitchen and hallway on the other side of the swinging doors. As she walked down the hallway, she thought about her bike parked outside. It was inside the chain-link fence, but she hadn't locked it. She wondered if Raúl kept the gate secure when he wasn't in the guard house. There were always speed freaks outside the gates.

She had almost passed the windows to the courtyard when she heard a clicking noise and a faint holler.

From behind the hollyhocks, a young girl did a military roll onto the ground. She was dressed in camo fatigues and held an air rifle to her chest. She crouched into position and took aim at another grouping of hollyhocks. There was a reverberation of compressed air, and then a sparrow dropped into the gravel.

Fenella guessed that this was Lexi.

—Invitation—

"An Evening of Compassion"

A Disco Spring Fling

The Blatchington Woods Hurt Diminishment Society's
Annual Gala and Charity Auction

Benefiting the Orphans of Iulia

Dance to the tunes of The Solid Moves Band and open your heart! Sign up to adopt your very own Iulian Child

Hosted by Thurl and Nina Rostunger at their newly remodeled estate, "The Confectionery"

Event Attire—Disco Black Tie

WHEN FENELLA WAS FOUR, LUCINDA GAVE BIRTH TO INA. Daen hadn't been making much money at the auto mechanic's shop in Barnby Dun, and when faced with the news of another baby on the way, he studied for and passed the Coast Guard Inspector's Exam, hoping to apply his mechanical knowledge to a more financially secure field. He had expected to find a job in the City, if not within Perdita itself. But near the end of Lucinda's third trimester, he had not been called back for any local interviews. Then a posting appeared on the staple-laden job board outside the front door of the local harbormaster's office for a government position inspecting commercial vessels in the Islands. He applied by mail the next day. Two days before Ina was born, he received a job offer.

Daen and Lucinda discussed the pros and cons of the move at the dinner table, prayed about it together, slept on it, and the next morning Daen listed an ad in the *Barnby Dun Soothsayer* offering an extended lease for their house and mechanic's shop.

When Lucinda and Ina had been home from the hospital for three weeks, Daen flew out to the Islands to look for a place to live before he started work. There were no takers on the mechanics shop in Barnby Dun, but Lucinda found a young professor from the University of Perdita to rent the house who agreed to water the front yard ferns and look in on the vacant shop regularly.

Nonna Agnelli helped Lucinda pack. They stored most of the furniture in the shop and shipped clothing and basic household items to the Islands.

During this time, Daen found an inexpensive white clapboard bungalow surrounded by banana and plumeria trees in an unincorporated village near a Loffer church. While it took close to an hour's time for Daen to get to work at the port in Sugar Bay Harbor, he and Lucinda wanted the same country tranquility they'd enjoyed in Barnby Dun and to have the girls brought up within a community of fellow Loffers. The small community of Cacao Beach provided such a location. It was on the west side of the Small Island. A volcano bifurcated the land north to south and the peak was high enough that residents on their side had sunsets, yet never sunrises. A month later, Lucinda and the girls flew out to join Daen.

The first Sunday, after they'd gone to church, and when Ina had been fed and Fenella was still clean in her church clothes, Lucinda took the girls down the street. She introduced herself to the neighbors while Daen installed some shelves in the living room. They moved methodically down the gravel road, knocking at each door. Dark, heavy-set women came out onto their porches and touched Ina's head.

Lucinda looked at her own shins that had been exposed to as much sun as the ferns on Barnby Dun's forest floor. She felt self-conscious wearing socks. After they had worked their way down Lord Monboddo St., Lucinda switched Ina to her other hip, crossed the street and knocked on doors back up towards the clapboard house. They finished by knocking at the house next to their own. The woman who answered the door held her Pomeranians back with her leg as she came outside.

"Oh . . . oh, how cute. We . . . we are . . . hi. We are the Lundgrens. Just moved in. Yes. Next door. I wanted to . . . "

"Wait please," said the woman. Then she went back inside and closed the door.

Fenella looked at Lucinda, who looked back at her and shrugged her shoulders. Fenella side-stepped and hugged Lucinda's leg. The barking Pomeranians grew loud again, and the woman re-opened the door. She handed over a pie tin filled with sweet rolls, each wrapped in a thick layer of plastic wrap.

"Goodness, thank you. Thank you so much. That is so nice. Honestly, we should be the ones . . . .what do you say, Fen?"

"What's your name?" asked Fenella.

"Oh, Fen . . . "

"Onishi," said the woman. "Mrs. Onishi."

"Glad to meet you Mrs. Onishi," said Lucinda.

Lucinda used the remainder of her first week on the Island to put the house together. She recruited Fenella to help her unpack dishes, hang curtains, and organize the kitchen cupboards. Fenella opened a box of kitchen utensils, and Lucinda found her cradling a large wooden spoon as if it were a baby. Lucinda brought out a marker and drew a face on the spoon's concave.

"This spoon is named Dolly," said Fenella.

Over the next few days, Lucinda and Fenella began to take turns spotting frogs that hopped around the back yard.

Lucinda noticed that she was losing her baby weight quickly. She forced herself to eat in the still air that closed in on the house like a sleeping breath. She reminded herself that breastfeeding meant she needed more fuel, more vitamins. In the afternoons, while Daen was away, she would write letters to the Agnellis.

> Sorry to hear that you've broken your hip, Nonna. So terrible. Call the sheriff if the Sweeneys disturb you while you're laid up. If you would, check on that professor at our house from time to time to see if he's watering the front of our house like he promised.

Other days, Lucinda would study her *Celestial Mandate*, underlining passages as she went. She weighed Ina every week and wrote the results on a chart she had tucked into Ina's baby album. She played jacks with Fenella on the back concrete, but Fenella would scream when a frog jumped close by. Many afternoons Lucinda caught herself, staring blankly out the back window as a light rain hit the glass, listening to the sounds of birds she'd never heard before.

They'd spent a lot of money on the move. Unable to find a cheap crib for sale in the neighborhood, Lucinda bought a full-sized used mattress for Fenella and Ina to share. When Ina learned to roll over, Lucinda wrote the date she'd learned in the baby album chart, and then placed a pile of folded blankets on Ina's side of the bed to keep her from rolling off. Most mornings, Ina had baby spit up next to her head on the mattress.

Early one morning, Lucinda came into the girls' bedroom and found a trail of ants marching into Ina's sleeping mouth, harvesting the regurgitated milk. She pulled the bed away from the wall, put insecticide in four pots, and set each bedpost in a pot. The next morning, she found ants dropping from the ceiling and falling onto the mattress beside her children's sweating heads.

She watched Fenella out the kitchen window as she began exploring the street. While playing in the front yard she met sisters who lived a few houses down. They introduced themselves as Okalani and Kiele. Fenella couldn't say their names. The girls climbed the gardenia tree in the sisters' back yard together and picked the buds off of the branches. White sap oozed from each stem where they had broken off a flower. Okalani told Fenella it was the tree bleeding. Lucinda shouted over the chain-link and told them to "Cut it out". All the girls came to Fenella's house and they took turns jumping on Ina and Fenella's double bed.

At night a gecko crawled from his home inside a crack in the pitched ceiling of the living room. He chirped along with the TV and Ina's coos, telling the Lundgrens stories of previous tenants, warning them of sticky doors in the house, spinning gecko yarns.

~~~

—*The Celestial Mandate, Illuminations, Book of the Serpent, chapter 1:1-5*—

WHAT ARE WE TO UNDERSTAND FROM THE BOOK OF RAM, OF THE BEHEMOTH AND OF THE CREEPING AND GNAWING CREATURES OF THE FIRMAMENT? WHAT OF THE BOOK OF BIRD AND THE GREAT FOWL OF THE ETHER? AND WHAT ARE WE TO KNOW OF THE PROPHESIES OF THE BOOK OF SERPENT AND THE GREAT AND TERRIBLE BEAST OF THE SEA?

BEHEMOTH WAS NOT AN OX, BUT AS JOB SAYS, CHEWS GRASS AS AN OX, AND ALSO HAS HORNS. HE IS THE SERVANT AND THE SUSTENANCE AND THE PRIZED TREASURE OF THE PEOPLE OF THE LORD. HE TRAMPLES THE MINIONS OF THE LEVIATHAN, WHO WRITHE AND SLINK AMONGST THE ROCKS AND DARK PLACES OF THE EARTH. THE BEHEMOTH SHALL GAIN STRENGTH IN THE LOINS AND IN THE SINEWS FROM THE HOLY SHADOW OF
~~~

THE MOUNTAINS THAT REACH TO THE HEAVENS: THE DOMINION OF ZIZ. AND ZIZ, THE MIGHTY WINGED ONE, WHO IS ARRAYED IN EXCELLENCE AND MAJESTY, WITH GREAT REACHING TALONS AND FEATHERS SO PRODIGIOUS THAT THEY MAY BLOCK OUT THE SUN. ZIZ, HAVING DOMINION OF THE AIR AND THE SUN, HE ALSO HAS DOMINION OVER BEHEMOTH, THE GRAZING PROVIDERS, AND ALSO DOMINION ABOVE THE CREEPING HIDDEN CREATURES OF THE EARTH. AND ZIZ REIGNS OVER THE BLACK TEMPEST AND THE LEVIATHAN WHO THRASHES IN THE DEEP.

AND BEHOLD LEVIATHAN, WHO SEEKETH TO LEAD THE PEOPLE TO INIQUITY AND TO HAVE DOMINION OVER THEM. THOSE THAT SHALL FALL INTO HER BLACK DEPTHS SHALL BE REPULSED AND SHALL HISS AND SHALL BE CAST INTO DESPAIR AND TORMENT. AND FALLING INTO HER LAIR, THEY WILL KNOW MUCH WAILING AND GNASHING OF TEETH, AND THE GREAT AND EVIL SERPENT WILL SIT UPON THEIR CHESTS AT THE BOTTOM OF THE EVERLASTING AND YAWNING ABYSS.

BUT WHOA, NONE IS SO MIGHTY AS THE DELIVERER ZIZ, WHO LOOKS UPON THE LAMB AND RAM WITH MERCY, BUT BRINGS THE TERRIBLE WRATH OF THE HEAVENS UPON THE HORNS OF TANINIM, AND WILL PLUCK THE FLESH OF THE WRITHING DEMON FROM THE SEA. AND LEVIATHAN WILL BECOME BOUND AND WILL TURN TO DUST AND WILL HAVE DOMINION OVER THE PEOPLE AND BEHEMOTH NO MORE.

—Scrawled on the Back of a Napkin From the Addled Egg Diner—

It’s useless. I’m drowning. Sorry about the party. You know I have a flair for the dramatic.

ঌ

FENELLA RODE HOME ON HER BIKE FROM HER FIRST DAY of work at the Rostunger's. Slivers of glass had affixed themselves to the sleeve of her sweater. An image of the cormorant with blood seeping up from under ash-colored feathers flashed again and again. She passed the homeless encampment. A woman was screaming, in her underwear. Fenella wondered if having money in itself was a bizarre state, if it cultured eccentricity, if it attracted moments of uncanniness, or if it was some combination of all three.

When she braked her bike at a stoplight, Fenella carefully removed the largest glass sliver from her sleeve. Then the light turned and she rode on, making sure to cross the embedded train tracks on Seahorse Road at a perpendicular angle so her tires wouldn't get stuck and make her crash again. The Schwinn's rusty gears squeaked mournful notes as she pushed down on the pedals. The tide was in and the rush of waves down at the beach drowned out the cries of the gulls picking at the trash cans on the Pier.

She stopped to open the iron gate to the Andromeda Apartments, then rode her bike through the courtyard lifting her right leg off the pedal and back over the rear tire, coming to a perfectly-timed running stop just before the steps that led to her apartment's hallway.

The Andromeda was built in the Hiberian style. At one time it had been used to house the mechanics and game stall barkers from the Amusements. Now, the entire building gave off a feeling of exhaustion. Stucco crumbled and mice gnawed at the sagging windowsills. The bell tower leaned unnervingly to one side, the result of a bombing by anarchists from an encampment in the Pobre Clarita Mountains some sixty years prior.

After the purchase of the building by the socialite Phoebe Carlyle, the state of the Andromeda only became worse. The apartments had been converted to a coin-operated electricity system, as tenants at the Andromeda regularly fell months behind on utility payments. TVs flashed at all hours behind cat-torn curtains and cigarette butts piled up in the corners of the hallways. Shouting matches could be heard behind the thin walls near the end of the month and after football games. Kids crouched under the stairways to draw penises on the walls in magic marker.

Fenella chained and locked her bike to a partial iron railing that edged the path in the courtyard, then walked up the sandy wooden steps and down a red-tiled hallway to the front door of her apartment. She pushed open the door, then gathered the mail and put it on the desk she'd recently found on the street.

After fishing in her pockets for coins, she deposited three dollars' worth of quarters into the black electric meter located in her closet, then walked to the other side of the room where a flimsy Masonite tower held the metal water heater tank. When she flicked the heater's "on" switch a low rumble sounded from its depths.

The tank itself had not been outfitted with a lid, and after suffering through several incidents of pockmarking caused by boiling water that leapt out of the tank, Fenella had painted a "scald zone" on the wooden floor in a red and white target pattern, denoting from past experience the radius best avoided. An old ship's former life jacket provided insulation for the tank. As the water began to heat, the stenciled "Miss Peony" on the jacket steamed out a salty, low-tide odor that permeated every corner of the apartment.

Fenella unbound her hair from the tight bun she'd fashioned at the nape of her neck, and then brushed it. It had become a lighter brown since she'd been spending more time in the Andromeda's courtyard. She took off the rest of her clothes and looked at her body in the bathroom mirror. Her skin was transparent enough that she could see blue branching veins across her breasts. She rubbed her forefinger across her teeth once or twice, and then examined the larger freckles on her nose that were converging into one large mass.

Filling the bathtub with hot and cold, Fenella could hear hisses as boiling water bounced from the water heater onto the floor in the main room. She slid into the tub and moved her neck around. Vertebrae pressed hard into the chipped porcelain and made dull crunching sounds beneath the water.

When the bath began to feel cold, the phone rang. As she grabbed a towel, she made out Benny's voice on the answering machine.

"Fen . . . Fen. Agghhh! It sucks that you have a job now. Hey, Walter and I are watching this movie called *Tabu*. It's silent, but you like Murnau, don't you? Walter's making weird, shitty food. And I have pills." Fenella picked up the handset.

"Ben. I'm here. I just got in."

"Oh hey, yeah, I see your bike down in the courtyard."

"Listen, I have to water and then I'll come."

"Ripping."

Fenella changed into canvas sneakers and the jeans and navy sweatshirt she'd always worn when she painted at the studio at school. She left her apartment and walked through the Andromeda courtyard, watching the sea wind roll cigarette butts around the pathways.

The landscaping at the Andromeda had also been left to wither and rot. Calla lilies had multiplied and spread until their thick stems choked the raised stucco flowerbeds that lined the perimeter of the courtyard's walls. Bougainvillea ran amok, its dense, woody snarls blocking light to ground floor apartment windows. A constant litter of pink blossom tissue covered the crabgrass beneath.

Three months after she had graduated from New Concepción College, when she was still unemployed except on the weekends when she helped at the register at her parent's Barnby Dun roadside shop, Fenella found herself sitting on the steps of her apartment as the summer shrieks blew in from the Amusements, looking at the crabgrass and the small piles of accumulated sand that had blown in from the beach. She'd been peeling off some loose black paint from the iron railing and then, almost without thinking, she'd gone back into her apartment, and grabbed a dull-edged knife from the kitchen drawer that her mother had once inspected and called "cruddy".

She'd begun by sawing through the calla lily stalks. Their watery pitchers were their own funeral bouquet. By evening, she'd cleared enough foliage to discover a small pond against the north wall behind the weeds and branches that had grown together tightly and spilled over the pool's edge. There were no tell-tale sounds of cycling water. When she cleared the dead limbs from the water's surface, a swarm of brine flies huddled within yellowed eelgrass released and swelled, causing Fenella to hold her breath as they scattered around her face. Bending down to inspect the pond more closely, she flinched at meeting the eyes of a beastly looking koi fish, who raised his head out of the water and parted his thick lips like a gargoyle.

After a visit to her parents' house, Fenella brought back some extra tools from the shed as well as three starter artichoke plants. She'd found a leaky brown hose by the Andromeda's meters and began watering the courtyard first thing in the morning. Afterwards, she'd make toast and eat it while sitting on the stucco retaining wall next to the pond, watching the koi lurch to eat the falling crumbs.

When the Amusements began to shut down full operations for the fall, Fenella took clippings from succulents around Perdita like she'd always seen Nonna Agnelli do. She planted urchin euphorbia collected from the front of the old Palace Saloon building, some prickly pears from a neglected patch by the Perdita Library's main branch dumpsters, and a number of aloes that lined the walkway to the Pier. Since spring had arrived, the feathered spires of the artichoke thistles reached close to Fenella's height. Waking up for her first day of work had made her skip this morning's watering.

Fenella's wet hair and the mist on her skin chilled her. When she finished watering, she got her pair of clippers from the kitchen drawer in the apartment and lopped off three riotous purple thistles. She grouped them into an arrangement and then scanned the water for the koi in the pond, but it had grown too dark. The purple whiskers of the artichoke thistle reminded her of the face of the koi, and the koi was the color of the ocean as the sun set across the street.

Taking the stairs two at a time, she went through the Andromeda's tiled archway, ringing the bell beside the mail slot that had a typed sign affixed with yellowed scotch tape reading, "2C – Fresnel, Kopek-Zuiyo". Fenella handed the thistles to a small-framed, black-haired man as he opened the door.

"Why thank you my dear," he said. He held them to his chest in an exaggerated bridal pose. "Sit down. Wally bought mock-duck in a can."

"That's so random. What do you even serve that with?" asked Fenella.

"Tonight, rice," he said as he led her towards the couch. "Wally, bring the Valium with the faux-fowl."

"Stop talking to me like I'm your bitch," said Walter as he stuck his head out of the kitchen. He took off his glasses and pinched his nose from epicanthic fold to bridge. "Hi Fen," he smiled.

"Hi, Walter."

Walter returned to the kitchen while Benny and Fenella fell into the brown mottled couch, and as the familiar and damp smell emerged, Fenella worried that Benny would now begin grilling her about her first day of work, and that she would have to attempt to describe the whole of the day, and she felt overwhelmed.

"Look out," whispered Benny into Fenella's ear. "Wally's got a nasty case of the morbids again." Fenella grimaced in sympathy.

"Benny," she said loud enough for Walter to hear, "I understand they're making socks without holes at a rather reasonable price these days. You should consider investing."

"Oh Fen, always bringing your bourgeois Loffer ways down from the mountains for the benefit of us all," he said.

Walter came from the kitchen with two bowls of food and set them on the ringed coffee table, then went back to the kitchen and returned again with three glasses of water and a pill bottle tucked into his front shirt pocket. He handed Fenella and Benny a glass each and then unscrewed the cap of the pill bottle and poured out a number of blue tablets.

"Miss Lundgren," said Walter as he placed two into the palm of her hand, " . . . and Lord Fresnel."

"Thanks," said Fenella before swallowing the pills with a few gulps of water. "How's your job at the library going?"

"Tell her Wally, tell her," said Benny, in an unnaturally high register. Walter scooped a forkful, then stopped and turned the fork over, letting the food land with an audible moistness. He let the melamine bowl drop onto the coffee table and folded his arms petulantly.

"Can you please shut the fuck up Ben? No one asked you, plus . . . "

"He just decided to stop going to work. Didn't you, Wally?" said Benny.

Walter hugged his knees to his chest and fell sideways into a fetal position on the couch. His oily black hair fell across his eyes.

"Fuck that job. God, Ben. Can we not talk about this right now?" said Walter.

"Can you both shut up? My day has been stressful enough already and I also don't want to talk. Start the movie Benny," said Fenella.

Benny pressed play on the VCR, which made a whine as it started the tape.

"I'll be right back," said Benny picking up the artichoke blooms. "There's a piss jar in my room that I think I can turn into a vase."

Fenella took her untouched food into the kitchen, then sat next to Walter on the couch. She rubbed his arm for a bit with her thumb until he sat up. Benny turned the water on in the bathroom, then came back out with the thistles arranged in a jar and set them on the coffee table before sitting down on the other side of Walter.

At some point Fenella became distracted from the plot of the movie. She watched the flicker of whites from the television around the room and then the running liquid patterns cast on the walls from the moon-backed windows as their breaths condensed and slid down the panes.

"Omigod Fen," said Benny. "There's fucking BUBBLES coming outta your mouth."

"You didn't rinse all the soap from the glass Ben," said Walter. "That's why you can't even call what you do washing the dishes."

Fenella looked at her water glass. It held a layer of thick suds midway down. She wiped her mouth off on her sleeve and lifted her head and put it on Benny's lap, closed her eyes, and immediately fell asleep.

❧

—Handbill—

SEARCHERS of BENITOITE!

Geomancy, Scrying, and Divination

—POSSESSOR of KEYS! GUIDED DISCOVERY—

—Mr. Olaf Ewerloff, Master Prognosticator of the City—

THOUSANDS of VEINS DISCOVERED!!!

Price Engagement Forty Dollars Only Most Reliable

—to be paid in specie, dimes and half-dimes only—

For further particulars, see Mr. Ewerloff IN PERSON

—At the end of Seahorse Rd, the steps of the

Harbormaster's office on Mondays in PERDITA

❧

ON HER SECOND DAY OF WORK, RAÚL ONCE AGAIN LET Fenella in through the gate of the Sugar Factory. She smiled and nodded to him, and he smiled back with a flash of his silver teeth. Fenella locked her bike against the chain-link, entered the Factory through the loading dock door, and found her way up through the series of stairwells and dimly lit hallways until she reached Nina's office. Taped to the door was a note.

Am sick today. Keep crushing on, N.

Fenella entered the office and put her backpack in the corner. She sat on the carpeted floor, surrounded by piles of paperwork and debris and began sorting. After an hour she had established a number of designations and had begun labeling stacks with sheets of notepaper placed on top that read "Receipts", "Bills", "Upcoming Invites", "Items for Purchase", "Gardening Club", "Financial Reports", "Medical", "Lexi", "Bridge", and "Requests for Donations" in her crooked handwriting.

By midmorning, the "Bills" pile loomed large. Occasionally, Fenella paused to stretch her legs and shoulders, get a sip of coffee from the thermos in her backpack and look out the bay windows as heavy clouds gathered over the restless Picaroon before returning to sifting through the strata of thick, scattered paperwork.

Through examination of the paperwork, Fenella learned that Nina had a number of doctors. She had two knee specialists, a dermatologist, several pain management physicians, a gastroenterologist, a neurologist, and a psychiatrist who had diagnosed her with mild depression. She learned that Lexi's tuition at the Blatchington Academy was over forty thousand a year and that her grades were poor. She discovered a receipt from the week prior from the La Oasis Spa for twenty-five hundred dollars' worth of services. She found an invitation for a benefit to support the fashion department at Fenella's alma mater, New Concepción College. She also found a number of unfinished handwritten letters addressed to Thurl. Fenella set them aside and tried not to read them, but they often began:

"Dear Thurl,
I am so confused . . . "

When the light from the windows had shifted considerably, Fenella heard a meow at the door, and when she opened it Lokum ran in. The cat splayed itself on top of the pile marked "Requests for Donations", while her bell tinkled. Fenella smiled and kneeled down to pet her Earl Grey head behind the ears. The cat purred at first and Fenella smelled her sooty, oily dander, and then, without warning, Lokum flipped and scratched and embedded a single claw into the top of Fenella's hand below her thumb.

Fenella gasped and retracted her arm, but the cat's claw remained hooked inside her flesh. Lokum's eyes widened a bit, but its expression remained calm and cold. Fenella took a deep breath in through her nose, feeling too intimidated in the surroundings to call out loudly. She grabbed ahold of the cat's paw, and firmly slid the curved, tense nail from her skin.

Fenella leaned back against the wall and pressed her thumb on top of the drop of blood that had formed. She took a few forced inhales, then stood up and opened the office door. Lokum swiftly left the room, with silent paws and a flicking tail.

By twelve thirty, the storm clouds were emptying a steady downpour into the Picaroon's currents. Fenella left Nina's office with her backpack, and after making a few wrong turns down corridors, eventually found her way into the elevator and down to the hallway that led past the courtyard where the hollyhocks were blowing violently. She pushed through the swinging door into the kitchen that echoed with heavy rain on the windows. The lights on the Turbinado sign were on outside. The smeary red of the "The Sugar on Top" in the rain matched the dried blood swoosh across her thumb.

She put her plastic food storage box onto the counter tentatively, and after looking back towards the kitchen door, she began opening drawers an inch or two to see if she could find the silverware. After the fourth drawer she found a fork, and then she sat at the kitchen counter, and peeled back the lid to her leftover capellini.

The kitchen door swung open suddenly, and Fenella stiffened, feeling guilty at having a borrowed fork in her hands, but she found no face behind the door. A rapid clink-tunk clink-tunk sounded on the floorboards and Fenella looked down to see a wide-haunched, saggy-eyed bulldog at the foot of her stool. The dog let his hindquarters fall as he snorted, and then he saw the fork in Fenella's hand and let his jaw fall slack. Drool oozed from the dog's jowls onto the floor.

Fenella set her fork down and looked out the window at a seabird who hovered over the river in the rain. The bird curled its wings and fell into a death roll, slicing the river's tumbled waves, then reemerged at the surface a few seconds later, with empty talons.

The kitchen door swung open again. This time, a lanky prepubescent girl appeared, barefoot and in pajamas. She had fleshy, curving lips and dark shocks of eyebrows over two mercury grey eyes.

"Oh, hello . . . Hi. I'm Fenella." Fenella wiped her mouth with a napkin and stood up.

The girl, surprised, gathered her hands to her face, then hung her index fingers from the corners of her mouth and smiled, showing a row of braces, slick and white-filmed from sleep. The girl cocked her right shoulder and hip back awkwardly.

"Lepsie," she said with her fingers still in her mouth. The girl suddenly jerked her hands down to her hips.

"Nice to meet you, Lexi. I'm working for Nina now. Is that your mother?"

"Stepmother," said Lexi as she shuffled towards the refrigerator.

"Oh, okay, so Thurl's your father. I haven't met him yet."

Lexi said nothing and opened the wide door to the refrigerator and plunged the top half of her body inside to search for something in the back shelves.

"Is this your dog here?" asked Fenella.

Lexi emerged from the fridge gripping a pint-sized tub with both hands.

"Yeth. That's Ashur."

"Oh. Hi, Ashur. Ashur looks hungry."

Lexi twirled her jumbled dirty blonde hair with one hand while opening a drawer with the other. She plucked out a soup spoon and carried the tub and spoon to a bar stool next to Fenella and sat down, smiling. Fenella looked at the tub. It was prepackaged chocolate frosting.

Lexi pulled off the top of the frosting tub and dug the spoon down deep into the glistening brown. She scooped a heaping boggy-sounding mound. The spoon slid into her mouth, then slid out again as her upper lip glided across the top portion of the frosting. She displayed the smaller, shiny mouth-shaped spoonful to Fenella.

"MMMMMmmmm," said Lexi, smiling again with a wash of brown showing across her teeth and braces.

"It's Tuesday," said Fenella. "You go to school, right?"

"I'm sick," said Lexi before she inserted the frosting spoon again. Her long toes kicked the underside of the counter happily as she pulled the now empty spoon from her mouth horizontally, as if it were on a well-lubed track.

"Oh. Well, I hope you feel better."

Fenella pushed her barstool away from the counter. Ashur stood back up on all fours and looked at Fenella, anxiously panting.

"I'm sure I'll be seeing you around."

"Yeth," said Lexi.

Fenella carried her uneaten pasta back down the corridor and up the elevator back into Nina's office. She looked around the room, which had only been cleared enough to make a small portion of the rug visible. The rain outside was clearing a bit, and she remembered Nina instructing her to get a new answering machine.

She left a note on the notepad on Nina's desk saying where she'd gone and that she'd be right back, and then she made her way once again through the bowels of the Factory, and unlocked her bike from the chain link.

"Be right back," she said to Raúl at the guard gate as she pedaled past.

Fenella pushed along the levee road, swerving now and then to avoid the tufts of wild fennel and the broken glass and needles left behind by the river's homeless and speed freaks. She crossed the Picaroon bridge and rode into the wet blurry gloss of Perdita's downtown. Three naked men leaned against the bike racks next to the head shop. Everyone walked past them, saying nothing.

Next to the Palais Royale Hotel was Jim's Electronics, which was designed to look like a Mayan Temple throughout. At Jim's Electronics one could purchase a new motherboard as well as a gallon of milk. Next to the entrance was a man holding a picket sign. He wore wraparound shades, had long hair, and all black clothing. A cargo van at the curb was pasted with the same verbiage as his sign. His sign read:

SNELLGROVE
HEXSNARFGATRILLIONS OF ALIEN
POPULATIONS ZEGNASITE
INFRAPASTURES
HORNED GOD

On the reverse of the sign:

FRIDA'S ALPENHAUS
2 4 1 DRINK SPECIALS
DURING OKTOBERBREAST

Inside Jim's Electronics, near the steps to the central temple, Fenella located an upper-range answering machine model with four separate mailboxes and forty minutes of recording time. It pained Fenella to extract her own credit card and push the box across the counter, but she felt that showing initiative with Nina would pay off in the end.

Fenella folded the answering machine receipt neatly and inserted it into the front pocket of her backpack, then she mounted her bike and pedaled back to the Factory, breaking a sweat in an effort to beat the clustering clouds propelled by cold sea winds.

"You've reached the office of Nina Rostunger. Please leave a message for her or her assistant Fenella Lundgren after the beep and we will return your call shortly."

It only took Fenella three tries at recording the greeting before she was satisfied that she had come across as articulate, efficient and poised.

—Translated Document Fragment Attributed to Reinaldo Morgante, Quartermaster of the shipwrecked Caravela Redonda, Nuestra Senora de Las Robles—

Translation by David Geldoff, Ph.D.

Department of Archaeology, University of Perdita

Carlyle Library, Special Collection Record Locator MS-3-30

". . . having been run aground some months ago while putting ashore here before sailing to the Islands. The location of our barque in the bay, silted up with great expedience, being abundant in fine sand, has accorded the land's ovine inhabitants to graze at a distance near to it. The vessel's bow has been upended to such a degree in the air that the natives who appear from the hillsides above us are delighted to no end by the sight. Don Gaspar Raoul Almeira de Saceda, our goodly captain, has been afflicted by the fever that has claimed so many of our men. The remaining eight in our party having taken refuge in a most flimsy shelter, pray daily for our deliverance and implore the most blessed Señora . . ."

THINGS HAD BECOME MORE DIFFICULT SINCE INA started crawling. Lucinda was reluctant to buy a playpen and so she did the best she could, leaving Ina in the middle of a spread blanket on the living room floor while she ran outside to line-hang a few diapers. Usually, Ina could only make it as far as the kitchen before Lucinda came back inside, but then, mopping, Lucinda began to find roach droppings where the linoleum curled to meet the rough cupboards. So, she was happy to spend twelve dollars for a wind-up baby swing at a neighbor's yard sale and keep Ina off the floor.

One afternoon, Lucinda folded laundry on the couch while Ina click-clacked, asleep in the wind-up swing. Lucinda was examining the stained neckline of Fenella's shirt when something black, like the shadow from the plumeria tree outside the window, caught her eye.

And then the black form came into focus. A centipede, the length of Lucinda's forearm and as thick as her thumb, groped with half its body, searching for a path with its hordes of legs and writhing antennae. The bottom half of its segments clung to the white aluminum leg of the baby swing. With each half-second rock, the thing reached closer towards Ina's chubby foot.

It was almost as if the swing had stopped, highest in its arc away from the centipede, and it seemed as though the shadows from the plumeria tree froze for a moment on the high shag of the rug. Lucinda found herself against the wall with Ina in her arms as the clacking sound of the swing was replaced by a deep pounding coming from the front of the house.

Lucinda navigated the perimeter of the room to open the door.

"I heard you scream," said Mrs. Onishi.

Lucinda hadn't realized that she had made any sound at all, but she noticed then that her mouth was dry. She nodded, and unable to find words, pointed to the insect.

"May I?" asked Mrs. Onishi. Lucinda moved out of the doorway. Mrs. Onishi entered and went to the broom closet undirected.

❧❧❧❧

Olaf Ewerloff and The Madeira House

By Branca Agnelli

Olaf Eklof Ewerloff had been a devout follower of Swedenborgianism in his youth, and was preternaturally enthused about the imminent second coming of the Lord. As a disciple of Emmanuel Swedenborg, he had discovered an organization to the universe. At the age of twenty-two, he emigrated to the City and found a position as a bricklayer. He rented a simple room near the Canopy district, and kept his money and his soul safely indoors after dusk.

His longing to convene with the mysteries of the divine eventually led him to the Barouche Café. Behind an innocuous looking door, mostly hidden by datura trees, the Barouche was not only a place for teetotalers, serving only coffee and chicory, but it was also a famed vinculum for spiritualists. Mediums, hypnotists, clairvoyants, automatic writers, and spirit guides gathered there for table turnings and rappings with the dead. It was at the Barouche that Ewerloff encountered the widow, Mrs. Harriet Delby Smimes, a noted mystic and practitioner of a religion of her own invention called "New Zoroastrianism".

Mrs. Smimes made her living as a "Consultant with the Holy Cosmos", though her foretelling was strictly limited to portending the most propitious orientation of houses. At the location for a planned abode, she would call upon "Mithra of Wide Pastures" and alternately break a swallow's egg to read the yolk, or toss three quartzite pebbles into the air to study their proximity from one another upon landing, thereby receiving the spiritual guidance by which to prognosticate. Her clients were then directed to build the entrances of their homes to face East or South or seaside, depending on the vitellus or rocks.

Ewerloff began his association with Mrs. Smimes when her popularity as a positioning interpreter was on the wane. The City's neighborhoods were rapidly filling in, and homeowners, no matter how attuned to alternative dimensional forces or how desirous of a spiritually prudent housing situation, had little choice but to build their parlors towards the established streets. Fewer clients were happy to be told that their sitting room windows should look onto nothing more than their neighbor's wall a few inches away.

Mrs. Smimes' husband had been buried for a few years, and perhaps that was why she craved the attention, but in return for pious courtship by the working-class foreigner Ewerloff, she provided him with a social base, tinged with the allure of mysticism.

As well as introducing Ewerloff to the finer points of divination, Mrs. Smimes instructed him on how to spot the "druj" which she defined as being "aberrant to the natural order". Drinkers, gamblers, women on bicycles, and meat-eaters were all considered "druj" to Mrs. Smimes. She and Ewerloff often spent Sundays together at the Barouche, sketching figures of Faravahar, the ancient winged sun-disk, and drinking chicory and chocolate. Mrs. Smimes, after a number of months, became weary of Ewerloff's company as he seemed to never tire of questioning the tenets of New Zoroastrianism. When the rappings at the Barouche became less frequent, Ewerloff, unsatisfied with his work as a laborer, and lonely now that Mrs. Smimes has ceased spending time with him, decided to move to Perdita.

He arrived in town during the Centrifugal Pleasure Way's first season, and immediately began posting bills near the village harbor advertising himself as a diviner of Benitoite strikes.

Ewerloff led clientele on long treks throughout the Pobre Clarita Mountains, often rambling and bivouacking for several weeks at a time. During these treks, Ewerloff would sporadically pause in a clearing and reach into his oversized carpet bag, bringing forth a series of small bones, which he claimed were the relics of the Magi. He would cast the bones on the ground, then cover them with a black silk handkerchief and with a fervent, furrowed brow, feel the bones through the cloth. He would do this repeatedly in several areas around the mountains, playing an occult version of "warmer, cooler", until he had decided on a spot that should be mined.

Those who hired Ewerloff marveled at his ability to keep clean in the rough, and he was noted for appearing to his companions every morning at dawn, freshly shaven, with alligator skin boots, a spotless cravat, and a top hat.

Despite his sharp appearance, the bones of the Magi proved unreliable, and Ewerloff rarely directed his clients to sites that yielded Benitoite. Pick and sluice weary miners brought charges, and Ewerloff was tried and convicted several times for false divination, for which he served numerous stints in the Perdita Jailhouse.

Upon release from his last sentence, Ewerloff returned to brick laying, and began working at the Madeira House construction site.

In August of that year, while an additional port wine cellar at the residence was being dug, several skeletons and spearheads were discovered in the pit, causing a stir in Perdita. Despite Gunnison Carlyle's impatience to finish Madeira and his prejudices against his neighbors, he called on Ephraim Geldoff's son, Professor David Geldoff, an archaeological expert and founding member of Perdita University, to investigate.

In addition to the human remains and spearheads, Geldoff and his team unearthed several pottery fragments and specimens of ceremonial jewelry that were identified as having been fashioned by Liwa Natives, the ancient inhabitants of the Perdita Coastal area. Geldoff also discovered a sea-chest of some antiquity that contained semi-preserved documents he attributed as belonging to the shipwrecked party of the privateer known as "El Terasque".

A botanist from the Academy in the City came to survey the site. Dr. Cecilia Easter catalogued the first pressings of Cirsium "Madeira", or Madeira thistle, a weed known to cause runny noses and blistered fingertips.

Because of the meticulous work by Geldoff and Easter, the work moved slowly, and Carlyle became increasingly anxious to complete Madeira House before his daughter Adelaide's upcoming nuptials. Finally, despite protestations by Geldoff and the University, Carlyle ordered the dig to be halted. He was quoted in *The Perdita Village Bugle* defending his actions, which by then were in opposition to local enthusiasm for the finds.

"After affording access of my land to antiquities workers for a period of fourteen months, I should have thought that my generosity at this juncture might have been pronounced exceedingly bountiful. My gaiety at the furtherance of knowledge regarding primitive peoples cannot be overstated. But while man cannot live on candy floss alone, neither can he be advanced with the earth turned topsy-turvy. I ask that the good men of the University, to whom I have yielded during these proceedings, now gather up their digging doodads and leave Ice Cream Hill to its Christian future."

Ephraim Geldoff petitioned Mayor Horsley, on behalf of his son, arguing that completing the dig was in the public's interest. Nonetheless, the Geldoffs were unable to garner the sufficient political will necessary to divide the mayor from his key campaign contributor. The village council ruled in favor of abandoning the site. David Geldoff collected the preliminary finds and installed them at the University. Gunnison Carlyle ordered the crews back to begin work once again on the cellar.

Leaving the rest of Liwa burial site artifacts lying beneath the racks of aging port at Madeira House did not sit well with Olaf Ekloff Ewerloff. Shortly after his construction foreman called Ewerloff back to work, Ewerloff dispatched a fiery declaration to *The Perdita Village Bugle.*

"After many invocations utilizing theurgical runes, monadic planchettes, and other implements of dimensional revelation, I can be of the utmost certainty that the ancient spirits of Ice Cream Hill, trapped as they now are under these most unholy of mortars, will never fail to cease their evil deeds while Madeira House yet stands."

Ewerloff was summarily fired. He returned to the Pobre Clarita Mountains living mostly off the land, sleeping in the hollows of the great trees that dwarfed his figure. He lost his immaculate habit of dress and grew a long and grizzled beard. His fingernails became dirty and he began to dress in rudimentary habiliments, often fashioning his own clothing from the deer or raccoons that he hunted with a crossbow.

His cadaverous figure would periodically appear in Perdita. He'd trade pelts for rough provisions, then wander Saceda St. for a number of days, shouting admonishments to the townsfolk to unearth the ancient spirits or incur the Madeira curse. Then he'd trudge up Ice Cream Hill and back into the mountains where his ungainly specter would not be visaged until months later.

⁂

FENELLA SAT ON HER MATTRESS, WHICH LAY ON THE floor of her apartment. She picked at the dirt underneath her fingernails with a paperclip. Weeding the Andromeda's courtyard and the constant scrubbing of her hands left them rough and dry. She pulled at a bleeding hangnail.

Earlier that day, Nonna Agnelli had driven down from Barnby Dun in her LeBaron to deliver Fenella some focaccia. Fenella had been sitting with the koi who peeked at her ardently, expecting crumbs. The koi's goofy, tough guy face made her think of her ex-boyfriend Ted. She always thought that the reason they had never worked was because he liked Miracle Whip and because he would put on his childhood record of "Macho Duck" to sing along to when he got drunk. Sitting by the pond, she realized maybe she'd called it quits because he whined when his mother asked him to mow the lawn on visits home.

Fenella brought Nonna Agnelli around the courtyard when she showed up.

"The building, it's a little cruddy, but on your budget it's a palace," said Nonna. Then she patted the top of Fenella's hand and told her to get some hand lotion. "It's a nice garden," she added. "The koi fish, they swim upstream, and that's what artists have to do." Nonna broke off one of the artichoke thistles with a liver-spotted hand and pinned it to her own lapel before leaving. Fenella slapped the dirt from her hands onto her jeans and went inside.

The gulls screamed from the beach. The phone rang and Fenella pushed herself forward onto her hands and then stretched her right hand to the receiver on her desk, using her left hand extended as a counter-balance.

“He-loo?” said Fenella.

“Fen. Listen. What are you doing tonight?” asked Benny. Fenella pushed herself off the desk with her scratched left hand until she balanced on her feet, and then she fell back onto the mattress.

“Um. I can’t say I’ve got a whole lot planned.”

“Fab. Okay, it’s Walter’s birthday next week, so I want to have a party for him here on Friday. I’ve notified the masses already. So, can I store some stuff in your apartment until then? Because, it’s a surprise.”

“Sure Benny, I . . . ”

“Okay, great. So also, if you could change into, I don’t know, like all black, that would be perfect. Like, now. And um, grab your icky knife. I’ll be down in fifteen.”

“Wait, what? Benny . . . ”

Benny had hung up. Fenella shook her head, then changed into a black T-shirt and black jeans. She grabbed her gardening knife from the kitchen and a square of focaccia. She sat back on the mattress and when she had finished the focaccia, a fist pounded on the door. Fenella opened it, and saw Benny standing in the hallway, also dressed in black. He was wearing black eyeliner and held a knife between his teeth while he snarled like a pirate.

Benny removed the knife from his mouth and wiped the spittle from the blade onto his black slacks that featured a large hole to the left side of the crotch.

“Vive les fronds!” he said.

“Excuse me?”

“Vive les fronds. We’re going to liberate palm fronds. I’m throwing a tiki party and I want to make the whole apartment look like a grass hut,” said Benny.

“Oh my. And where are we finding said fronds?”

"Are you blind? They've got those short little stubby palms all around the Amusements parking lot, and even more at the Ducale Apartments."

"Well, do you think I need a flashlight?"

"No, you're fine, come on." Benny and Fenella walked through the Andromeda Courtyard. The knives gleamed in the moonlight. Fenella stopped for a moment to dig at a weed along the courtyard path.

"Noooooo," said Benny, tugging her along.

They walked down Seahorse Road in the middle of the empty street, along the railroad tracks. White sequenced lights burst around the arcade building, down to the end of the pier and back, and up and down the domed roof of the Periwinkle Palace. More bulbs flashed and led the way along the tracks of The Kraken up to the coaster's peak. Then, the eyes of the giant black octopus that topped and intertwined with the coaster glowed red while a speaker from within emitted a base moan and three animatronic tentacles vibrated and curled around various tracks below.

It was too early in spring for The Kraken to run on a Tuesday night. The management kept the lights on until ten p.m. advertising that the Periwinkle Palace and arcade were open on weeknights. Fenella could hear the roar of the ocean, which meant that the Pier was mostly deserted, except for a handful of the University kids who came to the Periwinkle during the week to see obscure punk or garage bands at the Quay and to play pinball afterwards.

The vast Amusements parking lot was an open empty sweep of asphalt, punctuated periodically with tuffeted islands of short palms. Benny eased towards one of the low plantings in the lot.

"Keep an eye out for the dudes in the security trucks," he said as he began sawing the fronds from a palm bush. "Fuck. These fuckers have crazy sharp spine thingies. Be careful." Fenella hacked at a palm a few plants down.

"Benny, you ever see the parrots that live at the tops of the tall palms here?" asked Fenella.

"Parrots. What parrots? You're crazy."

"No, seriously Ben. They're like pets that escaped. But the climate is supposedly fine for them. They've set up regular little flocks. One flock lives in that big palm tree there. You can hear them in the morning mostly."

"You're on glue."

The two worked, sawing and cutting at the low growing palms, and when they'd pulled a good number, they dragged them into a pile towards the side of the parking lot closest to the Andromeda.

"We need more. Fen. A lot more. I want to cover the walls and ceiling."

"I have to work tomorrow you know. I've already been clawed by a cat today, and I don't really need my digits lacerated further by fucking palm fronds because you want to be Trader Vic."

"Look, we just need to get the bigger ones over by the Ducale and we'll be okay. And this is for Walter, remember, not for me. He's been having a very bad time, Fen."

"Ugggggggghhhhh . . . fine."

"I've scouted the Ducale," said Benny. "Lots of small bushy palms with big fronds."

"Cycads, I bet." They walked to the far end of the Amusements parking lot as The Kraken moaned periodically. In her apartment, when Fenella went to bed early it was often hard to distinguish among the low bass crash of the coaster cars, the deep moaning of the octopus, and the roaring of the ocean; they all became a single low growl that rumbled in her mattress.

The Palazzo Ducale Apartments were located on the opposite side of the Picaroon River mouth from the Amusements. The apartments were reachable from the Amusements side by a train trestle and a footbridge that spanned the lagoon of the outlet. On the footbridge, Benny picked up a few pebbles and threw them at a shopping cart that had been upended on a brackish sandbar beneath the bridge.

"You missed, champ," said Fenella.

They clomped along the bridge above the tule grass until they reached the far bank, then followed a dirt path to another bridge that arched slightly with carved cinquefoil rails. This bridge connected the Ducale's central plaza to the beach.

The Palazzo Ducale Apartments were a decrepit series of buildings that stretched into the lagoon. Narrow canals ran between the wings of rooms. The exterior plaster was painted in sun-worn Venetian frescoes and the hotel's window boxes displayed brittle stems, the dried paper beginnings of wasp's nests, and the crumbling huts of swallows.

The courtyard at the center of the hotel was a plaza interconnecting the various wings and canals of the Ducale. It featured chipped concrete statues of lions and various saints in between palms and tangled white wisteria that propelled a sweetish, overripe vapor into the thick night air. Several archways led off the plaza and the flaking words on their voussoirs denoted the names of the various walkways that had a wing of apartments to one side and a canal on the other. The lapping water on the plaza's lagoon front sent periodic odors across the flagstones like mussels gone off.

"Don't cut down all the fronds," whispered Fenella. "Just take the drier ones, near the bottom."

They worked silently around the courtyard, gathering fronds and placing them in a pile.

"Okay, that's enough Ben. We won't be able to drag back anymore."

"Last ones here. There's a bunch of good ones," said Benny.

Fenella followed Benny through the archway marked "Titian" and began cutting the fronds that framed a series of entry doors. As the Ducale rented apartments with kitchenettes by the day or week, its residents were even more notorious than that of the Andromeda. Fenella sawed anxiously, her throat tightening at every noise.

The walkway extended beyond the canal and building, ending in a dock that protruded into the waters of the river mouth. A thematic set of striped poles decorated the end of the dock, patinaed with realism by the droppings of Bonaparte gulls and brown pelicans. A storm lantern hung from one of the poles, casting a dim cone of light onto the cockscomb prow of a rotted gondola tied to the dock.

Benny gathered a pile of fronds and dragged them back towards the main pile they had left in the plaza while Fenella continued working down the walkway. A blackened figure moved in front of the lantern at the end of the dock. Fenella squatted behind a palm.

"Interesting hobby you've got yourself there," called a male voice. Fenella wondered if she should run.

"Doing a bit of gardening for the management," she said, standing.

"Yes. The management is very into upkeep here. They like to pay lots of overtime to keep the place in tiptop shape. Always bringing in night gardeners," said the voice as it moved closer.

Fenella grasped her knife tightly and turned to look back over her shoulder. Benny cowered on the other side of the archway. The man's face appeared in the moonlight. He was smiling.

"Don't worry," he said. The casual tenor of his voice and his face relaxed Fenella slightly.

"Good haircut," she thought. The man looked youngish, but it was hard to tell in the light.

"I can't imagine what you two are doing, but I endorse it nonetheless," he said. Benny speed-walked to Fenella's side.

"We're here per the explicit instructions of the management," said Benny.

"It's okay, Ben," said Fenella. "He doesn't care."

"Oh," said Benny. Fenella watched Benny's chin soften as he took in the man's features. "And who might you be?"

"Pierce," said the man.

"Well Pierce, I bet you'd like to know what these here palm fronds are for," said Benny.

"I would actually," said Pierce smiling. Fenella noticed how white and straight his teeth appeared in the moonlight.

"Well, you're just going to have to walk over to the Andromeda Apartments, 2C, Friday night, eight o'clock," Benny said as Fenella shot him a look of incredulity. "Eight o'clock sharp."

"Eight o'clock. 2C. Okay. I'd gather your clippings, though. Some advice. "Concussion Mania" is about to end and all the unsavories here will be coming outside for their smokes soon."

"Oh, thanks," said Fenella. "We'll go then." She clumsily picked up the fronds at her feet. "See ya."

She and Benny gathered the pile of fronds in the plaza, dragging the whole lot like sleds back over the Ducale bridge and the footbridge towards the Amusements. As they neared the main pile they'd left in the Amusement parking lot, Benny paused under a street lamp. He dropped his fronds to the ground and opened his eyes wide, then put a finger to his pursed lips and bent forward from the waist. He cocked his heel and looked back at Fenella between his legs.

"Seeeee yaaaahh," he said. Fenella laughed.

"Agh! Shut up!" In the Andromeda's courtyard Benny walked up the stairs and deposited his fronds in front of Fenella's front door.

"Why are you stopping there?" she asked.

"You SAID I could keep stuff here before the party. I can't very well explain all of these to Walter before Friday, can I?"

"Oh god. You're serious."

"Fen. C'mon. It's two days . . . Open the door. Sweetie. For Walter."

Fenella lay in the dark on her mattress trying to sleep and listened to the growl of the sea and The Kraken. She began to feel uneasy about the presence of palms piled high in her room. She turned on her bedside lamp and saw that a number of spiders had crawled from the foliage and gathered on the ceiling. She grabbed her pillow and comforter, and nimbly raced to the bathroom, where she shut the door and made up a bed in the bathtub.

DAEN WORRIED ABOUT LUCINDA. HE'D OFTEN FIND HER in their bedroom, not noticing that Ina had finished nursing. She'd push the food around on her plate at dinner, then would ostensibly do the dishes, turning the faucet on and off, picking up pots and pans to set them down on different parts of the counter, and then she'd leave the kitchen without having cleaned anything. She'd stopped doing laundry, or sweeping the floors. Then she stopped cooking. When he got home from work, he'd find Fenella standing on the counter, pulling things out of the cabinets.

Daen hired a local girl from the Loffer congregation to help take care of Ina and Fenella, even though they were short on cash because of the down payment he'd made on a used brown sedan. He thought that getting the family involved in more activities would help Lucinda to make friends. The Loffers were nothing if not good at keeping their members busy.

They went to a barbeque on the beach, hosted by the church. When they arrived, the young girls of the congregation were sitting around piles of banana leaves, folding and weaving them into mats. Fenella looked at the girls and scratched one leg with the toenails of the other. They sat on the ground near the edge of the larger group, where the crabgrass began to invade the sand. Lucinda moved their blanket around several times.

"The smoke, it keeps getting in my eyes," she said.

She pulled the locks of her wheat-colored hair to her nose, trying to better understand the moist sooty fragrance that permeated it. Fenella looked at Daen with wide eyes as the men of the church lifted an animal from the ground. Daen took her hand.

"Come on, let's say hello to the Priest."

Daen and Fenella wandered through the smoke and the crowds. Brown, barefoot children ran across their path from both directions. They found the Priest, a large Islander with calf muscles the size of melons.

"This is really something else," said Daen to the Priest.

The Priest laughed. "Stupid pig. I think he was maybe from a farm over the mountain there. Broke into my yard and dug up most of the yams before I shot him."

Daen saw Fenella watching the other girls who were dancing. She thrust her hips from side to side awkwardly, and mimicked the synchronized turns two or three seconds after the other girls completed them.

"Barbeque," said Daen to the Priest. "I thought maybe hot dogs or something."

AT THE START OF HER SECOND WEEK AT THE SUGAR Factory, Fenella pushed through the curtains of fog that hung from the banks of the Picaroon, locked her bike along the chain-link next to the topiaries and made her way into the series of dark hallways that led to Nina's office. She had memorized the way. Up to Five, left, left, around the Conservatory, right, then the fourth door on the right again.

Nina's bare feet were crossed over the surface of her cherrywood desk. She leaned back in her chair holding a phone receiver to her ear with her shoulder. She gave Fenella a wave of acknowledgement with a hand that held a clove cigarette, then took a drag. A long bluish plume of smoke curled around the oversized photograph of herself hanging above the desk. Nina spoke into the phone loudly, as if the connection was bad.

"Well Candy doesn't get it . . . Muffin, listen to me . . . We all know how hard you worked on that event . . . No, Muffin, it's true and everyone knows it . . . And the CENTERPIECES, just between you and me, were not the only thing talked about afterwards that Candy could have done better…and did you know that Candy's sister-in-law owns that floral supply place?…That's what I said . . . AND she failed to reveal that to the budget committee…right."

As she spoke, Nina picked at her toenails with a pair of nail scissors, extinguished her cigarette, and lit another. Fenella found that a few of the piles of paperwork she had filed had been scattered back around the room, as though Nina had been trying to look for something. Fenella busied herself re-sorting the piles while Nina continued talking. Lokum jumped down from a bookcase and slinked between the stacks. The smoke in the room began to burn Fenella's eyes, but she thought it might be rude to open a window.

An hour and a half passed and Fenella did her best to try be industrious. She'd finished re-sorting the paperwork, and began sorting the detritus. Paper clips in one pile. Personal care items in another. Shoes lined up in the corner. She expected when Nina got off the phone, they'd have a meeting. Fenella would explain her rationale for a new filing system, and after some discussion, she'd get to work putting the stacks of paper away in into the filing cabinets. She'd tell Nina that the glass people were on their way to fix the ceiling in the Conservatory, and that a check should probably be ready. She'd ask Nina how she liked the new answering machine, if it felt right. She'd retrieve the receipt for it from her wallet so she could be reimbursed. Then maybe they could discuss what her day-to-day responsibilities and duties were, and if there were any long-term projects.

"Well, I must have you down to my family's ranch. I'm taking it over you know. My uncle is in no shape…yeah. Well Dabney rides, doesn't she? You know, I bought two Andalusian sires last month. We're starting a yeguada. That's Hiberian for …well, we're going to breed and train them. Yeah, my uncle knows a few people . . . I will . . . I'll email you . . . Oh, plus that Hermès scarf . . . It's around here someplace. With the little red squiggles . . . Right . . . Did you know I'm thinking of buying a property out there? Oh HER? Did you know she was supposed to help me with the fashion line. Zip from her . . . She dropped the ball bigtime . . . Well, some people don't get it . . . No, she really just doesn't get it . . . She wanted to do this whole thing with snaps, that's all she'd talk about, snaps, snaps, snaps, but when it came down to it, and we were visiting the factory in the Islands, oh, huge disaster, didn't know her ass from a snap, I'll tell you . . . Okay Muffin . . . I'll call you . . . Yes . . . I'll call you . . . Yes . . . she really is a piece of work isn't she . . . yes . . . right . . . yes."

Nina set the phone down hard into its cradle. Fenella eyed her from the floor with an expectant expression, figuring that they'd finally be able to meet, get some things in order. Nina put her cigarette in a cup of cloudy greenish liquid that held several other butts, and then jammed her feet into a pair of plaid flats lying near the desk.

"Listen Lisa honey, I think Thurl's been expecting you at his office all morning. Did you see all that paperwork I had from Dr. Shah?" she said while fishing through her purse.

"Oh, I didn't know, but I have a stack…"

"So, I have to run to this appointment. Good job here. Sorry, but you know, I'm getting over this bronchial thing… so if you could find Thurl. We'll talk later, okay? And if you could make Lexi a dentist appointment. I think she has a cavity. Have you seen my keys?"

"Oh, I'm not sure, but . . . "

"Here they are. Aggh! This cat! Fur everywhere in here. Ask Catalina how often she's been vacuuming if you would. And if the cat's getting her hairball remedy. She should be getting it at least twice a week. And make sure it's the organic stuff, not that cheap crap from Meow Mart . . . "

Nina twisted her hair into a chignon and clipped it with a barrette from the desk. Then she opened the door to the powder room, pulled down her pants, sat on the toilet and began urinating. Fenella averted her eyes.

"You don't mind nudity, do you? I'm an equestrian and when you're on a long ride, well, it's just how it's done. I'm related to the President you know, and he pisses in front of all his advisors."

Nina pulled up her pants.

"So, okay, I guess I'll . . . "

"I'll see you this afternoon," said Nina. "No, you'll be with Thurl. Tomorrow then."

Nina was out the door. Fenella sat motionless for a moment looking at the smoke that hung in the air.

Fenella had no idea how to find Thurl or the East Wing. Since it was time for the glass repairmen to arrive, she hoped that Raúl would be showing them to the Conservatory, and then she could ask him if he knew how they were supposed to get paid, and where she should go to find Thurl. If Catalina was around maybe she could ask her if she knew what dentist Lexi went to. She wondered if making doctor's appointments would be a regular sort of thing.

Fenella gave Lokum a wide berth as she exited the office and breathed in the dark air of the corridor. She made her way down to the elevator where she heard faint barking as soon as she lifted the door.

In the Conservatory, workmen were busy carrying in ladders while Raúl held back a barking Ashur. Another man who Fenella had seen clipping at the topiary dolphins a few days back lifted furniture to make more room.

"Hi, Raúl . . . hi . . . " said Fenella.

Ashur came running toward her with wooden eyes. He drooled onto the carpeting and growled at her.

"So, do you have any idea how I should pay these guys? Does Catalina have a checkbook or something?"

Raúl gave Fenella a shrug and a close-lipped expression that hid his metal teeth. Fenella approached the glass repairman who was giving directions to the others.

"Are you Jorgé? We spoke on the phone?"

The man nodded and scratched his beard.

"The ceiling's taller than you said. I'm having to send one of my guys back to the shop for the bigger ladder."

"Oh, I'm sorry. I said it was just an estimate . . . but listen, my boss, who's the owner . . . she isn't here, and I know I was supposed to have a check for the deposit, but, I mean, can you invoice me so I can show her something? I'll do my best to have it tomorrow."

Jorgé sighed.

"I'll email it to that address you gave me."

"Great," said Fenella over Ashur's barking. "I really do appreciate it."

She walked back to Raúl.

"I need to find the East Wing? Can you take me to Thurl?" she asked. Raúl turned without responding, and Fenella followed him as he dragged Ashur away by the collar. They entered the dark corridor and halfway down, Raúl opened a side door and threw Ashur in. His barking gradually subsided by the end of the elevator ride to the ground floor.

Raúl led Fenella back past the staircase near the loading dock, then to another corridor and a second set of aluminum stairs. They climbed up three flights with echoing footsteps as the only commentary. Raúl pushed open a door that led to a suspended catwalk inside a multistoried room.

Below was a complex network of oversized stainless-steel vats connected by a series of pipes studded with levers and pressure gauges. Fenella assumed that it was all was the leftover workings from the sugar refinery, but then she heard the pipes gurgle and hiss, and saw steam escape from joints. She wanted to ask Raúl what this was all for, but he seemed annoyed and so she kept silent.

At the far end of the catwalk, Raúl pushed through another steel door and they walked through a single-story windowless room, outfitted with a metal desk and an industrial rolling chair that sat askew under an archaic time clock and a rack for punch cards. They walked through this room and through yet another door.

Filtered sunshine hit Fenella's face. Through a skylight, beams bounced off planted palms along the walls that had been papered in a subtle vine-print with hues of ochre and plum. The room featured a massive solitary carved wooden door at the far end that looked newly stained. It emitted a sweet acrid smell of varnish that hit high in Fenella's nose.

Raúl rang a buzzer next to the door and the sound of a small motor whirred above the door frame. Then the lens of a camera tracked them. Its iris opened wide and clicked once. There was a short pause.

Fenella turned towards Raúl with raised eyebrows, and then a compression sound and a release came from behind the door. It eased open a few inches. Raúl turned on his heels and walked back the other way, leaving Fenella to enter.

No one greeted her. She entered an enormous, vaulted room near the ceiling, on the uppermost landing of a highly detailed wrought iron staircase. A shadow passed over her head, and she lifted her gaze. The ceiling was constructed of glass and girders, and above was an immense Aquarium. Stingrays, damsel fish, and schools of bluefin tuna swirled in an endless expanse, while vines of kelp dangled towards her, beckoning her in Rapunzel fashion to simply climb up. She lost her footing for a moment, then steadied herself and proceeded down the stairs.

She took in the rest of the windowless room. It had the character of a Victorian ballroom. The walls had been papered in a red-flocked brocade while bulky crystal chandeliers hung from girders beneath the glass and lit the room meekly with blue gas flame. Black light highlighted the lint on her clothing.

There was a fireplace at one end of the room, large enough for Fenella to climb inside. Several more tanks of water lined the walls framed in heavy gilt as if they were pieces of classic portraiture. Even more curiously, the center of the room contained a series of raised garden beds. A network of irrigation lines fed the black soil in each, and as Fenella neared the bottom of the stairwell, she could hear the hiss of water emanating from the tendril-like water lines.

The immense body of water was so delicately suspended overhead it left Fenella feeling constricted, muffled, confined, as if she were in a submarine that had lost power and had come to rest at the bottom of the ocean. She stopped then, and because her feet ceased to make ominous and lonely clangs on the iron staircase, she became aware of the room's sound.

There were no cries of seabirds or the rolling slaps and knocking of buoys heard in Nina's office. Here, the high-pitched hum of irrigation lines combined with the deep-set rumbles and bellows of obscured piping in the walls. One of the girders overhead released a lament and Fenella instinctively raised her hand to her neck in a gesture of shock and looked upwards, expecting her eyes to be met with a deluge of water and the rubber bodies of eels and jellies. The chandeliers tinkled and swayed slightly, and then the room returned to the dreamlike drone of deep water. Fenella moved closer to one of tanks set into the wall.

A few crustaceans sporting vibrant blues, greens, and reds started, then came to a drifting stop, the frills of their appendages rising in the water like the orange paper manes of dragons in a Lunar New Year parade. Orange spots appeared beneath a pair of high green collars. "Peacock Mantis Shrimp," read the caption underneath.

Fenella moved along the wall and peered into another tank that at first seemed to contain only plant life until there was a cyclical fluttering, and then the equine profile of a seahorse appeared, though his body was comprised of plumes, reedy stems, and leaves. A darker companion to the seahorse made a movement then, displaying purplish black filament. He propelled himself by undulating small coquettish fans. The wall text beneath the read, "Leafy and Weedy Seadragons".

Fenella continued to move around the room. She examined the whipscorpions, glass catfish, the jewel fairy basslets, the bubble coral and the sea plumes. The adjoining wall held tanks of chocolate chip stars, mermaid's purses, leaping blennies, fluffy sculpins and fire urchins.

"Good afternoon," said a deep voice from the far side of the room. Fenella started. A bead of sweat ran between her shoulder blades, beneath the band of her bra.

"Almost a million gallons of water, circulated in from the ocean to provide the needed turbidity for the kelp, and suspended overhead in a completely secure way, even during a shaker, or so my engineers tell me." A towering older man with thinning gray hair moved further into the dim light. He let out a slight laugh. "Let's hope they're correct," he said before inserting a fat cigar into his mouth. It burned orange for a moment like the tips of the peacock shrimp's antennae. The smoke rose, drifting in the air currents lazily as if was contained in the liquid above.

"Are you Mr. Rostunger?"

"I am indeed. And I'm assuming that you're Nina's new girl, yes?"

"Yes. I'm Fenella," she said as she stepped forward, extending her hand. Thurl seemed not to notice, and he put his hand onto hips that stood almost mid-chest to Fenella. He looked towards the ceiling and exhaled once again.

"I have lots of difficulty sleeping, Fenella," he said. "When I sleep, I sleep shallow, you know what I mean?" Fenella nodded. "I don't dream," continued Thurl. "Not that I don't remember my dreams, mind you. It's that I don't dream at all. At least not while asleep. This water; these animals…they relax me."

"Yes, it's all very…dreamlike…yes."

"Yes," said Thurl as he abruptly lowered his sightline to meet hers. He removed his cigar from his mouth. "Well, why don't you come into my office."

Fenella followed him and the smoke that smelled like dirty candy. Thurl wore high-waisted pinstriped pants with a belt that exaggerated his gigantic middle, and he walked in a lumbering way, with stiff knees. He opened another carved wooden door at the darkest end of the room, and the two entered a smaller space, still lit partially and eerily with black light. It was filled with mounted trophies of African wildlife and dark-tanned leather furniture. An unblinking, blue, monstrous fish stood suspended in a tank above Thurl's desk, its jaws agape. And then a shriek from behind her turned Fenella's attention to the back of the room.

"Ahhh. This, is . . . Lucretia."

Thurl moved towards a black iron cage topped with a spire and opened its door. He took something from the pocket of his wool cardigan and fed it to a glassy oil slick of a crow, who met the treat quickly. Its black eyes widened and the feathers on the back of its neck raised as it screamed again.

"That's enough for now, Lucretia. Crows and ravens have very developed minds. Up there with primates and cephalopods you know. Pipe down if you would Lucretia," said Thurl. He shut the door to the cage, walked behind his desk and sat down, gesturing for Fenella to be seated on the other side in a club chair placed on top of a gazelle hide.

"This specimen," said Thurl motioning to the fish behind him, "is a coelacanth. A prehistoric fish, thought to be extinct until rather recently. It's a relation to the Eusthenopteron, that presumptuous creature who sprouted legs and came ashore to conquer land some three hundred sixty million years ago."

"It's all very impressive," said Fenella. She could feel the twisted horns and flared nostrils of the trophies that surrounded her closing in. For all of the luxurious touches, the room had the feeling of a bomb shelter. It felt as if the hot breaths of its hanging beasts had been captured and bottled between the walls.

"And so, as you can tell, I have a keen fascination for flora and fauna," continued Thurl. He ashed his cigar into a wastepaper basket beside the desk made from an elephant's foot. "I have become a bit too eccentric for my wife," he laughed. He then leaned forward. "I have other interests, though."

"Oh yes?" asked Fenella.

"Yes," said Thurl. "And that's where you come in."

Fenella edged near the tip of her seat and eyed the door. Thurl rose from his chair and turned towards the coelacanth as if he were addressing it.

"I like to construct and collect scenes."

"Scenes?" asked Fenella.

"'Vignettes' is more of an apt term. I choose the subjects from my memories, or from motifs and eras that appeal to me."

"And you collect them?"

"On video," said Thurl as he turned towards her once again. "I have a top-of-the-line set up. Nina said you had some experience with this . . . ?"

"Well, I went to art school. I made a few student films…"

"Marvelous. And you would say you have a strong connection to your subconscious, to thematic subtleties?"

"Well, I…I've had professors tell me that I have a good imagination if that's what you mean. As far as 'thematic subtleties', . . . if you mean if I have the training and discernment to view art critically, I can only say . . . "

"Yes. I can see that you'll be fine," said Thurl, taking a seat once again. "Two projects over the next three weeks. I have a series of rooms here in the East Wing. I've been putting together something of a back lot with the help of my other assistant. He'll be in soon enough. I'd like you to build a scene for filming. 'German Expressionist Dinner Party' is what I've decided the theme should be. But feel free to utilize sound. That's the only direction. Run wild. I'll have a credit card by tomorrow in your name for expenses. Raúl can help you with the carpentry. Bring in any actors you think you will need. Pay them a fair wage. I'd like to shoot on the 31st. Five minutes of material should be sufficient."

"Oh, well. German Expressionist? So, but, where . . . "

"I have a second task," said Thurl. "My daughter, Lexi She's turning thirteen next month."

"Yes, I've met her."

"Muffin Laidley has kindly offered to put an event together. She'll need your help though. Nina will put you in contact with her. And now," he said pulling a snorkel out from a drawer in his desk, "I'll leave you to explore the Studio Area, as I'm calling it. I've got fish to feed, pH balances to check, and these delivery men can't seem to get 50 lbs. of decapsulated brine shrimp eggs in before two p.m. to save their lives. This way dear, you'll find a door to the studio and the main Aquarium room right through here. I like to be left to my own thoughts while I work, so come and go freely, and I'll see you on the 31st."

Without waiting for a response, Thurl gave Fenella a brief pat on the shoulder at the threshold, then shut the door to his study.

"FEN! COME HERE A SECOND . . . FEN . . . OH, FEN. PUT ON A shirt. But first, no come here . . . Puele told me you've been picking flowers off the next-door neighbor's trees. Is that true? Don't lie to me." Lucinda wore a Loffer-style puffed sleeve cotton nightgown.

"Puele ties the curtains into knots to keep them open. Did you see?" Fenella scratched her shin with her toenail.

"We're not talking about the curtains, Fen. Did you pick the neighbor's flowers?"

"Yeah, but, but, but Kiele said it . . . "

"Hey. No more of that. I don't care what Kiele said. Be a good girl and help Puele make your lunch. And put on a shirt. I don't want to see you naked again when I come home from work or I'll have to give you a spanking. And I'll take away that spoon. We're gonna work on a rule list tonight. We'll put it on the fridge and draw pictures so you'll remember."

"I hate papaya."

"Eat your lunch today, Fen."

❧❧❧❧

Murder and The Madeira

By Branca Agnelli

Following the disruption caused by the discovery of Liwa artifacts in the cellar pit, the construction of Madeira House again came to a halt during the tumultuous period of Adelaide's illness and passing and Gunnison Carlyle's trial for the murder of Pickett Snellgrove.

Six months after Adelaide's burial, Gunnison took up the project again with renewed fervor. A new architect was hired to add additional wings to the house, and soon scores of new crewmen arrived at the Sea-horse Road railway station before trudging to the site on Ice Cream Hill.

Skilled craftsmen from the City came to adorn the estate's exterior with stone sea serpent grotesques. Inside, the staircase railings, newels, and balusters were formed into carvings depicting schools of fish and trailing kelp. The parlor's wall rosettes, frescoes, moldings and plinths were decorated with sailing ships, pineapples, blue whales, and the gambols of dolphins.

Then word spread throughout Perdita that the Madeira's new architect had been fired. Gunnison brought in another architect, as well as a new building adviser from the City, Mrs. Delby Smimes. For a time afterwards, little was seen of Gunnison outside of Madeira House. He ceased attending services at the First Christian Church. Mayor Horseley stopped receiving invitations to sample ports from the cellar.

The construction of Gunnison's house became both frenetic and capricious. Wings and turrets seemed to shoot up overnight from the estate, only to be dismantled again within a few weeks. Expensive materials were ordered, then left to deteriorate outside. Stained glass windows were installed, only to be obscured by new wings.

Legions of laborers who had been discharged without cause from the site became drunk at the Palais Royale and spoke of building hidden musket rooms and secret safes. They told of staircases in the house that led to precipitous dropoffs, and doors that opened into sealed walls, and of the library and kitchens that were riddled with spying nooks. Then the fired workers stumbled, whiskey-addled, to the Seahorse Road station to wait for the train to the City, only to see their replacements disembark when the train pulled in. Brawls following train arrivals became commonplace for the period.

Rumors spread throughout Perdita about the now-reclusive Gunnison Carlyle. It was said that he wandered through the labyrinthine corridors of Madeira House, attempting to avoid the apparition of Adelaide who appeared in white to wail of her fate. Ex-employees reported that Mrs. Smimes was the only person granted regular admittance to Gunnison's private rooms, and that she counseled and compelled him to continue the mad pace of building. It seems that the two came to believe that by constructing dead ends, odd angles and oblique additions within the house, they could outwit and neutralize the disturbed specter of his late daughter.

Proof of Mrs. Smimes' hold over Gunnison was confirmed when rivers of port wine appeared, rushing down Ice Cream Hill, dying the white blooms of the miner's lettuce along the road a burgundy color. Both Gunnison and Mrs. Smimes' names were added to the membership of the Perdita Temperance Society, and letters were dispatched to Mayor Horseley urging him to enact higher taxes on the beer halls along the Pier as well as the saloons such as the Palais Royale.

Mrs. Smimes ordered large quantities of Benitoite mineral ore to be delivered, as she believed that the gems were useful in communicating with the spirits. A set of rock walls went up around Madeira House, which displayed the dark sparkle of the gem specimens cemented into the masonry of the facades like many reptilian eyes, warning against entry. A high-spired circular séance room was constructed, and in the evenings, its chimney belched smoke tinged with blues and reds. The grounds around the house were permeated with the distinct odors of sandalwood and ambergris.

Then, an announcement in *The Perdita Village Bugle* appeared. The widow Harriet Smimes and Mr. Gunnison Carlyle of the Carlyle Lumber and Holding Company were engaged to be wed at the Adelaide's Quay the following Saturday. Debates swirled inside the beer halls and parlors of both Perdita and the City as to exactly which concoctions and incantations Mrs. Smimes had used to captivate and subdue the famously hotheaded and imperious lumber baron.

The next week, the Village Bugle described the scene after the ceremony, under the headline: "A Marriage to Quiet the Sorrows: The Houses of Trees and Spirits Join Hands and Hearts".

"Flocks of Perdita's curious gathered outside the bandshell of Adelaide's Quay during the nuptials of Mr. Gunnison Carlyle to the widow Harriet Smimes, formerly of the City. The jostling crowds sought the most advantageous view from which to espy the newlyweds upon the wooden sidewalk, which the groom had covered in carpet, so as to prevent his bride's slippers from becoming soiled as she alighted from a white carriage, fully draped in an orange blossom-colored veil. Few guests were granted admittance, but those among the lucky few were Mayor Wicksteed Horsley and his wife and children, the ever-sporting Mr. Cyril Legume, the distinguished chairman of the Board of Regents at the University of Perdita, Mr. Leroy Mill, and the proprietor of the Algerine Palace Hotel in the City, Mr. H.R. Collis."

During the ceremony spectators outside strained their ears to glean something said and the sun finished its day's long journey into the sea. Then the Adelaide's Quay Orchestra broke into the wedding march as the doors to the bandshell conch were opened. The newlyweds posed for a photograph on the steps of the shell. Mr. Carlyle appeared dapper, with closely trimmed mutton chops and a finely tailored suit, though it was noted that he had recently lost some of his famous stoutness of figure while having gained a considerable degree of whiteness to his pate.

"Mrs. Harriet Carlyle displayed a full, proud face, framed by the orange blossom Honiton lace bridal veil held in place by a crescent of diamonds," continued *The Village Bugle*. "The bride wore an Ondine silk dress of an ocherous, titian color, with small flounces at the bottom edged in silver. The train itself was perfectly plain, though the pointed bodice was of a sumptuous brocade."

The crowd cheered the couple, but soon broke into whispers, even as five hundred white doves were released into the air, when a grizzled man appeared at the periphery shouting,

"Curses! Curses to you and the house that imprisons the heavenly spirits!"

The disrupting man was quickly taken into custody by Perdita constables.

The couple then walked through the crowd to the street where they were met by the Carlyle carriage.

"The few invited wedding guests followed the newlyweds in separate surreys past the bejeweled gates of Madeira House for a private celebration. By all accounts, the event displayed a fanciful suggestion of Kismet," the *Bugle* reported.

The Carlyles soon resumed their cloistered life behind the walls of Madeira, where the incessant noise of saws and hammers kept time with creaking timbers and the shouts of laborers. Bricklayers, spending their pay at the Palais Royale, reported seeing Mrs. Smimes as being visibly pregnant, and in the spring, the rumors were substantiated with another announcement in *The Village Bugle* of the birth of a son, Emmet Floyd Carlyle.

A few years passed before the curious Carlyle clan was cast into the spotlight once again. Creditors to Carlyle Lumber complained to the authorities about debts unpaid, and another architect quit the Madeira House site and brought a lawsuit, claiming unpaid fees. Then loggers and flume workers at the Barnby Dun and Picaroon Jam operations went on strike demanding regular pay. Again, rumors surfaced throughout Perdita about the Carlyle Company's capital being used for the extravagant and excessive building at Madeira House.

The situation festered for ten months, and Perdita's citizens wondered if the lumber company would soon declare bankruptcy. The village of Perdita, despite negotiations by the mayor, was forced to place a lien on the Madeira House property for unpaid taxes. And then, as it had been the source for so much news of the mysterious Carlyles, *The Perdita Village Bugle* announced that the Carlyle Company's controlling interest in the Perdita Coast Railway had been sold to the Geldoff and Rostunger families. Within a few weeks, the Carlyle's creditors were paid and silenced, and the work of embellishing, demolishing, and expanding Madeira House continued.

It so happened that the Perdita Coast Railway owned large areas of land on either side of the train tracks up the coast. It was also known that the City had been running out of graveyard space and was looking to export their dearly departed. The Geldoffs and Rostungers struck a deal. Visitors to Perdita were now greeted with the solemn monotony of military headstones, Collis family crypts, and early New Calfian tombs on either side of the train when they approached Perdita. The farmland for the famed "Pogonip Artichoke" disappeared.

ঌঌ

THE ISLAND HOUSE PULSED WITH THE SOUNDS OF THE gecko and the scratching of the birds on the roof and the writhing of centipedes in the walls. Fenella bit into her toast. Daen had cut up an orange for her before he left for work, but the fruit flies were already at it. Lucinda came from her bedroom carrying Ina on a bony hip. Ina's cheeks were flushed. She'd had a constant heat rash for weeks but she'd been crying less since her first teeth had pushed through the gums like the white tips of the bamboo orchid bulbs in the backyard. Tiny whorls of hair were plastered to her head in the heat.

Lucinda shuffled across the floor and opened a cupboard. A cockroach fell out onto the counter, followed by a plastic jar of chicory that landed with a hollow base note on the floor. It kept rolling long after Lucinda's shriek, until it found the low point in the linoleum.

The family stared at the jar of chicory for a moment, and then Ina began to cry. Lucinda took her back into the bedroom and Daen left the kitchen. Fenella got out of her chair and gave the chicory jar a half-hearted push with her bare toes. She decided to go out and see if anyone was on the street.

Lord Monboddo was quiet, and so she walked on the gravel shoulder of the road, jumping back and forth over a trail of fire ants along the way. She knocked on Okalani and Kiele's front door, and their mother answered.

"The girls can't play," she said. "They're practicing ipu."

"Can I watch?" asked Fenella.

"No," she said.

Fenella walked back to the back steps of her own clapboard house and sat down on the lowest stair. She scratched her leg with the toenail of her bare foot, and then began picking off peeling bits of white paint from the step and throwing them into the grass. She could see Mrs. Onishi in her backyard, weeding a flower bed.

"Come here," Mrs. Onishi called. Fenella jumped off the steps, but approached with trepidation.

"Do you know what this is?" asked Mrs. Onishi, pointing to something with a short-trimmed nail.

"No."

"It's called a darkling beetle. See this over here? This is a monkey pod caterpillar."

Inside, the gecko squeaked a canticle from the rafters that Fenella could feel on the back of her neck. She leaned over to examine the caterpillar with hands on her bent knees. A fire ant crawled across her foot in the crabgrass.

BENNY HAD COVERED EVERY INCH OF THE WALLS AND ceilings with palm fronds. He'd arranged them in layers and used nails to attach their woody stems to the Andromeda's aging plaster in his apartment. Bits of chalky wall littered the stained brown carpet.

Benny had scoured the barrels of the Bargain Trough, a thrift store by the University, and found several tablecloths and kitchen curtains with tribal or island style prints. He'd thrown them over the sofa and hung them in the doorway between the living room and kitchen and tacked them onto the bathroom door. The fabrics let out unwashed smells of hamburger dinners and sweat.

He'd put blue and red and yellow silk handkerchiefs over all the lamps and had arranged bunches of plastic flowers, from a stall run by Gran Columbiana ladies at the drive-in flea market, into tropical groupings he placed on the tables. He used some smaller blooms to make leis, spaced on strings preschool-style with bits of plastic beverage straws he'd swiped from the Addled Egg Diner on Saceda Ave.

A vintage 45 woozed scratchy ukulele on the record player as Benny dumped "High Seas Admiral" brand rum from a plastic jug into a punch bowl. He added a six pack's worth of Punchie Quench into the bowl along with a can of pineapple bits in syrup. Fenella was impressed with his effort.

"I brought the peanuts," she said as she came through the door and surveyed the scene.

"Cool. Find a bowl in the kitchen," said Benny. "There's good rum hidden in the coffee can if you want a nice starter drink before the hoards arrive."

"Thanks," said Fenella, adjusting her breasts in her bikini top. "Do I look lame?"

"You're expecting the Ducale dude to show up, aren't you?" said Benny as he popped a pineapple chunk into his mouth.

"Where's Walter?" asked Fenella.

"In his room. Getting ready, I guess. I think he's planning some sort of entrance." Benny's tiny body gyrated some oversized hula moves in front the punch bowl table. He was dressed in a blue and white striped shirt and white short shorts so small Fenella guessed they were from the girl's section at the Bargain Trough.

"Is he still morose?"

"No, things are looking up. I'd say he's more in a truculent state. He complained all morning about my hammering the palms into the wall. I tried to get him out of the house. So much for the surprise."

Fenella pushed through the curtain adorned with masks and spears and entered the kitchen. She reached into the cupboard for an orange melamine bowl, inspected it, picked at a few mystery bits at the bottom with her fingernail, then emptied the peanuts into it. She found a lone highball glass in another cupboard and tossed in a few salty-smelling ice cubes from the freezer in. She heard a knock at the front door, then hurriedly peeled back the plastic lid of the coffee can and took out a small bottle of Sugar Island Rum and poured four full fingers. She found the dregs of some orange juice and two maraschino cherries in the fridge and stirred the cocktail with her forefinger.

As people came in, she handed them red plastic cups and filled in on changing the records when Benny bummed a smoke off someone. Every once in a while, she darted into the bathroom to fuss with her bangs in the dirty mirror, and to check her teeth, and inspect her nostrils. She gave a pained look to Benny when he asked her to get more ice from the corner store, pointing to her breasts in their orange floral bikini top, but Benny returned a look to her, and so she shrugged her shoulders, grabbed her purse from behind the couch and headed towards the door.

When she returned to the apartment, people had filled up all the standing areas. Benny had surf guitar on the record player, and only laughter could be heard distinctly above it. Fenella held two bags of dripping ice to her chest as she navigated the crowd in the living room. She made her way into the tiny empty kitchen and dumped the ice into the sink. Then she inspected her bikini top, which she found to be soaked through. Her cold nipples shot painfully from the fabric. She puffed hot breath on the ends of her fingers, and slipped them into her bra top, trying to smooth her nipples down.

There was a rustling at the kitchen doorway curtain, and Fenella removed her hands from her top and looked for something to fiddle with on the counter.

"Hey," said a voice.

She didn't move for a moment, then turned and saw Pierce in the doorway with a section of pineapple perched on the rim of his red cup.

"Oh hi…you came," she said.

"Yes. It appears that I have." There was a silence for a moment.

"Pretty frigid for the tropics, isn't it?" he said. Fenella felt the color drain from her face. She wondered if Pierce was an asshole.

"I don't do High Seas Admiral myself. Why don't you chuck that, and I'll fix you another," she said as she lifted the lid to the coffee can.

She made him a drink using the last of the Sugar Island Rum and a half a can of Punchie Quench.

"This will hurt less in the morning," she said as she handed him the drink.

"Thanks," he said. "I never caught your name."

"Fenella."

"So, Fenella. The Andromeda . . . think it will last through another earthquake?"

"Not bloody likely, but I'm up to my eyes in loan debt, so what can I do?

"So what's your excuse for inhabiting the charming Ducale?"

"I'm a student," he said.

Fenella examined his face in the light. He had olive skin and dark eyes that took her in unflinchingly.

"Oh yeah? What year?"

"Er. Post-doctoral." Pierce's eyes smiled at her from over the rim of the cup.

"Oh God! How old are you?"

"Thirty-two. Is that acceptable?"

"That depends. Got any hair growing outta your ears yet?" she asked.

"Hmmm. I haven't checked in a while. Take a peek and let me know, will ya?"

He bent down towards her. Fenella could feel his breath on her bare shoulder and could smell his freshly showered neck. She held his earlobe between her fingers as she pretended to examine him, and felt the urge to bite it.

"Other side," she said. "Hmmmm. All clear for now."

"What a relief. It's never occurred to me as something I should be searching for."

"So. God, post-doctoral work . . . what's your discipline?"

"Neuroscience. And I'm telling you the truth because I like you. I usually say that I study Autonomy or Reverse Engineering."

Fenella laughed and smoothed down the back of her hair. "A scientist. Not my forte. Just a poor artist, myself."

"Art looks like it pays as well as science research," said Pierce gesturing around the room with his red cup.

"Oh, this isn't my place. I live downstairs where everything is altogether chic." The record stopped. "Come over here with me while I change it," she said.

They went into the crowd and felt the heat of standing bodies. Someone's plastic grass skirt brushed against Fenella's shins below her pedal pushers and she slipped her foot from one of her plastic flip flops and scratched her leg with her toenail. She picked an album by the Mukoos with a cover that advertised the hit single, "Mean Sea". She put the record on and turned back towards Pierce. Benny shouted from behind the punch bowl.

"Fen! FEN! Get Walter the fuck out here already." He raised two plastic jugs of High Seas Admiral to show that they were empty. Fenella nodded.

"Hang on a sec," she said to Pierce. "I have to extract the birthday boy from his room. He's a little shy." Fenella knocked loudly on Walter's door.

"Walter! Your party's raging without you."

Fenella put her ear to the door. She turned the knob and pushed, and then found herself staring at Walter's legs which swayed in time to the reverbed Fender chords. She took in Walter's blue temples and the veins in his forehead, until Pierce rushed forward, grabbing Walter's legs to lift him up.

❧❧❧❧

The Rise of Lofferism

By Branca Agnelli

Little is known about Ewerloff during his time alone in the Pobre Claritas. Miners who came into Perdita reported seeing him from time to time, and one summer, during a forest fire, he joined a volunteer crew that burned a break around the Picaroon Lodge and downtown Barnby Dun. He made an appearance every six months at the General Store in Perdita to buy cornmeal and miner's britches, but mainly it seems that he lived as a solitary mountain man and trapper for a period of close to three years.

Then, near the summit of the Teonchee Pillar, not far from the big United Mine, he came across some glyphs on the side of a rock face. The glyphs, now known to the University of Perdita Archaeology Department as being of Liwa origin, depicted several figures of sheep, akin to the Big Horn subspecies common to the mountains. On an adjoining cliff Ewerloff found similarly carved depictions of the sun, water, a bird, and a character resembling a shark.

Some months after the discovery, Ewerloff came down from the mountains into Perdita. He carried his customary stack of pelts and bundles of smoked fish, but this time, he also carried a crude manuscript, bound in buckskin, which he held aloft in both hands as he progressed along Saceda Street.

"The Word has arrived! I have the keys to the New Word!"

He traded his skins and pelts to the typesetter at *The Perdita Village Bugle,* in exchange for the first 100 printed copies of his tome he called "*The Celestial Mandate*".

Ewerloff's "Celestial Mandate", or "C.M.", was divided into several sections, or books. The first book of *The Celestial Mandate* consisted of Ewerloff's personal account of his discovery of the Pobre Clarita Mountain glyphs.

I SAT FOR A MOMENT, RESTING TO SIP WATER FROM MY CANTEEN BESIDE A SHEER FACE OF GRANITE. PRESENTLY, AS I LOOKED ACROSS THE WIDE EXPANSE OF CREATION, I FELT A PRESENCE, AND A RUMBLING IN THE GROUND THAT GRABBED AHOLD OF MY ENTIRE PERSON. I CLUTCHED MY CANTEEN AND SATCHEL, THINKING THAT A GREAT TREMBLOR HAD STRUCK, AND THAT I WOULD SURELY BE CRUSHED BY THE ROCK ABOVE ME, BUT WHEN I OPENED MY EYES, THE SHAKING CEASED, AND BEFORE ME I BEHELD A FAIR AND DELIGHTSOME ANGEL, WHO EMITTED A BRIGHT WHITE LIGHT OF CRIPPLING INTENSITY.

I COWERED CLOSE TO THE ROCK FACE, SURE THAT I WOULD PERISH FROM THE MAGNITUDE OF SUCH INTENSE SPLENDOR. 'MY NAME IS FEE JEE,' SAID THE ANGEL. 'FEAR NOT! YOU HAVE BEEN CHOSEN FOR A MIGHTY AND WONDROUS PURPOSE.

The C.M. asserted that the Ancients had "**RECORDED THESE KEYS AND SIGNS ONTO THIS HOLY PROMONTORY**" and that the glyphs, "**LOST TO MAN SINCE ANTIQUITY**" were "**THAT WHICH MUST BE HONORED TO BRING THE GREAT HORMAZD TO HIS SECOND REIGN.**" Ewerloff recounted how Fee Jee ordered him to accept his "**DIVINE DUTY TO REVEAL THE HOLY SECRETS SO AS TO BRING ABOUT THE SECOND COMING OF THE REDEEMER.**"

The second book of the C.M. contained Ewerloff's "illumination" of the Holy Secrets. The book was broken into chapters, named after the figures Sun, Water, Bird, Sheep and Serpent.

"**SHEEP**" stated that the animals are "**GOD'S LIVING REPRESENTATIVES HERE ON THE MORTAL PLAIN, TO BE KEPT AND PROTECTED BY GOD'S PEOPLE. NEITHER SHALL THE RAM'S BLOOD BE SPILLED, NOR SHALL THEIR FLESH TOUCH THE LIPS OF MAN**."

Despite Ewerloff's reputation in Perdita as an eccentric, as well as the fantastic declarations made within *The Celestial Mandate*, the six months that followed the publication of the C.M. saw the conversion of as many as seventy-five individuals to the sect he had formed around the book. Ewerloff called the congregation the "Perdita Penultimate Christian Church", however by the first anniversary of *The Mandate*'s publication, the villagers of Perdita, in a truncated corruption of Ewerloff's name, began to refer to the group simply as the "Loffers."

The next year, with collected funds from the church's membership, Ewerloff was able to purchase a fifty-acre parcel in the Pobre Claritas, and the congregation soon moved to the site. The Loffers began living in as collectivist vegetarians. They built simple, clean redwood cabins from their timber, and constructed a central chapel with a Benitoite encrusted sun sculpture that hung above the nave. They rose before dawn, and sang together as they worked on their gardens and made only necessary trips into Perdita.

Ewerloff set about anointing several priests to who he conferred "the gift of phrenological interpretation". The "gift" allowed the priests to discover sin among the followers by conducting scalp searches for abnormalities. When sin was identified, the offending Loffer would be made to lie in the Picaroon tributary streams to cleanse themselves, often for many hours. There were reports in Perdita of Loffers dying from hypothermia in this way.

Due to the many sheep that the Loffers kept grazing on their land, the communal camp of the Loffers came to be called the Mowed Over District by the residents of Perdita. The sheep in the Loffer camp were not only regarded as holy and worshipped as such; their wool became the economic backbone of the Loffer economy. Loffer wool was of high quality, and the Loffer weavers, knitters and dyers became especially adept.

The development of the "Loffer Loom" enabled them to effectively compete with the large-scale Power Loom operations in the City, as it could create more intricate and complicated woofs and warps. Loffer-manufactured sweaters gained widespread fame and effectively became the evangelists for the community. Many of the Loffer converts had originally come to the farm to purchase wool or finished sweaters, but stayed, lulled into joining the working hands as they sang their simple hymns.

ALL IS MIGHTY IN THE SUN-LIGHT
GENTLE IS THE LOVELY AIR
WHEN THE SHEEP HAVE SET TO GRAZING
NEVER SHALL WE HAVE TO FEAR!
FOR THE WATER RUSHES O'ER OUR MOUNTAIN
AND ALL IS CLEAN AND BRI-GHT
HERE WE WORK AS HORMAZD'S CHILDREN
TO CRUSH THE SERPENT IN HIS LAIR

ONE SUNDAY, LUCINDA CALLED FENELLA.

"Hi, Hon. How are you?"

"Okay."

"And how's the job going?"

"A little weird. But I've got rent sorted, so that's good."

"That is a good thing. Self-sufficiency is very satisfying . . . sooooo. I don't know what you've got going on today. It's been a while since you've been here. How about after we go to church, I come down there and pick you up for dinner. You can bring your laundry with you."

"Um. Yeah. Okay. So, what time do you think?"

"Oh. Two, I guess. The last of the asparagus is in and the first of the artichokes. I thought I'd make some pasta."

"Sounds good, Mom."

Fenella hung up the phone, left her apartment, and climbed the stairs to apartment 2C where she let herself in. Benny was laying on the couch. He wore black pants and a black shirt with a silk-screened neon green question mark on it. Palm fronds had come unfastened from the ceiling and littered the floor.

"You working at Mystery Manor today?" asked Fenella.

"Yup. Me and this bottle of Adderall will be serving lemonade to tourists all day," said Benny who kept his eyes closed as he patted the bulge that rattled in his pants pocket.

"You heard from Walter's parents?"

"Briefly. He's in a lockdown place in the City. He'll be there for God knows how long. They said they'd pay his rent here until he gets out, and they're going to put him on a leave of absence from the master's program."

"And no word on how he's doing…"

"No."

"If you need help taking down all these fronds…"

"I don't care about them, Fen."

Fenella let herself out and went back into her apartment. She found an issue of *Splice*, an art and music quarterly where her old pal Marvin had found a job as a contributing writer. She took the magazine to the ledge by the koi fish and rolled pieces of gravel around the concrete with her toes as she read an article about the history of Cabaret Voltaire. Then she watered the courtyard and went inside and brushed her hair and put on a clean white shirt. She put new band-aids on the blisters on her heels, then slipped into some shoes before returning to the courtyard to wait until Lucinda came clanging through the Andromeda's gate.

Fenella tossed her laundry bag into the back of the pickup truck and then climbed into the cab. She and Lucinda drove down Seahorse Road until they reached Saceda Avenue which followed the Picaroon away from the sea and into the mountains.

"They've really done a nice job with that octopus on top of the coaster," said Lucinda. Fenella looked at Lucinda's hands on the steering wheel and noticed how thin they had become. Raised blue veins stretched weblike over the top of them.

"I heard they're really promoting the remodel too," Lucinda continued. "TV and radio in the City. Should mean extra business at the stand this summer."

"That's good," said Fenella.

"I got a letter from your sister yesterday."

"What'd she say?" said Fenella as she closed the air vent on her side.

"Well, all of Gran Columbiana is having a very hard time you know. Not that those people had much to begin with. So Ina's seeing some very tough things. The people she is able to reach are responding really well. It's awful when a family has so little and the father drinks up what is left. Lofferism, despite your objections Fen, does teach people to act responsibly. Hard work. Self-sufficiency. Community."

"I'll give it that," said Fenella.

The truck lurched as it moved into a lower gear near the top of Ice Cream Hill.

"Crap," said Fenella as they passed Mystery Manor. "I should have asked if Benny needed a ride to work. Too late now."

"The boy with the roommate in the hospital? Awful," said Lucinda.

Fenella and Lucinda said little else as they traveled through the mountains. The trees closed gradually overhead, tightening their hold on the road. Fenella checked her wispy hair in the flecked side mirror, rubbed plaque off the front of her teeth. As they pulled into the Lundgren turnout, the cicada-like buzz of Daen's chainsaw could be heard. Lucinda shut off the truck and Fenella hopped out and slung her laundry bag over her shoulder.

Daen wore plastic protective goggles. He pursed his lips and grimaced as he worked the chainsaw amidst a cloud of red dust. A bear grasping a salmon was beginning to emerge from the redwood. When Daen saw Fenella, he shut off the saw, and blew his nose into a tissue taken from his back pocket.

"Gearing up for the season, huh?" said Fenella.

"Yup. We need a good one," said Daen, walking towards her. "I need to get over to your place and check out the new stuff they've done to the coaster."

"The octopus is huge," said Fenella, nodding.

Lucinda, Daen, and Fenella walked along the agapanthus-lined path from back of the stand that led to the shingled house. They reached the front steps and Daen kicked off his heavy boots. They went back into the kitchen and Lucinda took Fenella's laundry bag from her, while Daen washed up.

"I'll get this started for you. I've got some snickerdoodles for you in the deep freeze down there too," said Lucinda.

When Lucinda's footsteps down the basement stairs quieted, Fenella turned towards Daen who was seated at the kitchen table, examining his hands.

"She's really gotten into this cookie thing," said Fenella.

"Yup. Nonna Agnelli's about up to her eyeballs in them. She's too nice to say no."

"She should fill them with arsenic and bring them over to the Sweeney's," said Fenella. Daen smiled.

"We'll sell the cookies at the stand this season. It gives her something to do besides stained glass. You know, there's lead in that solder. Can't be good for her. She's forgetting things."

"Yeah. She should probably not be doing that," said Fenella.

"And how's the job going, Missy?"

"Oh. You know, weird rich people and their weird problems. I'm still figuring it all out."

"I'm glad you were finally able to find something, pay rent on your own. Your mother and I wondered how you'd be able to pay off those loans with an art degree. You ever wish you'd listened to Dad and gone to the technical school? There's good security in medical billing I hear," said Daen picking a toothpick from a small jar and placing it in his mouth.

"No, Dad. I have not wished that."

Daen got up and turned on an oscillating fan on the counter by the back door. The air lifted tufts of his hair, revealing the thinning spots on his head.

"I'd stick with the steady job for a while kiddo," said Daen leaning against the kitchen counter, crossing one of his long legs over the other. "I bet there's some opportunity there. Remember, hard work will pull you through about every time. I don't know what kind of people they are, but I bet they respect diligence. Keep your nose clean and your head down, and you'll pull through alright." He turned the toothpick around in his mouth, then took it between two fingers.

"It must be nice to have that kind of confidence," said Fenella looking at the creases next to her father's eyes.

"Confidence? Barely making the mortgage. Time you knew it. We'll be renting both your room and your sister's. Thought you should hear it from me first."

"Only fair," said Fenella. She kicked at the linoleum. "I'll help if I can, Dad."

"You worry about yourself, especially those loans of yours. You happy, Fen?"

"I don't even think I know what that means," said Fenella.

Daen lowered his voice. "You know in your heart why you feel lost. Fen, if the Church is wrong, I mean, what do you have to lose? You'd have led a good decent life that would have saved you from sorrow. When have I ever steered you wrong Fen?"

"I'd rather be tormented than accept a lie, Dad. And I never said I was tormented."

Lucinda's footsteps echoed on the basement stairs. Fenella got the milk out of the fridge and poured herself a glass.

FENELLA AND PUELE RARELY SPOKE. PUELE WAS A NATIVE Islander. She hid her emotions from Daen and the children with a studied indifference. She deftly swept the dust from the corners and shushed the gecko so that Ina could sleep. She sprinkled cinnamon and hand soap shavings on the trails of ants.

After arriving in the morning, Puele would tie back the front window curtains into great bulking knots. When the breeze filled the front room, she'd get Ina out of bed, feed her in the kitchen, then take off her diaper and let her crawl around on the back grass naked. Before Puele, neither curtain tying or outdoor nakedness had occurred to Fenella as even being possible.

Puele had very few rules. She forbade Fenella from climbing the poles that held the clothesline, and she warned her against plucking the flowers off Mrs. Onishi's tree. Her silence on most other things granted Fenella autonomy. Fenella returned the favor by giving Puele the same wide berth she gave to the centipedes.

Fenella developed her own daily routine. After Daen had left for work, and Puele and Ina had gone into the backyard, she'd crack the door to her parents' room, and hold her breath while peering into the darkness. Then she'd wander inside, arms outstretched, feeling her way towards the bed, smelling Lucinda's closeness. When she found the comforter with her fingertips, she would grasp the folds with both hands and search with her toe for the box spring she would use as a foothold to climb. Fenella would lie with Lucinda in the bed quietly, feeling Lucinda's chest rise and fall. Sometimes she would suck her thumb. Lucinda had stopped telling her not to.

When she got hungry, Fenella would leave Lucinda's bedroom and go barefoot to the yard to see if any bananas had ripened. If there were none, she'd go back inside and drag a chair from the kitchen table to the counter, scramble up, and pull bread, cinnamon, and sugar down. She'd place the bread in the toaster, then climb down and push the chair over to get butter out of the refrigerator.

She'd eat her cinnamon toast on the back steps, while watching Puele and Ina on the lawn, and after she'd finished, she'd watch the ants that formed on the steps around the toast crumbs and sugar crystals as they carried bits off to cracks in the concrete.

After eating, Fenella would go out to the street to see if Okalani and Kiele were playing, but she no longer knocked on their door.

Once, when Fenella was playing jump rope on the street with five or six other girls, their mother had come outside, smacking the dust from a cream-colored sole, and called out "Punchie Quench!"

The other girls ran into the house, grabbing cups. Fenella tried to follow, but as she put a bruised toe on the grooved and splintered threshold, she was met by the mother's open palm.

"You can drink from the hose," she'd said to Fenella.

Now, after breakfast, if Okalani and Kiele weren't playing on the street, Fenella would often spend a while examining the wound on her big toe as she stubbed it every few days running barefoot on the concrete out back. Then she'd travel through the back yard, picking up rocks and comparing the insects she surprised underneath. She still liked to pick plumeria blossoms off Mrs. Onishi's tree. She'd rub the petals on the insides of her wrists, and behind her knees like she saw Kiele do once, and then she'd squish the stems between her fingernails. After a while, she would return to the banana tree, where her candy-colored plastic tricycle was parked.

Fenella had wanted a Hefty Spin tricycle for her birthday. Lucinda found one at a garage sale. The plastic streamers on the right-side handle were thinner than the left, and the front wheel's tread had been worn down. Fenella would turn the hollow plastic Hefty Spin upside-down on the concrete and then pump the pink pedals with her hands, calling out,

"Ice Cream! Ice Cream!"

Then, she might relocate a beetle with a stick and place it on one of the pedals, slowly turning them again, chanting, "Ferris Wheel! Ferris Wheel!"

By this time, it would be getting hot, and Puele would take Ina inside. Fenella often followed them, spending time looking at pictures in Daen's encyclopedia, listening to the slow tock-tock of Ina's swing, the dull scratches of birds landing on the roof, and the longing warbles of the gecko.

FENELLA SOON LEARNED THAT A LARGE PORTION OF HER job involved wiring funds; to the horse stables, to foundations like the Hurt Diminishment Society, the Friends of the Madeira House Garden

Club, and the Foundation for the Orphans of Iulia. Often, there was not the tens of thousands of dollars required to do so in Nina's bank account. "Borrow from the margin," was always the reply, which Fenella discovered was akin to having a credit card if you had a lot of stocks.

"The bankers called. They said we're at the margin limit."

Fenella had just entered Nina's bedroom. The decor was based on the Versailles the Hall of Mirrors, except that television screens appeared from behind the mirrors when turned on and could be viewed from Thurl and Nina's merengue-like bed. One television played a gem shopping channel, another romance movies, the third; cartoons. Lokum sat beside her on the bed licking the upturned lid from a pint of chocolate ice cream. The empty pint had been turned into an ashtray.

"What do you mean?" said Nina. "Well ask Thurl then! Tell him we need the money for Lexi's party. Do his office paperwork for him, help him take care of his fish. That will make him happy. I need to wire funds to the vet at the stable right away."

Fenella arrived at Thurl's office like a supplicant, with Nina's bank statement in hand.

"The German Expressionist film is coming along very nicely," she said to him. Spittle collected at the corner of his mouth as he perused the document.

"Very well. I'll have my bankers take care of it. But let's have the film by the end of the month."

Fenella's carefully sorted piles in Nina's office were scattered each night, and every morning, Fenella began the Sisyphean task of reordering documents-by-date into the manila folders that lay slack-jawed on the partially revealed Tibetan rugs.

Fenella was on the floor putting back together Lexi's school folder when a woman entered. She was so small that she looked as though she had been pinched from all directions. She had thighs as wide as a man's upper arm, clockwork-like ankles and wrists, a chin like a pinball. Designer brocade darted under her child-sized bottom like a neatly wrapped gift of stationery. She seemed devoured by the occasional chairs around the room. She had a stiffly coiffed pixie cut that reflected the light from the Picaroon off of its ashy hues.

"Aren't you cute," said the woman as a way of greeting. "Muffin," she said extending her hand, and a pile of gold bangles rushed from her elbow to her wrist and threatened to crash onto Fenella's forehead. Muffin stopped them at the last millisecond with a cock of her thumb. Fenella stood up and took Muffin's hand and stood, feeling large, feeling sweaty. "Nina says you're going to be my little helper for Lexi's party, yes? Here's the theme. Lexi wants to do Asian."

"Asian what?" asked Fenella.

"For a theme."

"Like the continent."

"Yes, for the party."

"Not just a cuisine."

"No."

"Oh."

"I've hired some acrobats already," said Muffin.

"Asian acrobats."

"You know it."

"Are we talking Chinese or Korean acrobats?"

"What do you mean?"

Fenella thought about what she might have to do going forward working for Nina. Ethically questionable was beginning to seem like an understatement. She thought about the empty jar on her kitchen windowsill, where she kept spare coins for her electricity, and the overdraft notices from 1st Concepción Bank. How each thirty dollars felt like a wound that she could not heal from. She thought about Lucinda's drawer in Barnby Dun when she had found the cruddy knife to take home, and how the drawer had been stuffed with coupons for five cents off soup, thirty cents off taco seasoning. And she thought about Benny drinking High Seas Admiral to deal with Walter's hospitalization, and then these people and their dumb party seemed like the thing to cheer Benny up. It was just another ridiculous way to make a dollar, like Benny's job at Mystery Manor. Still, she pictured her old Professor Charles, with raised hog's back eyebrows, viewing her with a mix of amusement and disdain.

Fenella looked at Muffin in her pearl earrings and ballet flats and sat back on the top of Nina's desk and said, "You want me to order some Chinese lanterns?"

"Aren't you sweet," said Muffin. "After we build the pagoda, we'll need lots of lanterns."

FENELLA HADN'T HEARD FROM BENNY IN A FEW DAYS. Lexi's party and the planning for Thurl's set overwhelmed her. She'd been coming home, dropping quarters in the electricity box, taking a bath, then eating a cold sandwich while standing over the kitchen sink, catching glimpses of her pathetic reflection in the window.

When Benny did call, she was relieved. The Andromeda courtyard needed watering and weeding, but she didn't feel like it, and attending to Benny eased her conscience.

"Hey, put a sweater on. I need you to help me with something," he said.

"Your voice sounds hoarse."

"Yeah. I'm not feeling so good. I'll be down in two secs."

Fenella answered the door, and Benny stood unshaven and bleary eyed. He held a small grey plastic box in his hands.

"What's that?" she asked.

"A mouse."

"Okaaaay."

"It's a humane trap. I caught it in our apartment."

"I'm still listening."

"So, like, where would you go to . . . ?" Benny paused and scratched his face, ". . . let it go?"

"Oh Benny . . . okay, let's walk." Fenella grabbed her purse, and then Benny followed her through the courtyard and out the gates of the Andromeda.

"I gotta stop at the bank on the way back and get a roll of quarters for the electrics. I've called in sick the last two days so I don't have any tip money, and it feels wrong to raid Walter's change drawer while he's gone," he said.

"What's wrong with you?" she asked.

"A cold I think."

"Too much stress over Walter and too many pills and cigs and booze I'm guessing."

"Maybe."

They walked down Seahorse Road. towards Saceda Avenue. The fog was rolling closer and Benny cradled the grey box in both his hands and stopped talking. Occasionally he coughed into the sleeve of his sweatshirt. They made their way through a crowd on the sidewalk smoking cigarettes outside the Palais Royale, and crossed to the smaller streets lined with chestnuts as the streetlights blinked on, casting them in sodium yellow. Fenella stopped in front of the Perdita Library.

"They'll be safe in the ice plant I'm guessing," said Fenella. "Plus, the librarians eat their lunches on the front steps there sometimes. I used to see Walter and his buddies put unfinished sandwiches into that garbage can there all the time. And Branca…"

"Mice don't eat books, do they? I mean, you don't think they'll be able to get inside there?"

"Benny, jeeesuhs! What do you want?"

Benny didn't meet her eyes or her question. He coughed again into his sleeve, then took a few steps into the ice plant. The plant made crunching noises under his Converse like the sounds of small bones. He knelt down and opened the door to the grey box, and after a while a brown mouse ventured out, blinking and reaching on its haunches unsteadily. It didn't run into the foliage as Fenella had expected, but turned and stared back at them with a moist twitching nose and wide eyes.

"Here, this oughta get you situated," Benny said, and he pulled a handful of oyster crackers from his sweatshirt pocket and set them in the ice plant. The mouse sniffed the crackers warily.

"C'mon," said Fenella. "The bank's closing soon."

The Loffer Matter
By Branca Agnelli

Ernst Schleswig was a professor of comparative philology at The University of Perdita at the time when Olaf Ewerloff's *Celestial Mandate* was published. Schleswig's newly completed paper had just been read to the University's faculty. It was entitled, "The Upsurge in Spiritualism: New Zoroastrianism and the Barouche Café, A Case Study". It had been received enthusiastically.

After reading *The Mandate*, Schleswig sent an undergrad with a letter to Ewerloff requesting an introduction. He was especially interested in the newly purchased farm by the Loffers in the Pobre Claritas. The boy returned to Schleswig's office one month later, dirty, with a prominent gray hair that sprang wiry and conspicuous among the darker hair of his twenty-year-old head. He refused to speak, but placed a Liwa arrowhead on Schleswig's desk, and went immediately to the registrar's to withdraw from his courses.

Schleswig put the word out on Saceda Street that a reward was to be offered should he be notified the next time Ewerloff came to town. He didn't have to wait long. Within the week, Ewerloff began preaching and holding a copy of *The Mandate* aloft in front of the Palais Royale. Schleswig convinced Ewerloff to come to his office for an interview. After dinner together, Schleswig offered to have Ewerloff stay with him at his home, and he interviewed him extensively for the better part of two weeks.

In the spring, Schleswig presented a paper on the subject of *The Mandate* at the annual Philology Colloquium in the City attended by his colleagues from around the world. Schleswig's presentation had been billed as a highlight of the event, as *The City Times* had recently run a series called "*The Loffer Matter*", and *The Mandate* had gained a wide exposure.

"There has been a long history of competing translations of the Scriptures," began Schleswig, "including, but not limited to large discrepancies between the Masoretic, Septuagint, Hebrew, Greek and English texts. The enduring altercation regarding the rejection of John, for example, stretches back to the Alogi who attributed the words to the Gnostic heretic Cerinthus. There has even been prior argument as to the correct translation of "the Lamb of God", as some scholars have maintained that while the literal translation of the Aramaic "talya" is "lamb", it commonly meant "male child" at the time it was written. Additionally, the Aramaic for "ram; being "d'kar", can mean "male" as well. Also, there is the inherent difficulty in translating the simultaneously independent and inseparable Hebrew preposition "min", meaning "from" or "out of", though certainly it cannot be construed as "is". The idea of "God is the Lamb" is reminiscent of several competing theories throughout Christianity of the anthropomorphic vs. symbolic Agnus Dei. We find a continuance of this line of thought within the Loffer community.

The Celestial Mandate aside, in regards to the assertion by Ewerloff that the Bible promotes vegetarianism; there is ample evidence throughout the Good Book, especially within the Pentateuch, for animal sacrifice. That a retranslation of the texts could lead to such a thing as vegetarianism is wholly unfounded, though it is interesting to note that there exists a Hebraic tradition of vegetable words having wide symbolic meaning. "Carrots", for example, is "gezer", in Hebrew and resembles the Hebrew word "gezerah" or "decree". The word "kra", Aramaic for "squash", has been linked to the Hebrew "to tear". "Kartie", Aramaic for leek is related to the Hebrew word, "koret", meaning to "cut off", as well as "khareit", meaning "to decimate". All are examples in favor of Ewerloff's assertion that in the Ancient World the scope of common vegetables did indeed have a far reach.

Furthermore, while there is no support whatsoever to Ewerloff's linkage of the word "d'kar" to that of ramps or wild leeks, it does recall certain historical instances of the lamb being combined with flora. The "Scythian Lamb" or "Vegetable Lamb of Tartary" is only one such example. Another ancillary fact worth noting: when the Children of Israel left Egypt, leeks happened to be one of the foods mentioned as being sorely missed.

Notwithstanding, and most importantly, after interviewing Mr. Ewerloff in great detail, a crude transliteration on the part of Mr. Ewerloff of "ram" to "ramps" is most probable explanation for his *Celestial Mandate* assertions, as I find him to be not only completely unschooled in any language, but rather lacking in cognitive ability. My conclusion, therefore, is that while Mr. Ewerloff's manuscript is briefly amusing, the thought that he could offer any new insights into the Holy Book beyond that of heresy is simply nothing short of preposterous."

The day after Mr. Schleswig's remarks at the conference, the following headline ran in *The Perdita Village Bugle*:

"U of P Prof. Backs Loffer's Barn Yard Deity"

The subsequent opinion piece railed against Schleswig's paper, which had the audacity to discuss the existence of multiple and less than literal translations of Scripture. The population of Perdita was enraged, and the controversy was fueled when, at a town hall meeting called to discuss concerns the burgeoning community in the mountains and its involvement with the dark arts, Mayor Horseley referred to Schleswig as a "Loffer apologist". As the sententious Mayor Horseley also served on the University's Board of Trustees, he had little trouble convincing the other members that using taxpayer funds to support such a character as Schleswig was tantamount to "administering kisses on the very mouth of Mephistopheles". Mayor Horseley's views were met with success. The University declined to offer Schleswig tenure, and his reputation was irreparably damaged. Horseley won reelection to the mayorship in the fall.

The Loffer community, in the subsequent years following Schleswig's exegesis, thrived. Ewerloff rapidly evolved the belief system of the Loffers through a series of reported "dream-visions" where the angel Fee Jee visited and instructed him. He expanded the newly emphasized "Bird" and "Water" chapters of *The Mandate*. Flight gained an ascendancy in the Loffer cosmology. The new sections of *The Mandate* instructed the Loffers to build "heavenly wings, such as that of the Spiritual Dove", which they were to use to "find and destroy the Great Beast of the Sea"; enabling "the Day to end all Days". This resulted in the Loffers clearcutting their land in an all-out effort to build wooden flying prototypes that Ewerloff promised would one day be used as reconnaissance vehicles over the ocean.

During this time the Loffer community also gained a high-status convert in Peony Rostunger, who had been married to Ormand Rostunger, of Rostunger Shipping, for close to five years. Peony contributed a large amount of funds to the church that they used to build a large temple called the "Holy Corral". She also organized a proselytizing trip to the Islands, and a number of Loffers were able to secure free transport aboard one of the Rostunger's ships. The trip was to be a mixed blessing for the Loffers, as it led to many converts on the Islands, but also the sudden death of Peony as a result of an allergic reaction to the sting of a *Vespula glassinae* wasp, common to that area.

Ormand Rostunger was beset by grief and enraged at himself for indulging his wife by allowing her to participate in such a fatuous pastime as religion. He attacked the community by paying *The Perdita Village Bugle* to run a series of stories alleging widespread bestiality in the Loffer compound. The Loffers were then forced to pay ruinous sums in a legal effort to defend themselves against the accusations. To further complicate matters, as the Loffer sheep were enabled to live out their lives free from the threat of slaughter or sale, the population of the herd grew to surfeit, and the Loffers required additional land to graze. Mayor Horseley affected a halt on Loffer real estate purchases, and the Loffers suffered enormous losses to their stock as a result of starvation, which also ultimately decimated their sweater production abilities.

Ewerloff became highly agitated over the crisis in the Mowed Over District and began to call for increased efforts to locate the "Great Beast of the Sea" in order to bring about the "Day to End all Days" before the community was bankrupted. The increased flying machine production only had the effect of straining the Loffer resources further.

After a series of desertions by Loffer priests, Ewerloff staged a great demonstration in an effort to maintain power. He announced that he had a vision in which the Great Lamb revealed to him the proper building specifications for the flying vehicles. He built a wooden machine accordingly, and on the following Grazing Day he led the Loffers down to the White Cliffs of Perdita, strapped on two large wooden wings, and after a lengthy scalp searching by the remaining priests, leapt off the cliff where he promptly crashed in the sea and died.

As it turned out, Ewerloff's final act was favorable for the preservation of the Loffer religion. His martyrdom consolidated the community, and allowed power to pass to the much more phlegmatic Horace Almond, a phrenological priest who became the new "Head-Butter". Horace enacted a "Decree of Reconstructive Diaspora", allowing the Loffers to cease living communally and to find outside work. He also found a buyer for the ruined Mowed Over District property in the newly formed Judgement Day Libation Deliverance Commission. The sale of the land stabilized the church financially and was integral to their eventual success.

WHEN THURL LEFT HIS STUDY IN THE AQUARIUM INSIDE the East Wing of the Sugar Factory, Fenella looked back at the coelacanth in the tank, its black maw seeming as though it could suck all the furniture and the glass-eyed heads and the crow and Fenella into itself. Lucretia shrieked again and Fenella heard clopping sounds as if someone were dropping walnuts along the cement floors leading to the study, and then the carved wooden door reopened and a pair of animals entered. They looked like very small deer, closer in size to Nina's cat Lokum than to the dog Ashur. But they moved daintily, up on tiny quick legs and hooves, appraising Fenella with cartoonishly large black eyes and oversized rabbit-like ears with conical tufts of fur between them.

Then the deer creatures parted and a very small boy entered the room. He was barefoot and naked except for a basket over his shoulder and a loincloth. The diameter of his eyes seemed relative to that of the deer. His white skin was luminous. He looked at Fenella briefly, then bowed his head and silently stepped towards Lucretia's iron cage. Reaching into the basket, he proffered a few pieces of cheese that the crow snapped from his fingers. Then the boy held out his hand and presented several bits of meat which the bird met with another rapturous caw and machine-precision darts of her beak.

The child approached and Fenella put hand to her neck.

"Me name Vaclav," said the boy.

"Hello, Vaclav." The boy ate a spear of asparagus. "Aren't you cold?" asked Fenella.

"I like," he said. "Warm here. Always cold before."

"Oh. Do you . . . live here?"

"Yes." He gestured towards the deer. "This called dik-diks. Thurl gave. This Dusan." He reached into the basket and held a spear of white asparagus. The dik-dik ate from his hand. "And this Kasimir."

"They're incredible," said Fenella. "And so cute." She reached out her hand hoping they would approach. "So, who are your parents?"

"Thurl is guardian," said Vaclav.

Fenella walked towards the desk and put her hands on the leather blotter.

"Why haven't I met you before Vaclav? Have you been at school?"

He motioned for Fenella to follow him. They left Thurl's study with Dusan and Kasimir's hooves snapping on the cement like rubber bands. She followed him back into the large room with the staircase and Fenella once again took in the expanse of the vaulted Aquarium.

Vaclav pointed to the raised beds.

"I grow here," he said brushing his fingers in a circle on the soil. "Asparagus. They like," he said pointing towards the dik-diks.

He went to the side of the large fireplace and turned a brass key in the wall. The fireplace flared to life and the flames warmed the air above Fenella's head. From underneath the stairs, Vaclav pulled several piles of thick blankets and cushions. He dragged them across the floor and set them down in front of the fire. The dik-diks knelt on the folds, their eyes closing as the warmth and light of the fire spread across their espresso-sized haunches.

Vaclav seated himself and patted a cushion nearby. Fenella lowered herself onto one. Vaclav rifled through the blankets until he retrieved a notebook with a pen stored in the metal-spiraled binding.

"The woman. In cold place. She show letters. Now Thurl show letters," he said opening the notebook offering his handwriting to Fenella to inspect.

"You're not in school."

"I like here. Come, see."

He held her hand and led her to the small door next to the fireplace and pushed it open. Fenella stooped beneath the iron stairs and entered the simple windowless kitchen beyond. Vaclav opened a mini fridge. He gently touched the milk, the eggs, the lettuce, the bread, the bananas, the cheese, the brown-papered steak. Then he opened a cupboard and presented rice, cereal, and a plastic tub of almonds.

"You can see?" he asked.

"No. I…VaHclove. Vahclav. Are you allowed to leave? To go outside? What I'm asking about is Thurl. Does he stop you from leaving? Do you see anyone else, like ever? Does he hurt you?" She lowered her eyes to his loincloth. Her mind traced the distance to the Aquarium's door, the camera, Thurl's size.

"I like here. I happy. Dusan, Kasimir and Thurl here. Thurl show me letters. I read. Come here, you can see."

Vaclav took Fenella by the hand again. They left the dik-diks by the fire and reentered Thurl's study and passed the coelacanth and Lucretia's cage and then exited through a door on the opposite side of the room.

A sound stage opened before them. Above hung stage lights from trusses. Two blue spotlights guided them onto a set. A row of ornate columns were placed in front of a multi-storied wall with clerestory windows. A segmented brass telescope protruded from the upper story window. A painted backdrop of a city populated by smokestacks was propped to the side and a structure of a metal-riveted rocket ship stood next to a compact-sedan-sized, painted-foam moon carved with a smiling face.

"A Trip to the Moon," said Fenella. "Mèliés."

"Yes," said Vaclav. "Me and Thurl. We build. He let Vaclav be," Vaclav held up a velvet wizard's hat and robe.

"Come," he said. He switched on a few more lights and the yellows turned the blues to daytime. He took her through a maze of tools, lumber, saws and paint cans. They paused at a table with a sewing machine and bolts of cloth placed beside.

"I can," said Vaclav touching the machine as they walked on.

At the far end of the stage was a black portable structure with windows, elevated off the floor with two-by-fours and accessible by a few industrial steps.

Inside Vaclav turned on more lights to reveal an equipment and control room. Cameras, power cords, ladders, and lights were piled haphazardly along one large wall, while a bank of Beta decks, switching panels, and monitors lined the other.

Vaclav reached over into the library shelf of D2 tapes and pulled out one labeled "The Alhambra" and put it into the deck. An establishing shot of the actual Alhambra in Granada appeared on the control room monitors in grainy black and white, followed by a series of shots of fountains and roaring water with the water soundtrack bumped up prominently. Then within the film, Vaclav appeared in front of a small palm tree as a tiny, robed, Moorish prince and recited:

If I could be any of the things that this world that moved
I would be a rat and come chewing up on you
And if when you're with me things come a bit unglued
Well, you know what happens when it bends and skews
And all of the blue scorpions lose their sting
And petite-fours lose their filling
And all the bones are calling after you
And all the tiger teeth are there for you
And all the blackened paisleys are a ruse.

"I'm guessing Thurl wrote the words?" asked Fenella with her eyebrows raised. Vaclav nodded.

"He said lullaby, nursery rhyme." Vaclav pressed his hands together and made a pillow, and rocked them back and forth under his ear.

"Clearly," said Fenella.

Vaclav ejected the "Alhambra" tape and put in another labeled "Maharajah" in black Sharpie.

"It's almost like our rich boss identifies with monarchies and hierarchical societies. How droll."

An establishing shot of Mysore Palace appeared. Blurry shots of flowers, blinking white Christmas lights, then Vaclav, seated in a throne, dressed in regal finery.

"I see that Thurl has a formula for his scripts," said Fenella. Vaclav, on camera, began his recitations once again.

If I could be any of the things that you do right
I would tumble round with you and be your faithful bike
And if the last time gutter boys screamed at you at night
Well, the sun always hides from my sight
And all the dirt and all the crumbs for you
All the scratching ants are after you
Doorbells filled with whiskey dear for you
And three-hearted octopi for you
Lapis lazuli shoes and rings for you
And bass bouncing downtown dear all for you…

Vaclav pressed stop. He went to reach for the tape marked "Aztec" but Fenella stopped him.

"This one says 'Lumiere—like Man Bathes in Sea". You have a Lumiere set?" Fenella asked. Vaclav nodded. "Amazing. Can you take me there?"

❧❧❧❧

Kiele and Okalani were jumping rope in the street.

"You want to play Church at my house?" Fenella asked them. "We have a lot of bread. We can use thimbles for the water."

"Okay," said they said.

The girls went into the Lundgren's kitchen. Puele was in the backyard with Ina. Fenella got a cookie sheet, a bag of white bread, and tore the bread into pieces and dropped them onto the sheet. Then she went down the hallway and opened the door to her parents' room. It was dark and she could hear Lucinda's soft breathing. A breast pump lay sideways near the bedside table.

Fenella slid open the closet door and behind a pair of rain boots that Lucinda had worn regularly in Barnby Dun, was a sewing basket. Fenella uprooted three large thimbles from fabric folds, then held her breath as she crept noiselessly into the hallway.

"Oh Mighty Father," recited Fenella in her room as she waved her hands over the torn bits of bread, "winged Ziz, we eat this as your Son the Lamb eats of the grass upon the mountain. We pluck the ramps from between the rocks, and we remember you, oh Father, until the day that we ascend."

"You know the whole thing?" asked Kiele. "Only my dad knows the whole thing."

"Shhh," hissed Fenella, putting her finger to her lips.

Fenella stood up and carried the tray across the room to the girls who were seated on the rug. Kiele and Okalani picked a single piece of bread each and put it in their mouths, chewing slowly with arms folded. Fenella ate a piece then walked ceremoniously back to the other side of the room, near the window. She placed the cookie sheet next to her dollhouse, then grabbed an orange plastic pitcher with both hands, and attempted to pour water into the three thimbles.

The water spilled fast between Fenella's toes on the carpet. Fenella took a stuffed plush alligator from her bed and placed it onto the green carpeting, stepping on the alligator's long body, soaking the water into its tail. The alligator's black button eyes bulged as she stepped on him.

"Oh Mighty Father of the Ether. We drink this water and remember that while it nourishes the Ram, it hides the Great Destroyer. We know, dear Lord, that your eyes can penetrate the depths of the sea, and that the blood of our fathers will not be in vain. We know that you will nourish and strengthen us, so that we may return to you, triumphant."

Fenella opened her eyes. Kiele was playing with a rag doll, moving its arms up and down, while singing indistinguishable words.

"You're not paying attention," said Fenella.

"I think we have to go home for lunch," said Okalani.

"Wait, but…I thought we were going to play jacks. Plus, do you hear that?" asked Fenella.

"Hear what?" asked Kiele. Fenella tilted her head towards the window.

"The winds. I think a hurricane is coming."

"Oooooh, I hear something," said Okalani.

"Well, we better get ready for the storm," said Fenella. Kiele shouted as she jumped to her feet.

"Yeah! Let's get ready!"

"Well," said Fenella, twirling a lock of her hair, "We have to make sure that the winds don't blow the door in."

"Yeah."

"So, I'll lock the door, and then we'll pile up all the toys, to keep the wind from getting in."

"Yes. Keep the wind out." Fenella pushed the button lock on the doorknob.

"Help me move the dollhouse," she said. "Then we'll move the bed."

The girls pushed the bed along the carpeting with their backs and stick-like thighs. Insecticide from the pots around the bedposts spilled with each push and filled the room with a smell that made Fenella's head feel light.

"Now we've got to weigh the bed down," said Fenella.

They put a bag of jacks and the wet alligator and Dolly the spoon, and Fenella's piggy bank, and her crocheted wall hanging of a sheep and all of her clothes from her dresser on top of the bed.

"Fenella!" called a muffled Puele from the other side of the door. "Fenella! Kiele and Okalani's mom wants them home."

"They can't leave until the storm is over," called Fenella through cupped hands, then quietly to the girls she said,

"It's going to get really cold when the winds come."

She went to the closet and pulled down the comforter she had used on her bed in Barnby Dun.

"I think we should all get under here."

"Fenella!" called Puele. The doorknob made repeated small clicks. From the living room, the gecko chirped.

"Open it! They have to go," pounded Puele. There was a swift kick to the bottom of the door.

"I don't know how to unlock it!" shouted Fenella, spreading the blanket on the floor. "I can't do it!" then, quietly, "We have to hide from the big storm." Fenella heard Lucinda's voice in the hallway.

"What's going on? . . . Fen! . . . Fen! Unlock this door!"

"Fenella, we have to go home," said Kiele.

"Not until the hurricane goes away. It's much too dangerous. Don't you hear the wind? The rain has started too. You'd better get under here with me. Sometimes the wind can take the rooves off houses, you know."

There were several more kicks to the door. It rattled and shook in its frame. Then the hallway became quiet. The girls looked at Fenella and then each other, and then Kiele said,

"Our mom told us that people like you brought the fruit flies."

Fenella pulled the comforter over her head and stayed there, breathing in the dark until she heard a metallic scrape from the window. She peeked from under the comforter. Mrs. Onishi's hand slid the window open. In her other hand she held a screwdriver.

"That's how you open the windows from outside. All the neighborhood windows are like this," said Mrs. Onishi. Lucinda bounced a crying Ina in the yard behind Mrs. Onishi and Puele.

"Unbelievable Fen. Look at this place," said Lucinda.

Puele hoisted herself onto the windowsill, put one foot inside, and then jumped into the room. She picked up the dollhouse and set it aside angrily, and then pushed the bed away from the door. Kiele and Okalani followed Puele out of the room.

HAVING RECEIVED THEIR COFFEES IN TALL GLASS MUGS and situated themselves within an alcove of the Ferula Coffee House, Pierce and Fenella sat stooped with backs pressed against the hard wooden splats of their chairs, Pierce examining the faded finish of the table, Fenella the bits of brown and white floral wallpaper that had peeled back from a corner.

"Thanks for meeting me," Fenella began. "Sorry that the party we invited you to was like…kind of intense. I guess I wanted to thank you for what you did that night."

Pierce's hands were fine-tuned, Mediterranean-tanned. He liked to pinch his thumb and forefinger into the flesh beneath the thumb of his opposite hand, on the pressure point, in an attempt to cure an almost ever-present headache. The squeezing of the pressure point became a nervous tic. Colleagues mimicked it at cocktail parties to do impressions of him. Pierce had a thin physique, that of a bicyclist to the passing eye, though he spent his time hiking and climbing rocks solo in the Pobre Claritas. His fingers were well-conditioned from constant pinching. He was able to find crevices within the rocks and he could hoist his light frame up easily. Pierce had full eyebrows, with several prominent hairs between them, and clear fine-pored skin. He held his arms open to a degree when he sat, as if taking in the table, as if presiding, as if gathering, as if he was too big for his shoulders, as if the wispy black hair on his head had worn his brain out and the headaches had forced his palms and forearms akimbo.

"They have some really excellent new classes of antidepressants on the market now," he offered.

"I think that Walter's on them all," Fenella returned, wavering in her closeness to him suddenly. She wanted comforting, a commiseration, not an explanation, not a lesson by someone who was a neurological "authority". This is what Daen had to offer in times of strife. "Answers", most likely from *The Celestial Mandate*, but rarely commiserations.

She scratched her nose, further eroding the makeup that she had carefully applied prior to their meeting. The bike ride, the steam in the coffee house, and the discomfort that she felt that caused her to touch her face repeatedly, and the foundation on her skin slid away; and her freckles, having been born long ago on the Sugar Islands, revealed themselves. She felt thick and stiff with the coffee in her belly and the feeling of the bikes's resistance still in her thighs, like one of the redwoods outside the window, yet foolishly young with the allure of her mascara having flaked off and her wispy, childish eyelashes that only underscored her hangnails, her clumsiness, and the way she mumbled when she was insecure. Fenella tended to sit with her lips apart like she was constantly taken aback, which Lucinda had chided her for since early adolescence. Fenella moved and spoke with the wariness and distrust of someone who has lost the religion of their family early in life and has not found anything to replace it.

"Come back to the Ducale? Let's get by the water. It's stuffy in here," he said.

Fenella was surprised, though she agreed and they finished their coffees and she unlocked her bike out front, and the pair walked back through downtown under the redwoods and the chestnuts and the walnuts and the jacarandas until they found the path to the beach. The fog had lifted and the day's heat bounced off of their heads and gleamed off of the handlebars of the bike. The seagulls screamed over the Addled Egg Diner and the Knickerbocker Theater as they passed.

"Can you get your bike over?" asked Pierce. Fenella nodded and he walked behind her as she carefully navigated the bike over the narrow footbridge that ran parallel to the train trestle over the Picaroon. When they arrived at the Ducale, he had her place her bike inside his apartment with a one-word excuse; "vagabonds". She assumed that they'd sit by the dock and that he'd prescribe various methods of treatments that she should suggest to Walter; cognitive behavioral therapy, cutting-edge SSRI's, meditation, yoga, electrotherapy. Instead, he led her further down the Ducale dock until they arrived at a wooden boat with an outboard motor tied to the striped piling.

"Surplus," he offered as a simple explanation. The two climbed into the boat and Pierce took a key from his pocket for the padlock, and then they were released from the mooring, and the two shoved off into the Picaroon.

For every sandhill crane they spotted as they motored upstream, the two navigated around another mired shopping cart, or bit of flotsam that looked as if it were from a crime scene. Single shoes passed them by instead of fishes, cardboard boxes peeked at them from the rushes instead of turtles. A flock of ducks came towards them timed to the shouts of homeless people living under the Saceda Avenue bridge.

Gradually though, they left Saceda Avenue behind. They passed the Addled Egg Diner, the Bargain Trough, Jim's Electronics, passed the inlet to the Sugar Factory's canal, and with Madeira House a spot in the distance on Ice Cream Hill, the sounds of cars quieted. The noise of rushes in the wind picked up and the water became clearer. Pierce navigated up the Picaroon further, past the Loffer Cemetery, and then into the forest where the shadows fell on them like cold compresses. Finally, the rocks began to scrape against the bottom of the wooden boat.

"I suppose we are here," he said.

Pierce tied the boat to a dogwood hugging the bank and began unbuttoning his shirt. The Madeira thistles menaced around the water's edge. Fenella's tongue dried and thickened and she began imperceptibly shifting her weight towards land and an exit. Pierce continued to remove his shoes. Fenella eyed the river down the banks. They were covered in deep thickets. She looked to his face for an explanation. Pierce removed his white athletic socks. Fenella reached into her purse, wrapped her fingers around her keys, took deep breaths. Pierce removed his pants and boxers in two confident, unhurried yanks, then jumped into the Picaroon.

"Good amount of this water is snowmelt," said Pierce to Fenella who remained in the boat, studying her shoelaces.

"Oh yeah?"

"So, they've found that cold water is great for your sympathetic nervous system," he said treading water. "And you and I just went through something kind of stressful." The clouds opened and the sun shone on the swimming hole, deep and green, warming Fenella's shoulders. "Also, this icy water is making me look effectively like a castrato, and it's Perdita, so why don't you swim, already." He put his hands together and made a squirt gun. The water made an arc over his head.

Pierce had already overstepped boundaries like a mouse in a kitchen cupboard. Mentioning her nipples at Walter's party. And this. A man takes a woman alone into the woods? What would Nonna Agnelli say? Fenella blamed herself. She had no voice to tell him to turn around. She cut off the blame like a fish head, because men, in the Loffer tradition, could not be expected to have social graces. Still, because the feeling was still so painful, she placed it onto a passing leaf and watched it float down towards Perdita. Fenella supposed there was an enormous possibility that he, like so many men, especially those sheltered in academia, was a dude who did what he felt. Fenella had worked for a professor in college, who had been highly eccentric, and the behavior tracked. It was an entitled, yet absentminded impulsivity. Fenella thought about taking the boat, to show Pierce, to teach him, though she wasn't sure that she could navigate around the shallows, and getting stuck and embarrassed, well that was almost worse.

Fenella was self-conscious about getting over her formerly prudish Loffer ways. The religion had preached modesty her whole life, yet it was true, here in Perdita scores of nudists laughed and cavorted below the White Cliffs. Every new moon the Wiccans gathered in their birthday suits for their esbat at the Teonchee Pillar. And there were three naked guys downtown. They just hung out. Nudity was everywhere in Perdita.

She wanted Pierce to like her. She didn't want to do anything to spoil the moment. Fruit has a very short window, Nonna Agnelli was fond of saying. It was as though Pierce was taking large stones from the river and putting them into the boat, filling her hopes about him with dark, cold water. She looked at his nimble fingers treading in the river and there was certainly attraction, though more than that, Fenella, as the first in her family to graduate from college, could not help but view Pierce as an authority because of his level of education. She was afraid of Pierce and what his intentions might be in the water, though she was more afraid of herself, of her own wholesomeness, of her own residue of naïveté. To hesitate now would be to give into the hoary paternalism of Lofferism after so much rejection on her part. She felt the rubber of the boat, dry-weathered wise, almost inhabited; its nose bobbing side to side like a divining rod.

Fenella untied her shoelaces first, holding onto the side of the boat for steadiness, as it rocked beneath her hand. She took off her shirt and bra, conscious to avoid Pierce's gaze, and she imagined a folding embroidered screen between them with peacocks and asters. She removed her pants and underwear. She gave her thighs a squeeze for courage and then she stood up and smiled, because she felt that she ought to, just before her freckles hit the water.

He made no effort to touch her. The makeup on her face washed downstream to collect against the shopping carts and single shoes and High Seas Admiral bottles. They swam around like a pair of timid dace hunting in the rocks, two unhitched reeds whirling in the eddies, a couple of flecks of pyrite flowing to the sea. She looked at the water in his curly-haired scalp. He pointed out a biplane on the horizon. The water and air temperatures merged.

Afterwards, they lay on the rounded rocks by the dogwood, drying themselves with droplets of water still on their backs and buttocks.

It was at this point, with Pierce stripped of his button-up shirt, with his authority-taut arms shivering, that she could bear to ask his opinion.

"Neurology. That's what you study, right? I have this boss. He has this sleeping disorder. He needs these weird videos. No, nothing sexual. To sleep. He says they're for relaxation. Fish too. He says fish relax him. Have you ever heard of something like this?"

Pierce rolled to his side and supported his head with his elbow.

"Who do you work for?"

"These people named the Rostungers."

Pierce laid back onto the rocks and put his hands over his eyes.

"I know them," he said.

FENELLA WAS AT WORK FILING IN THE OFFICE WHEN Catalina came to the door.

"Missus Nina wants to see you," she said.

Fenella found her in bed, slumped over her laptop, a clove cigarette in her hands, still smoking.

"Nina? You wanted to see me? Nina?" Nina's eyes rolled open slowly. She leaned her head back.

"Yeah. Yes." Nina took a drag from her cigarette with her small fingers. Then closed her eyes for another minute.

"Nina?"

"Yes. Yes!" she sat up. Adjusted the pillows. Took a drink of the cold coffee on her nightstand. "Honey, I need you to go to the store for me. I need a "N" key, and an "I" key, and a "P" key, and…" she turned the laptop towards Fenella. The keys had been melted from her laptop keyboard. A cigarette shape was burned into a hollowed out "Q".

"I don't know if they sell individual keys . . . "

"Go in the office and get me my bottle of pills," said Nina.

"Where are they?"

Nina retrieved a small, brass key on a necklace around her neck and handed it to Fenella. "It's in the locked filing drawer labeled 'Tampons.' Get the Dilaudid. Don't look at me like that, Dilaudid, is so, so safe. They give it to mommies with babies." Fenella thought about Benny and how he probably wished he was a mommy with a baby right about now. "And I have spinal stenosis."

Fenella wondered how long she'd been using this line, or which one of her friends had actually had spinal stenosis. Fenella had filed medical paperwork with letters denying Nina medication after test results showing no indication of "spinal stenosis".

"And call my banker," continued Nina. "I want a full audit. There's at least 500k missing from my accounts. And I missed the Board of Trustees Meeting at the Academy," she said with her eyes closed, leaning back into the pillow.

"It was in your calendar," said Fenella defensively.

"How can I get into my calendar if it has no KEYS!!!" she yelled. "I obviously cannot work without a computer. I don't know HOW I'm expected to WORK without a computer! AND before I forget, next time I fly commercial to the Islands? Make sure there's chicken. The last time I had to fly commercial, they ran out of chicken and they gave me beef. I hate beef."

Fenella nodded, her arms full with the computer and the melted keys. And the key from around Nina's neck, which was warm and smelled like Wellspring skin creme.

—Journal entry –

Therrl get fesh. Moor fesh evrie day. Fesh look Vaclav. Vaclav look fesh. Sum time, niiit time, Vaclav cook fesh on fihyeh. Moor fesh look Vaclav. Dusan en Kasimir look bak fesh.

PIERCE AND FENELLA'S HAIR WAS STILL WET FROM SWIMming in the Picaroon. After docking the boat at the Ducale, Fenella entered Pierce's apartment to retrieve her bike. It was a standard bachelor apartment. Bare plaster walls, a soulless black leather couch, a TV that was too large for the room. Pierce opened a kitchen cabinet full of mismatched commemorative souvenir cups.

"Can I get you something to drink?" he asked. He opened the refrigerator. It looked mostly empty. "What do I have? Um. Water, milk, some oldish wine . . . "

"Are you hungry?" asked Fenella. "Do you want lunch? Let's have lunch. I can make you lunch." Pierce nodded, looking relieved. They exited the apartment, walking Fenella's bike through the Ducale's courtyard, and back over the Picaroon's trestle footbridge to the Andromeda Apartments.

After dropping a few quarters into the meter, Fenella brought Pierce into her tiny kitchenette. She began looking through her cupboards.

"Would you like some soup? I have soup, popcorn…" Fenella offered. Pierce frowned.

"You're not going to use a microwave, are you? I haven't used a microwave in years." Fenella began to regret baring her vagina on the rocks while they dried off.

"Oh wow. Um, hang on, let me get a pot."

"Ha, ha, just kidding. I'm not anti-microwave. I even wear real deodorant!" He lifted his arm. "I guess it washed off. But no. My old housemates totally banned microwaves from our apartment."

"Sounds housemate-y."

"They wore natural deodorant too which is like wearing nothing at all, and why? Because the aluminum in regular deodorant will give you cancer? Where is the data on that? I need the science. And have you ever tried to use vegan floss, i.e. non-beeswax, coated with something and mint? It shreds between your teeth so that you need regular floss to floss that floss out. "

"Oh yeah, that's the worst."

"So can we?"

"Can we what?"

"Have microwave popcorn too?"

"Of course. Although first you need to clue me on all the deets."

"The deets?"

"About Thurl. And how you know him. Like, what's up?"

"So first of all everything I tell you, I shouldn't be telling you. It should all be private under HIPAA. So you heard nothing, yes?" Fenella nodded and turned to put the popcorn in the microwave, relieved that she'd had quarters in her pocket to feed the meter.

"Thurl came into the clinic and we studied him. We studied him because he doesn't sleep. Or eat."

"Or so he says?"

"Nope, we observed him."

"So, how can he?"

"We don't know."

"Do you know about the films? Did he tell you about the films he uses?"

"No. No idea," said Pierce. "Illegal films?"

"There COULD be some labor laws, and there's this orphan, but like, it's not what you're thinking. It's some sort of meditation technique as far as I can tell. I'll show you."

"Interesting," said Pierce.

"So can we?" said Fenella.

"Can we what?" said Pierce. The popcorn popping reached its zenith.

"Go to the Sugar Factory tonight so I can show you some freaky shit."

"Of course," said Pierce, moving towards Fenella, rubbing his thumb over her shoulder, made smooth and cold from the Picaroon.

Fenella decided she would wait to find out if Pierce was an asshole until after they had sex. She had never waited that long in high school or college, and now that she needed help with the Rostungers, it hardly mattered. And yet she could not wait to see his face as it registered the blue flashes from the Aquarium.

❧❧

THE FLIES MOVED HEAVILY. FENELLA SKIPPED BREAKFAST. She peeled off her pajamas and let them drop by the banana tree before sliding into the Hefty Spin and steering it across the crabgrass and the cracked pavement onto Lord Monboddo Street. As she pushed the trike up the hill she could not feel where her skin ended and the air began. She felt as though she might be able to swim through the bathtub-like temperatures that lay between herself and the mynas and the bulbuls in the trees.

With Dolly resting between the small of her back and the hard plastic seat of the Hefty Spin, she pushed down on the pink pedals with enough force to turn her toe knuckles white. She rode along the gravel until the rise became steep and the front tire made a sound like coughing. Then she stopped to dismount and pushed the trike to the top of the hill.

During her few months on the Island, Fenella had built callouses on her feet. Her stiff patent leather Sunday shoes were much worse than the sting of hot concrete or sand the rest of the week.

She came to the furthest point she had been to on Lord Monboddo Street, then pedaled past it. Small sugar cane fields and farmhouses appeared, partitioned by mailboxes on cinderblock mounts. She lost herself in the low tumble of hollow tires on gravel, coming out of her reverie only to adjust the position of Dolly at her back or to scratch her peeling nose. The fields became larger and longer and the wind whirred through the cane in irregular waves like the dives of her butterfly kite.

Fenella saw a mist of water coming from the blowhole of a whale-shaped sprinkler on a lawn. She left the Hefty Spin where the gravel met the patchy grass and dipped her stubbed toe into the spray while she took in the unbalanced frenetic motion of yard ornaments with her sweaty eyes. The red hats of gnomes mixed with the yellows of giant daisies. Ladybug whirligigs spun and wooden bird wings flapped. The motion differentials made Fenella feel as though she was still pushing rhythmically on the pedals of the Hefty Spin. She touched the raised white nodules on a giant clay mushroom, peered down into a miniature well, and stroked a ceramic donkey. Shells hung from the porch of the house bounced against cut bamboo and it felt as though the clattering happened in her ribcage.

She walked across the beaded blades of grass towards a farm house, climbed the concrete steps and pushed the doorbell with the tip of Dolly's handle. Her heartbeat quickened and she lowered her stare to the rough edges of the doormat while scratching an itch on her calf with the toenail of her other foot.

When the door opened, Fenella expected an adult, but seeing no one she dropped her chin and found a face level with her own, with red freckles and red eyelashes and white lips spread across gap teeth.

"Oh," said Fenella. "Can you wait for a little bit? I'll be right back."

Fenella turned and ran down the front steps without looking back and jumped into the Hefty Spin. She extended her legs until the space at the small of her back became tight and Dolly hardened against her vertebrae. At the top of the rise, she picked up speed. She took her feet off the pedals and put them on the handlebars where the pink streamers whipped them. The pedals mixed in time with pounding of her chest and lungs. When the Hefty Spin lost momentum at the bottom of the hill, she caught the pedals swiftly with her tattered toes and pushed into her thighs until the burning reached deep into her cricket legs.

She left the trike on the front lawn of her house and began to put her clothes underneath the banana tree back on again, shaking out her corduroy shorts to make sure no frogs had climbed inside. Dressed in a baseball shirt with a cracked iron-on featuring a rainbow and the words

"Dream to Believe", she tucked Dolly into the elastic of her waistband and stepped into canvas shoes left on the back steps. Then she pedaled back up the rise and past the fields to the house with the lawn ornaments.

There was a damp spot from sweat at the small of her back when she knocked again on the blue wooden door. The red-haired boy reappeared and smiled.

"Come in," he said as he moved back to let Fenella inside. The boy with the freckles did not ask her name.

She followed the boy into his room, which had thick, dusty carpeting and a slot car racetrack that went up onto scuffed walls. The boy demonstrated the speed of each car, pulling back on them one by one until they clicked and whirred like lizards on the banana tree. He showed her how to place the cars on the track.

A woman with blonde hair and paint-stained dungarees entered the room.

"Who's this?"

The boy hunched his shoulders.

"I'm Fenella."

"Oh," said the woman. "Well, would you kids like some Punchie Quench? Yeah? Come on into the kitchen then."

They went down the hallway and into a kitchen with dirty cupboards and linoleum printed to look like red bricks. The woman took out the same orange plastic pitcher that they had at Fenella's house, and poured Punchie Quench into plastic cups imprinted with pictures of hamburgers with wings.

"Want ice?" asked the woman.

Fenella shook her head no.

"Okay Andy, have fun with your friend. I'll be in the field."

The woman opened a sliding glass door, stepped into some flip flops and disappeared into the waving green. Fenella and the boy held the cups with both hands and gulped Punchie Quench, staring at each other's faces over the rims of the cups and licking the red from their upper lips.

"Ahhhhhh," said Andy when he'd drunk half the glass. "I like you," he added, in a frog-throated way, and continued drinking.

Fenella was silent. She shifted her toes inside her moist shoes.

"If you like me, you'll drink through your nose," she said.

The boy looked uneasily at Fenella and the Punchie Quench in his glass.

"It's not hard," said Fenella.

The boy put his white nostrils to the rim of the cup and crossed his eyes as a wave of red rushed towards him. Then he snorted and choked and his eyes filled with water. White and red flashed beneath his freckles. He began to cry. Fenella's eyes flicked towards the sliding glass door.

"Andy? Andy?" called the woman through the glass doors.

"Shut up," said Fenella. Her shoes began filling with more sweat. "Stop it."

The boy cried harder. Red punch mixed with snot and tears. It ran down his upper lip and dripped onto the linoleum. Fenella pulled Dolly from her waistband and held the spoon over her head.

"Shut up!" she yelled, and then she brought the spoon down onto the boy's head. He cried louder. Fenella turned her face and saw a flash of the woman's blonde hair through the cane. Panicking, Fenella opened the door of the broom closet and kicked the mop bucket to the back. She grabbed the sleeve of the boy's tee shirt and held Dolly over her head again, threatening.

"Get in!"

The boy screamed, yet allowed Fenella's hand to guide him into the closet. She shoved him backwards and closed the cupboard door, and with terror in her stomach, ran out of the kitchen, out the front door, and pedaled down Lord Monboddo St.

The wind began to pick up. By the time she reached home, Puele had shut the windows and untied the curtains.

—Found letter—

Dear Walter,

I think Madeira House has gotten into my veins. Veins like the one Bronislaw Dudek slashed apart. Writing you from the lemonade stand at Mystery Manor, my place of employment, my minimum wage captors. Tourists are coming for titillation. They want the story of the gore. And lemonade. But Mystery Manor will always be Madeira House, not the Amusements.

It's 10 a.m., right after the Mystery Manor gates open. The fog around Ice Cream Hill has not yet burned off. The damp carries the smell of my unwashed uniform to my nose. The smell has notes to it from pills and speed. Everyone has to make it through the day, so don't preach Wally. What do they have you on in that hospital, hmmm?

The tourists start to come into the main courtyard. You know how we were talking about telling the locals from the ones who are out of state the other day? Locals from Perdita and Barnby Dun are hikers, surfers. These out of towners are mostly ovoids with sport sandals. Loud talkers. Shitty tippers. The sound of all of the tourists is a kind of high-pitched buzzing, it feels like I have tinnitus. EEEEEEEEEEEEEEEEEEEEEEEE they all say. LEEEMOONAAAAADE they shriek.

In my head, Bronislaw Dudek appears with his ax from the shadows, clearing the courtyard again until the sounds of the birds come back to life. But even my dark, drugged self cannot wish for it too deeply, because there is some kind of knocking about that house that I can feel all the way over here in my lemonade cart. And it doesn't want to leave me out.

A thin-lipped and wide-hipped woman with a shirt that says "Always Late but Worth the Wait" approaches me. I see the remaining gems cemented in the top of the Manor walls reflect a new patch of sun into her glasses.

"Nine dollars for frozen lemonade? What's in it, gold?"

"Actually, dead babies," I say. She looks at my earrings, and the tattoo on my hand. Remember when I won the drag contest at Sancho's and you talked me into getting the crown inked? The crown is a little stand-in for you. I always think of you when I look at the crown, not me. The woman looks at my name tag on my work jersey.

"Salvatore, huh?" I wonder if your superior would like to hear from me, Salvatore." She waddles away.

I switched out my nametag for a fake one. Salvatore quit weeks ago.

Yours,

Benny

FENELLA HADN'T HEARD FROM BENNY IN DAYS. HE wasn't answering his phone or door. She called Mystery Manor to see if he'd been to work.

"No," said a man. "And if you do talk to him, tell him we've got his final check waiting for him."

Fenella walked barefoot up the tiled stairs. Grains of sand stuck to the bottoms of her feet.

She banged on the door with her fist.

"Ben! Ben! C'mon!!! I can hear you coughing!"

She waited. The only answer was the deep-chested cough. She moved down the hallway to the glass-louvered window that opened into the apartment's kitchen, and pressed her fingers down on metal that held the sides of the glass slats, prying the oxidized and salted hinges in towards the sink.

One by one, she lifted the sections of glass up and out of their slots, turning them delicately on the tips of her fingers until she could slide them towards her chest in the hallway. She slowly placed each piece of glass onto the tile until a cracked pane broke in her hands. She let it fall and scatter into smaller pieces amongst the sand. She removed her sweatshirt and placed it gently in front of the window, standing on it to protect her bare feet.

Her shoulders scraped against the sharp metal hardware as she hoisted herself through the window and into the sink, where her hands grabbed a soft, dry mound of used tea bags. The apartment was dark and the smell was fetid. Flies coasted and circled around her ears and ankles. She opened the refrigerator for light, but the bulb did not turn on. Benny had not fed the meter.

Her eyes adjusted to the minimal light coming from the hallway. Used dishes were piled on all the countertops and the oven. She made her way slowly through the living room, stepping on heaps of blankets and clothing that lay on top of decayed palm leaves, then passed through the open doorway to Benny's room, feeling flies scattering from her toes.

Benny lay on his mattress on the floor, without a sheet beneath him. He used a cardigan as a blanket. He didn't meet her eyes, but coughed again, a grating staccato ending in a rattle that pulled his body into a fetal position.

Then she noticed the mice. Ten to twelve were splayed stiffly on the carpet next to mattress, all impaled with sharpened pencils. The mouse closest to her foot twisted in and around the wood, stiff claws reaching for its insides. Others stretched outwards, haunches open to the ceiling.

"Benny. My God . . . "

Fenella brought him towards her by the shoulders. Her thumbs pressed into his small, tight pectoral muscles, slippery with sweat.

"Pneumonia, I think. Just a guess," he whispered. "I can't walk around anymore. I can't get out of bed."

"And these . . . ? The . . . pencils . . . "

"I woke up one night and felt something wet on my feet. A mouse gave birth in my fucking bed, Fen."

She looked over to a crumpled floral sheet that had been removed from the mattress. In the folds, tiny pink mice were dead, surrounded by streaks of dried blood.

"Why didn't you call?'

"I did, Fen. You were working I guess?"

Fenella lifted his torso to drape across her shoulder. He was slight in the best of times. Now he felt hollow.

"I took all the pills I had," he said. The smell of his hair up close made Fenella's stomach lurch. "I'd get to sleep and they'd wake me up running across the keys". He gestured weakly to a vintage toy piano placed near a guitar amp and mixing board that leaned against the dented wall. The top of the piano featured a faded pink lamb, hopping joyously over a yellow musical note.

"I felt them in the dark, running across my chest and legs." He paused again to hack and wheeze over her back. "They scream at night Fen. I could reach my can of pencils. It was all I could do."

Fenella lifted Benny. She helped him, and they made their way delicately through the apartment and out to the hallway, where she set him down on the tile against the wall once they were past the broken glass. Her nostrils savored the sea air greedily.

"I'm gonna wash you off downstairs, and then we're going to the fucking doctor."

"With what money? And then . . . like, what? You have your job and . . . I can't even get up to put a goddamn quarter in the meter . . . " Thick tears began to land on the grains of sand.

"Calm down, Ben. I've got some leftover codeine," she said, taking his shoulders in her arms once again. "I'm taking you somewhere without any electricity meters. You'll be better, Benny."

SINCE MEETING THE RED-HAIRED BOY, FENELLA NO longer rode the Hefty Spin up Lord Monboddo. Kiele and Okalani's mother told Fenella herself that her girls would no longer play with her. And so, Fenella began to spend her days building houses out of twigs for the ants in the backyard, or she folded banana leaves to make hats. She listened to the gecko chirp. Sometimes she breathed on the outside of Lucinda's window, though the curtains were drawn, and drew a heart on the pane that sweated and bled in the humidity.

She still liked to climb Mrs. Onishi's plumeria tree to pick blossoms and rub them on the insides of her wrists. She did this when Puele had closed the curtains and couldn't see her do it.

The day was rainy. The showers lasted longer than the usual five minutes of downpour that came around two o'clock and moistened the pavement. That day the birds were muted in the drizzle and the ants retreated into the stepping-stone cracks. That day, the smell from the plumeria tree reminded Fenella of the peaches in Barnby Dun, Ina's baby powder and the suntan lotion in the medicine cabinet here in the Islands. All at once.

The smell bore Fenella into the boughs of the tree and she sat for a while, breathing in the perfume without picking a bud, watching the raindrops gathering on the waxy green leaves. She looked through the branches back towards the side of the white clapboard house and at her parents' bedroom with the curtains closed. The window reflected the tree and the rain back to her. Above her head, a tangle of wasps wove themselves together as the hairs behind her neck.

She heard Puele calling for her from the back door. It was getting later. She'd want Fenella in the house before Daen came home. Fenella stretched a bare foot down to a lower branch. She barely felt the ball of her foot glide along the wood before she found herself lost in the untied curtains. Lucinda's window had opened, and the warm breeze blew the fabric around her face. It covered her whole body. It wrapped Fenella in the tender smell of grass and soap.

The soap smell became stronger then, and the cloth retreated from her body. The soap took on a form, a hard bar that wedged itself between her ribs and lungs. There was the feeling of cold rain, and then her skin leapt into tiny fires, fires everywhere, on her eyelids, her palms, the back of her knees. Fenella felt as if she were on the scraped Ferris Wheel pedal of the Hefty Spin.

She felt the fabric return, bundling her. She became weightless and the bar of soap dissolved into her stomach. The fabric felt heavy this time, stifling and coarse.

Lucinda and Mrs. Onishi stood above Fenella. She was inside the white clapboard house, seeing their faces and also beyond where the light blurred into the popcorn ceiling.

Mrs. Onishi was unwrapping a blanket from Fenella's body. Lucinda's sagging cheekbones scanned Fenella's torso. Her bony hands wiped tears away from Fenella's temples.

"You knocked a wasp's nest down, sweet pea. You fell right on top of it."

Mrs. Onishi brought over a blue ceramic jar.

"Volcano ash," she said. "Mix it with baking soda and another part vinegar."

Lucinda spent the evening outside of her bedroom, applying thick layers of bubbling mud paste to Fenella's skin.

Fenella could hear Daen bouncing a wailing Ina behind a closed door in the back bedroom.

The smell of vinegar and eggs disappeared when she felt Lucinda next to her. Lucinda was peaches, and baby powder, and grass and clean sheets.

❧❧❧❧

VACLAV HELPED FENELLA PUSH THE CASKET FROM THE Cabinet of Dr. Caligari set, strapped onto a dolly with mover's belts, into the Aquarium supply elevator.

"You're looking better Vaclav," said Fenella. "You're taking the vitamin D pills? And you're taking Dusan and Kasimir to the roof for sunshine too?"

Vaclav smiled and nodded.

"I need to figure out a way for you to get to a dentist too . . . somehow. We've got other things to think about tonight though."

They reached street level, heaved up the cargo door together and pushed the casket into the night air and the Factory parking lot. Benny's right cheek and lips were splayed across the passenger window of Raúl's pickup truck, his breath fogging the glass around his mouth.

"Get ready with the cabinet Vaclav," said Fenella.

Fenella opened the pickup door and eased Benny down into the casket, propping his head with pillow from the Maharaja set, and covered him with Caligari's cloak. She tucked the bag of prescriptions dispensed from the Perdita Free Clinic beside Benny, slammed the truck door closed and motioned Vaclav back toward the hulking Factory cargo bay.

It was in the box of the elevator when Benny finally took a long look at Vaclav in his tunic. There were dark circles under everyone's eyes from the utility bulb overhead.

"Who the fuck, Fen?"

"Vaclav. He's sweet . . . and pretty much . . . illegal or something. He's very healthy though, considering, I mean, I think he is. I don't get the idea that he's been chained down here for years or like straight up, classically abused. Look Benny, it's weird. I probably should have gone to the cops by now, but I'm trying to sort out how this should get resolved."

"Fenella?" asked Benny, "why are you taking me to a torture dungeon?"

"No, Ben. It's different than that. It's much weirder and more complicated than a torture dungeon. And there's free electricity."

"Kill me already, Fen. Close the door to this, holy shit, you've already putting me in a fucking casket! Bury me alive. Harvest my withered organs. But give me another swig of the codeine and some more of the Zithromax first."

"Ben, it's fine. Relax. Shut up."

They wheeled Benny to the Mèliés set. Fenella took his shoulders, Vaclav his legs, and they lowered him down onto the giant foam-painted face of the moon. Dusan pushed his nose into the room and Vaclav followed him away.

Fenella spread the black cloak on top of the moon, and positioned Benny's sacrum into the depression of the moon's eye socket, his shoulders and head cradled by the bridge of the oversized nose. She covered him with silks from the Maharaja set and placed a Moroccan tea tray on top of a Maharaja pillow to Benny's right.

"How much codeine did you give me, Fen?" asked Benny.

She arranged the prescription bottles on to the tea tray and Vaclav reentered the set with a steaming mug of broth.

"Thanks, Vaclav. Go eat your dinner, but do you mind bringing some crackers back in here before you go to bed? I want to stay with him."

Vaclav smiled with his eyes and noiselessly slipped away.

"This is where I work Benny. It's basically a little film studio. Vaclav . . . he's sort of adopted, and he helps me. Don't worry about this place, Ben. There's no mice. It's safe, it's quiet. I can look after you here, Ben."

Fenella turned on a warm steam vaporizer behind a painted chimney that filled the set with a fine mist. She flicked on the shooting star projection that lit the back wall, then wrapped herself in a faux Dalmatian skin wizard's robe and curled up beside Benny in the moon.

—The manifesto of the Judgement Day Libation Deliverance Commission—

> It is with profound conscience against the colonization and ongoing enslavement of the inhabitants of the Islands for the purposes of Sugars that we, anarchists, the true pacifists, side with the resistance and condemn the property of the Imperialist powers at the Andromeda Apartments. We cannot separate our fate in San Califia from that of our brothers and sisters across the way in the Islands. The silencing of the bell tower of control will ignite a worker's revolt. It is merely one method of anti-authoritarianism.
>
> Signed,
>
> Jimmy Chapman

❧❧❧❧

The Perdita Village Bugle

Turbinado Sugar Factory to Cease Operations

by Susan Finkelstein

May 2nd—

Carlyle Industries and Rostunger Limited is confirming that it will cease operations at the Turbinado Sugar Factory. A statement by the company says the decision is in consultation with all stakeholders. The next meeting is for Wednesday, June 19th when the unions and worker delegates will meet with the company.

"After more than 80 years of continuous processing of cane from the Islands, the production facility on the Picaroon has become obsolete," an anonymous rep for Carlyle Industries stated.

A spokesman for Rostunger Limited also said the group is facing trade pressures from foreign producers flooding the market with excess sugar. "Turbinado is no longer the sugar on top," the spokesperson said. The plant closure will mean the loss of 600 jobs in Perdita.

❧❧❧❧

FENELLA LED PIERCE DOWN THE STAIRS. AT THE BOTTOM, she held his hand and pointed upward to the Aquarium above their heads. She watched his eyes and chest fill full as he took in the immense, suspended ocean, and then their breaths synchronized to the vast rhythmic water pumps embedded in the walls of the Sugar Factory.

Vaclav and the dik-diks stood by the leafy seadragon tank. He held a basket of his white asparagus, freshly picked.

She smiled at Vaclav, took a single spear and put her fingers to her lips. Vaclav led the dik-diks away into the blackness, the plinking notes of their hooves echoing softly into Fenella and Pierce's ears.

She showed him the Dr. Caligari set first. He wandered up the crooked black and white stairs that led to the solid yet seemingly endless depths of the village backdrop. When he stopped and seemed to register something of the scene in his face, she climbed towards him. He took both her hands firmly and brushed her closed eyelids with his thumbs.

They walked through the rest of the German Expressionist Village to the Alhambra set. Fenella pushed a button behind a tiled archway and the fountains began to flow. She pulled him down onto the steps of the center fountain.

He began to trace the outlines of the Moorish tile with his fingertip. Fenella held out the spear of white asparagus. He bit the end and swallowed.

She removed his shirt and drew invisible lines around the muscles of his chest with the rest of the stalk. She poked it gently into his navel, then lightly tossed the stem into the gurgling fountain. Fenella leaned forward and slowly bit his bottom lip.

They undressed along the garden pathway lined with false bougainvillea, and when they reached the Murnau set, they fell into the Polynesian sand. He slid one hand inside her until she reached out and grabbed a paper palm leaf, and ripped it in half.

Fenella climbed on top him and re-synched with the rushing bellows beyond the walls. The sounds of water surrounded them, and the tiny jungle seemed to pulse and sway and tilt with their movement.

When Pierce came, he collapsed into the sand. Fenella kissed his nipples and chest, then buried her nose for a moment, under his Adam's apple, as if to breathe his very life in.

"Now I can begin to explain all of this," she said.

ఴ

ON LUCINDA'S INSTRUCTIONS, PUELE TOOK FENELLA AND Ina to their local beach at Misri Bay late one afternoon. Puele grumbled as she applied the "white people stuff"; sunscreen that had come to her with sand pre-embedded into the rim of the cap. The thick zinc-and-sand mixture created a sandpaper effect on Ina's tiny legs. Puele held her whitened palms up to the sky in exasperation.

"Do not get wet before I get this awful cream on you," she commanded to Fenella. As Fenella waited, she studied her arms and legs. She still had purplish marks from the wasp stings. Mrs. Onishi's volcanic mud had only helped to a limit. A white man walked by in a white T-shirt. The T-shirt had the outline of a naked woman and the caption, "Take It to the End Zone."

"We are not a sport!" yelled Puele.

Once smeared in zinc oxide, Fenella left Puele and Ina and went to play by the cliffs framing the Bay. She poked at the kind of mussels that shot back water when you stuck your fingers into them. And soon she followed bits of shells that led her to the sea's edge where the waves tickled her toes. A bit of kelp floated in, which was an entire Atlantis, and when she reached down for the king's mussel great-ships, she was splashing mid-waist. She waived to Puele on the beach who stared at her but didn't wave back. The oranges of the sunset began to touch the water and Fenella's little red swimsuit.

And then, a balloon came floating in the water, ahead towards the horizon. It was unlike any balloon she had ever seen. This was a blue beyond Ina's baby eyes, beyond the cat's eye marble in the cookie tin with her baby teeth. This balloon reminded her of the rope that came from the mama cat she had found in the forest in Barnby Dun, how it followed the kitten into the cedar shavings next to Daen's work shed. The balloon pulsed in that same way as the rope from the cat. So blue it was purple underneath.

It was out of place in these large foamy waves, a delicate thing like this. It was so fragile compared to the jagged cliffs, she worried it would pop. And the balloon was happy. Fenella was sure of it. It seemed to have come all the way from Barnby Dun and Perdita, when Daen would take her to the Amusements and she'd ride the little whale ride. It was next to the balloon kiosk, where the man would inflate the color that she wanted and she'd always choose blue because it was the same shade as the stained glass in her bedroom that Lucinda had made; ocean waves fit inside an octagon shape in the redwood frame above her picture window.

And so this balloon seemed a friend, something on the island that had escaped her thus far. She swam towards it in her red little swimsuit and distantly, she could hear Puele shouting at her from the beach to stop, to come back, and her thoughts were that Puele had no interest in letting her have fun, in letting her have a balloon; and it made her more determined that the balloon should be hers and hers alone.

She reached the balloon. It was like she was transported from the Islands altogether. It was instant, powerful. The balloon had saved her from her loneliness. She no longer had to think, although she was conscious of some sort of a buzzing in her toes and it reminded her of being in between radio stations or going over rocks in roller skates. These were very distant thoughts. Once she'd stuck one of Lucinda's bobby pins into an electrical outlet and perhaps she felt that way now, though the feelings were so potent that memories were wiped out even before they began. There was pain. The paint peeled off the sky. The water became dry. Then a more peaceful rhythm drifted and washed over Fenella. It swayed and rocked in time with her body, tick, tock, tick tock, like Ina's baby chair. She saw the rainbow whirligigs and the freckles on the red-haired boy and the sap on Okalani and Kiele's fingers and then something caught her beneath the knees and shoulders like the U-shaped branches of Mrs. Onishi's plumeria tree. And then a low sound, deep, that Fenella felt in her musculature, something that almost woke her from her reverie and brought to Fenella's dream-mind the fog horns from the ships that would carry from Perdita all the way to Barnby Dun.

Presently, Fenella became aware of an eye. It was slitted, like her cat's eye marble in the baby teeth tin, like the dash in a phone number. But the eye itself reminded Fenella of the picture of the moon of Ganymede, the large satellite of Jupiter. There had been an oversized photo of Ganymede in Fenella's science book in Barnby Dun. And this eye seemed as wide and luminous and mottled, then smooth and blue, then rough again like the turbulent sea. Indeed, the eye seemed a planet. It was larger than Fenella's whole body. Fenella had a small memory of the grit in the cap of the sunscreen. The thought was small like the teeth in her tin until she realized the feeling of the grit was on her legs and fingers. Then there was some certainty that the tumbling had stopped. The eye of Ganymede disappeared, replaced by the earthly moon, and suddenly, the hands of strangers.

"She ruined our day at the beach," Fenella heard Puele say.

"You live across the street from the beach." said Lucinda. She had come.

Fenella felt warm if still wet under a blanket. A man looked at her hands. There looked to be burn marks all over them. Mrs. Onishi was there.

"May I?' she asked Lucinda. Lucinda nodded, moving Ina to the other hip, and pulled Puele over to the side of the ambulance.

"You are very lucky," said Mrs. Onishi to Fenella turned her hands over delicately. "To be saved by Akkorokamui."

—Journal Entry—

The nieu vuman show me moor vriting. She chik teese and bones of Vaclav. She look en I's en ask about Therrl. Vaclav sho her master contrawl ruum. patch bay. moniters. aspekt rashio. rezolushun. Vaclav favorit? the wipe.

Nieu man cauf like en kold plays. Loocreeza hate.

THE CURTAINS WERE UNTIED FROM THE WINDOWS AND packed neatly into a box with an address marked "Barnby Dun". Fenella played jacks on the floor with a bright red ball while Lucinda made a "For Sale" sign for Ina's swing chair. The gecko in the ceiling sang farewell arias and the ants and cockroaches marched along the seams of the house in triumph, jubilant that they had won the battle.

Mrs. Onishi came over with sandwiches in sweet rolls for lunch.

"I can't thank you enough," said Lucinda, "for everything." Mrs. Onishi nodded her head and smiled. She sat down on the floor next to Fenella. Fenella missed the ball and it rolled back towards Mrs. Onishi who caught it, smiled, and held it tightly in one hand to her chin for a moment.

PIERCE CALLED FENELLA TO CHECK ON HER.

"I need to clean Walter and Benny's apartment before his parents bring him home from the hospital," she said.

"That place is a biohazard. I'm coming over," said Pierce.

Walter had declined to come home to his parents, citing the well-known general Kopek-Zuyio household malaise as being not conducive to his overall wellbeing. Pierce fixed the window in the kitchen that Fenella had broken while getting to Benny. The management at the Andromeda was useless after all. Fenella and Pierce set mousetraps, bleached surfaces, and retired the toy piano to the dumpster.

"I'm sure Benny can find another way to achieve a juvenile affect in his music," said Fenella as she wiped her hands on her jeans after she'd pitched it in. She was happy to have a paycheck, to be able to feed the electricity meter in Benny and Walter's apartment, to wash their sheets for them. She and Pierce scrubbed the bathroom and washed the windows and put the dishes away. Fenella lit incense, placed calla lilies in jars around the apartment, and for Walter, she bought a little green and yellow canary. It sang miniature descants of cheer and life's fervor. She hung a Victorian-style cage by Walter's window for his homecoming.

On Sunday, Walter's parents drove up with him in their full-sized luxury sedan. They seemed uneasy at the Andromeda. Afraid to touch anything. When they reached the front door, Fenella put her hand on Walter's eyes to surprise him as Pierce unlocked the door with Benny's keys.

"I've actually never seen it so clean," said Walter's mom.

"It actually smells good in here," said Walter. Pierce and Fenella looked at each other, pleased.

"And in here . . . " said Fenella leading Walter to the bedroom. The room was quiet. Fenella had hoped the canary would be singing. Fenella led Walter to the cage. The body of the canary remained on its perch, rigid, immoveable. Little feet grasped the perch tightly. Underneath, mouse droppings mingled with the millet.

"There's no head on that bird, Fenella."

Fenella was silent for some time.

"I need a dancer in a film I'm making, Walter," she said, taking his hand. "You'll need to move temporarily."

"When I dance, I look like a badger trying to squeeze through a cat door," said Walter.

"So will you do it?" she asked.

"Well, I guess I haven't unpacked yet," he said.

CHORUS:

Straight by the Picaroon
with can and fork in hand
the rushes hide the loon
no sleeping on the land

We scrape and poke and brawl
Under bridge tie-off, spike
Young Fenella, fair and tall
the coxswain, creaking bike

Two wretches drain slowly
House of Andromeda
And what of the study
by our strong Perseus

BOOK TWO

❧❧

—*Journal of Walter Kopek-Zuiyo*—

May 30

Outside, Perdita is howling. The streets are filled with homeless people. They scream and cry and no one knows what to do or can seem to help them. Every hour, those with homes face the prospect of losing electricity, heat. Mice invade every crevice and no one can keep out their tiny bodies. The sea makes its way into every fiber of clothing.

As for us, we're quite fortunate. We're comfier than thousands. It's quiet here in the Sugar Factory except for the creaking of girders and the occasional releases of pressure from valves in the Aquarium. We should be saving our money but Benny, Queen that he is, keeps buying Gucci shit online so I don't know if we'll ever get together another deposit for an apartment. It's so stupid that we can't think past this gingerbread house.

June 2

Dearest Diary,

We are living and working in the German Expressionist Village set. Me and Benny sleep behind a little cottage backdrop. The first thing I did was to help Raúl here at the house build actual rustic little beds for us all to sleep in that do double duty as furniture for the film. Fenella had us stitch little patchwork comforters for ourselves. She wants everything just so. We have regular sewing circles by the fireplace at night with Benny hemming then hawing over the right colors for our patches even though we're shooting in black and white. Vaclav is always sitting near at our fabric scraps while petting his weird deer pets.

June 10

Now that we've been in the Sugar Factory for a bit, I should tell you about our life here and what Fenella has us doing. It's so much better than daily group at the psychiatric hospital, if even more strange. I'll start with the night since it's always night in the windowless Aquarium.

6:00 p.m. Peter the chef usually sends food down to us via Raúl. We're usually building sets or shooting at that time but Fenella always makes sure that we stop to let Vaclav eat and rest. She gave us a lecture (while looking at Pierce) about how we should all be looking after the weird waif. Is the romance is already beginning to crack? She's talking about "learned helplessness" when finding misplaced things on the set.

9:00 p.m. We shoot our last shot for the night. Currently, Benny is playing "Cesare", inspired from "The Cabinet of Dr. Caligari" in our German Expressionist Village set. Fenella puts makeup on him, but he is already empty looking. Why bother?

Vaclav and his deer thingies get to sleep somewhere by the staircase and the asparagus beds, (where do they poop?) and the rest of us have a few glasses of whiskey around the Méliès set moon. I sneak out to take my Fluoxetine, Bupropion and Citalopram. There is another fish tank in the bathroom. A fluffy sculpin, or "Lizard fish". Two little combs on the top and bottom of its body like it's here to be a stylist. Complexion while brushing teeth: Blue.

11:30 p.m. Benny and I are in our little peasant beds behind our quarter of a peasant house, much warmer than we were when we were in our real peasant beds and our real peasant house. Voices come from the Mèliés set. A flood light with a blue filter like a snow forest; on, then off. Fenella is working on tomorrow's production schedule. We hear her close the door to the control room.

June 15

Dearest Diary,

New problems afoot here in the gingerbread house. Fenella has wondered if yours truly would not be better cast in the role of the modern Francis than Pierce. Pierce all George Washington teeth. Fenella stiff smiles, wide berths, high eyelines. An hour later Pierce accedes and then an hour later he is back to being Francis. Mood: Happy. I did not want to be Francis. It's back to scraggly Dr. Caligari for me.

Peter sends down lunch; carrot ginger soup with crème fraîche and chopped chives. Said that outside the Factory gate this morning was a o.d. and he had to call an ambulance.

Benny is menacing as Cesare, all angles and sinew and greasepaint on our geometrically absurd set with circus tent tops spinning like whirling dervishes. He is performing well because he is feeling better. Finally, Benny is sleeping at night. It wasn't so long ago that he was a murderous somnambulist in real life. Well, he killed mice.

Lucretia the crow teases Benny. She swoops over at breakfast time and pecks at the foam on his latte. "Papa, I want espresso!" we tease him.

Skin: Bad. New medication is causing zits.

Mood: Improved. Less dreams of suicide as a door.

June 20

7:30 a.m. There is no need for an alarm clock here in the Sugar Factory. Lucretia the crow begins diving in cursive caws, waking us from our prop-bed slumbers.

Fenella and Vaclav have already been up. She is teaching him to read. We should be reporting the Rostungers for not sending Vaclav to school and instead we are flouting child labor laws ourselves by using him as an actor in our films. Vaclav seems to be having a wonderful time. We push the thoughts of our greed, our culpability, out of our minds every time they enter. We hang on to his smiles like the handholds in Benny's old Dodge Dart that used to squeal around on Ice Cream Hill. All blind corners this.

Breakfast. Breakfast is a busy time in the Factory, full of clinking dishes and commotion. Preferences for the crew/house are as follows:

Vaclav and his deer pets all enjoy a blend of müesli and fruit.

Fenella has what she calls "the jet set". Coffee, coffee cake, and coffee.

Pierce has green tea.

Benny has Fruit Loops and Tang.

I have a stack of 3 pancakes, bacon, toast, and orange juice.

Lucretia has bits of dissected mouse and sunflower seeds.

My parents have called almost daily wondering what life is like, living with the famously wealthy Rostungers. The truth is, we've never seen them. Fenella goes up to work sometimes in the main part of the factory/house but the rest of us stay down here. Mom is disappointed. The Kopek-Zuiyos were always big on name dropping.

I opened the pages of a book that I brought from our apartment at the Andromeda. Near the spine was a solitary mouse turd. It struck me how here in the factory we are surrounded by animals; dik-diks, fish and mollusks, a crow, but the absence of mice has had such a stabilizing effect on me.

9:00 a.m. Fenella is working on editing our shots from yesterday. Benny as Cesare holds a knife. The knife's tip graphically ends where a crooked path begins and continues, upward, bisecting the film's frame in stark black and white. His high-contrast form now bleeds like ink across the blades of plane. His refulgent eyes sink into saucers of powdered kohl and a tiny town the size of a tea cup behind him begins to rotate. The knife's edge scrapes into the village walls.

"Why the knife?" I asked. "Isn't this supposed to be a relaxation film?"

"No," said Fenella. "It's supposed to function like a dream."

"Let's cut in some sounds of a weeping gull," said Pierce. "Research shows there is auditory content in 80-94% of dreams. This should not be a silent movie." Poison dart arrows shoot from Fenella's eyes. Bad times ahead for Pierce. Taking the director's seat. He's a regular Joe Mankiewicz.

10:00 pm. In all probability, we are in deep shit. Imagine it. Making experimental films in a Sugar Factory under an Aquarium with an Iulian orphan for the Rostungers! There will be some price to pay. We think of nothing except the relief that living rent-free brings us. We live from day-to-day making art and stuffing our gurgling bellies.

June 21

It was midnight, maybe one. In the far corridors of the Aquarium wing, Benny and I could hear Lucretia chewing on bits of words, eating them, turning them electromagnetic. The bellows of the Aquarium's gills heaved and hummed and the sound was like being inside a giant nautilus. Shuffling footsteps down the hall. I look at Benny trying to blend into his patchwork squares. We hear the steps near the control room. Our blood slows. I clench my toes inside my socks. The studio lights switch on. A man like Boris Karloff stands before us.

"Thurl Rostunger here. I require a film." Saliva runs from his mouth in thick threads.

FENELLA LEARNED ABOUT COLOR FROM LUCINDA WHO took her sorrow and put it into the hot shop in Barnby Dun where she plunged a blow hose into the howling, leaping furnace and pulled out molten glass. Lucinda found a way to collect the oozing things, let them harden, crack them off at crucial points. She learned with every unintentional shatter to release a little more within the places in her stomach that so resembled shards of the failed works that she swept from the shop floor. She blew and rolled and fit the hot sand and silicon dioxide into all kinds of forms. Rainbows, suns, sailboats, cirrus clouds, and stars. Crimson, gold, and magenta, spun from the places of blackness. And the frit, graphite, and vermiculite reached into the rotten parts of Lucinda that had been yanked and cut and burned and through an alchemy the wounds were cauterized.

Fenella saw Lucinda's work in Perdita; in the peacock window above the doorway of Calpurnia's Shoes, the San Marzano red of the lamps above the tables in Giuseppe's, the flecked crystal-cut doorknobs at the Ferula Coffee House. Each reborn grain of sand became part of her cellular build. She became a crane, an old-fashioned rose, a sea creature tip-toeing on the continental shelf.

A funny thing; when Fenella heard glass break, at a dinner party or when it tumbled out of the recycling bin into the dump truck, it was the sound of Lucinda's heart; her mother's light breaking apart into a prism. It was the shattering of she who has put her organs on the outside of her body. It was Ina, Fenella, the sailboat made from medium topaz frit, lead solder, and the pain of women.

Then the light shifted and like a clip from a pair of lead nippers, all was changed. The sun, master rod and tube, lit a flat plane of marsh. Sea glass, limes, celery, spring grass, the skin of a caiman.

❧❧❧❧

—*Written on Toilet Paper in Cell*—

The Sweeneys have always had a clean line to
the forest and being the oldest, it's pure in me, Gary.
I heard the hum of the minerals from inside the guard

gate at Madeira House. At night, when I drank beer by the hole in the chain link, the coyotes up in the Pobre Claritas howled because they heard it too. Not even the blue jays came to peck at the gems in those walls. Those gems are like eyes, eyes that see everything, like the time I held Denise's head in the Picaroon too long for the first time. Like the time I skinned my first dog.

At first, I only noticed the ashes and the litter around from the handicappers. Then I started to snort my crystal in the seance room. Did it off the old marble mantle. The room, it started knocking like a bass amp in the back of a GTO.

I liked to bite this one spot on the side of my thumb and taste that bittersweet taste. Then I'd rub the blood on the perimeter walls a little, for safety. In my guard house I used to pull out the panties of the girl with the small tits, and think about my tube sock around her neck. I'd get short on beer and I'd wait until it got dark, hoping some kids would want to party.

❧❧❧❧

—Handheld Sign on Saceda Ave—

IMPEACH
REMILLARD
INTERGALACTIC
NETWORK TELEVISION
GENPROTACTUITION
SCABIES

~on reverse~

Have You Had
Your Coffee Today?
The Addled Egg Diner
235 Saceda Avenue

—*Video Diary*—

The film begins and the subject looks unsure as if it has or has not been recording. The camera is handheld, shaking noticeably, turned around upon holder.

"This is Thurl Rostunger. April 8th." The voice is muffled and distorted in the camera's microphone. A line of drool eases out the corner of Thurl's mouth. He readily brings a handkerchief to blot it away, and then the camera whirls in a dizzying, nauseating whoosh of a pan, landing upon an oil portrait hung in a hallway. The portrait is oversized, the woman featured appears domineering. She is framed within jungle foliage, birds of paradise accenting the feather in her hat and the point on her umbrella—which is assisting her precarious balance upon two tiny boots and a small foothold above a waterfall. Near one of the birds of paradise, a singular wasp hesitates above the stamen. Thurl's heavy breathing in the camera's microphone can be heard.

"Peony Mecklenberg, wife to Ormand Rostunger, my great grand-parents. Commanders of the Ocean! Shippers of the Seas! Merchants to Magnates!" An intermittent electronic tone interrupts Thurl. Another wild pan of the camera. Blur, then focus on a monitor mounted from the ceiling. The gray-greenish image is of the courtyard of the Sugar Factory. A woman, in her twenties, pushes a bike through the gravel. She stops, slides her shoe off her heel for a moment, rubs it with her thumb and forefinger, then slips the shoe back on, and pushes the bike out of frame.

WHILE THE SUGAR FACTORY WAS AN ESPECIALLY CAVERNous domicile, the Rostunger household had long been a place where persons were lost or forgotten, or went mostly unnoticed. Prior to living at the Factory, Thurl and Nina lived in a traditional craftsman style home near Ice Cream Hill, in the exclusive Blachington Woods neighborhood. The mix of magnolia trees and wisteria disguised the enormity of the home's size from the street. The property had three separate entrances; one for the main house, one for the guest house, and another for services, which meant that people often came and went without being seen.

One spring, Thurl attended a fundraising event and struck up a conversation with Haustrian conductor Manfred Umlaut from the City's Metropolitan Symphony. Mr. Umlaut mentioned that he was due for a sabbatical, and Thurl invited the conductor to stay at their home in Perdita for the summer. Mr. Umlaut accepted.

By the appointed date in June however, Thurl had entirely forgotten about his invitation, and he and Nina had long since departed for their summer home in the Islands.

"I am expected by Mr. Rostunger," Manfred said to Catalina when he arrived.

Catalina took his bags without comment. She was not surprised that the Rostungers had failed to mention that a man would be staying at the house while they were away. Catalina regularly roused Nina from bed, telling her that persons insisting that they had confirmed appointments had arrived at the house.

"Sweet Jesus!" Nina would yell, and tear into the shower, shouting at Catalina to bring tea and stall them in the sitting room as long as possible.

During his summer at the Rostunger's, Manfred Umlaut lived quite comfortably. Catalina tidied his room daily, and Peter happily cooked for a new and grateful face who spoke to him while he sautéed and ate casually at the kitchen counter. In early September, two weeks after returning from the Islands, Thurl encountered Manfred reading serenely in the great room.

"Extraordinary," Thurl remarked when he discovered how long Manfred had been there. "Just about anyone could live here unnoticed."

Peter had been caught out several times at the Blatchington Woods house making tacos for one when a group of twelve guests appeared at seven expecting cocktails and a multi-course dinner. As a precaution, Peter now cooked for close to ten people every night, though no one ate his food with any regularity. Most days, he'd wait until nine, and if no one unexpected appeared, he'd give a portion of the extra food to the bulldog Ashur, then dump the rest into the garbage. If he was feeling particularly tired, he'd freeze some Beef Bourguignonne and try to cut back on the portions he prepared for the rest of the week. It was usually during these times that a visiting dignitary pulled up to the house.

When Thurl unexpectedly put the Blachington Woods house on the market, he told Nina that he wanted to get more distance from his ex-wife Birdie Oberlander. Birdie had purchased a home in the neighborhood with her new husband, Sergio, who, at the time of her marriage to Thurl, had been her personal trainer. Nina was outraged that Thurl could even consider living outside Blachington Woods, which she considered to be social suicide. They feuded for several months until the house sold. It was then that Thurl told Nina of his Sugar Factory purchase and his intention to inhabit it.

Nina considered divorce and made a call to her attorney. He advised her to get an updated report from her banker before proceeding, and so she made a call to 1st Concepción Bank.

"Nina. I've been trying to get in touch with you for ages," said the banker.

"Oh. Well, we were at the Island house all summer, Carl."

"Nina . . . it's April."

"Right."

"Nina, listen. About your account. You're overdrawn by 300K."

"What! Thurl gives me 50K a month, Carl."

"Nina, I'll be happy to meet with you any time this week and we can go over the statements line by line. But please believe me when I tell you that Thurl's monthly transfer only covers the interest on your loans."

In the end, Nina agreed to put up with the disgrace of living in a converted Sugar Factory. After all, she merely had to wait until her elderly parents passed away to inherit the balance of the Carlyle Corporation and the Madeira Mystery House, which had proved to be quite a popular destination for tourists. And Thurl was not in the best of health either. Cementing her decision to stay married was Thurl's conciliatory offer during one of their marriage counseling sessions to pay off Nina's margin loan debt, and to increase her monthly allowance to seventy thousand. To pacify Nina further, Thurl had his architect send Nina the preliminary drawings of the Moorish room, and suggested that she host the highlight of the Perdita social season, the PHDS gala, at their new home.

The entire idea of hosting the Perdita Hurt Diminishment Society's annual gala on a rundown industrial property was at first, perfectly ridiculous to Nina, further proof that Thurl had gone completely off the rails. His offer to contribute an additional four hundred thousand towards her chairmanship however, proved irresistible. She'd take the money and tell the PHDS she was contributing two hundred thousand towards the chairmanship and use the balance to pay off her credit cards, and the rest would get her through fall fashion week in the City. Thurl would never be the wiser. They kept separate accountants, and Thurl was obviously no longer playing with a full deck. As far as the feasibility of pulling off a successful social event outside Blatchington Woods, well, if Nina's mother Phoebe Remillard Carlyle endorsed the event, who was Candy Thorson to argue with her? She'd usher in a new era of casual elegance for the Perdita patriciate. Maybe she'd even get a feature in the *Coastal Gentry Quarterly*.

Nina was quite unaware of the plight of the orphans of Iulia or even that they were to be benefited by the PHDS fundraiser. Her involvement as chairwoman simply involved her monetary contribution and the choosing of a theme for the event, which she called in to the Hurt Diminishment Society's Undersecretary, Muffin Laidley. It had been Muffin's idea to host a benefit for Iulian orphans. Muffin had attended a dinner party at Fabiola Guelphe-Finkelstein's, where she had been introduced to Fabiola's brother-in law, Larry Guelphe-Finkelstein, who had served an ambassador to the Iulian region for several years immediately following the Gossamer Revolution. After her conversation with Larry and a few subsequent phone follow ups, Muffin launched an adoption awareness campaign within the Hurt Diminishment Society.

The whole of Blatchington Woods RSVP'd to "An Evening of Compassion: Disco Spring Fling", not only because of the immense curiosity about Thurl's seemingly mercurial purchase of a former factory to live in, but because of the great satisfaction they felt at seeing the Carlyle heiress ensconced in such an unlikely residence. And everyone wanted to say they were involved with the Iulian Orphans since the cause had been featured in an article in *Coastal Gentry Quarterly* earlier in the year. Candy Thorson had said herself that the Iulian orphan cause was "this year's juvenile diabetes for sure."

There were several reports that Nina seemed "out of sorts" during the Evening of Compassion. During the auction Nina repeatedly outbid herself to win the services of Blaine Dwyers, a professional playdate coordinator, for Lexi. Candy Thorson reported seeing Nina vomit into one of the arabesque tiled fountains in the Moorish room. Later, while having a conversation with Tinsley Walters, Nina asked if it was "hot in here?", then proceeded to tear off her pantyhose in shreds, and then stuff them into her rock-candy martini. It was after this point that Nina decided to pledge another fifty thousand and add her name to the Iulian adoption list at a table manned by Fabiola Guelphe-Finkelstein.

The confusion about Vaclav probably stemmed from an unlikely coincidence. Muffin Laidley dropped Vaclav off at his new home, the Sugar Factory, at the same time that Blaine Dwyers arrived to coordinate a play date for Lexi. Catalina promptly showed the two visitors into the Conservatory, where they sat at a table across from one another exchanging nods, while Catalina went to Nina's room to wake her up.

"A little boy and a Blaine Dwyers have come Missus Nina."

"Oh, she already brought a playmate over. Fabulous. Show them into Lexi's room Catalina, if you would."

"Mrs. Nina, Lexi is at Positive Body Image Camp. You remember? She thinks it's called Super Camp."

"I completely forgot. Look, tell Blaine I'm not feeling all that well and I'll call her later."

Catalina dutifully reported the news to Blaine back in the Conservatory.

"No problem," said Blaine with a wide-eyed full-toothed smile. "I simply wanted to drop off a list of potential playmates for Mrs. Rostunger to review. She can call me on the number at the bottom when she's made a selection and I'll review activities with her at that time. Don't worry Catalina sweetie, I'll show myself out. Thanks so much. And what an adorable looking child this is – one of the Guelphe-Finkelstein's? I do all of Candy Thorson's playdates you know. Sweetie," she said patting Vaclav on the head. "Give your full name and phone number to Catalina and we'll look you over, how does that sound?"

Catalina and Vaclav smiled at each other. Blaine tapped her nails against the patent leather of her purse as she showed herself out, heels hammering across the marble floor. Catalina, confused that Blaine had left without the child she apparently arrived with, pointed towards a chair, and Vaclav sat down again. Then Vaclav, suddenly remembering something, opened his small satchel and retrieved a stack of paperwork addressed to Mrs. Rostunger, which he handed to Catalina. Catalina walked back through the corridor to Nina's office, where she discovered Nina asleep on a chaise lounge with Lokum laying on top of her feet. After trying to gently rouse Nina without success, Catalina placed Blaine and Vaclav's letters on top of a precariously high stack of papers on Nina's desk inside a box marked "In.", then left the room.

A short time later, the top portion of the paperwork slid off the desk and into a wastepaper basket below. Along with Blaine and Vaclav's letters, an invitation from Nina's mother Phoebe for the upcoming Gardening Society Meeting at the Palais Royale Ballroom also fell unnoticed into the garbage can, which caused no end of hell for Nina at a later date.

Meanwhile, Catalina, who was unable to communicate with Vaclav in either Spanish or English, got him to follow her into the kitchen where she made him a tuna sandwich that he poked at nervously. He showed signs of being tired, so Catalina took him to a newly created guest room on the east side of the Factory.

❧❧❧❧

AFTER GRADUATING FROM THE BARNBY DUN SECONDARY school, Fenella accepted a partial scholarship to New Concepción College in the City, a small liberal arts school located near Norton Park. Daen took her to her new dorm room in Beardsley Tower in the City at the end of a carved bear delivery. She nursed a severe redwood splinter wound in her thumb throughout the first week of school.

Originally, she had intended on becoming a theater arts major. She filled her schedule the first two semesters with pre-requisite courses in playwriting, stagecraft, and acting. Fenella had enjoyed a measured confidence in her acting ability. She'd played Emily Webb in the Barnby Dun Secondary School's production of "*Our Town*" and was described in the Barnby Dun Soothsayer as performing "instinctively". During her first semester at Concepción, she'd had fun playing a maid in a bedroom farce, mostly because Lenny, who played the part of the cad, was a home brew enthusiast who regularly brought growlers of steam beer to share with the cast in the south quad after rehearsals.

It was during a student production of "*The Green Cockatoo*", that Fenella began to reconsider her studies. The week before the play opened, Jason Cusk, who had the role of Henri, joined a handful of other cast members when they took Fenella aside in the wings.

"Look. I know you don't like me," said Jason, "but you're going to have to get over it. It throws everything off to have Leocadie behave that way to her own husband."

"Yeah," said Carrie Ann in the costume of Severine. "I mean, look at him for God's sake." She grabbed Fenella's face between her hands and stared into her eyes. "Really look at him. Look!!! Omigod, she can't even look at me . . . There's going to have to be some kind of intensity there,

Fenella. I'm standing here right now because your distance is hurting the whole production." She clicked her character shoes on the wood for extra emphasis.

Fenella was stunned. She realized only then that she did, in fact, have a mild disdain for Jason Cusk. His mannerisms were goofy. He was pudgy and had a lot of dead skin on his forehead and nose. The realization that her unconscious emotions were so apparent shook her. She finished "*The Green Cockatoo*" to the best of her ability, and at the end of the semester changed her major to Film Theory.

As part of NCC's work-study program, Fenella obtained a job through the college as a clerical assistant to Professor Charles, who taught courses in medieval history and literature. She worked fifteen hours a week for him in the anteroom of his office, located within the Humanities building, doing filing, correspondence, and scheduling.

The Professor visited the office once a day for about half an hour, and two hours on Thursdays when he met with students. His inner sanctum contained an extensive display of medieval art and artifact along the walls, kept in shadow by heavy tapestries over the windows. Hieronymus Bosch prints, thumbscrews, claymores, haubergeons, pikes, judas cradles, and glaives were illuminated only by a circular, low-hanging, iron studded chandelier, lit by candles, surely in violation of the college's fire code. Part of Fenella's job required her to replace the candles once a week. She would push the only usable piece of furniture in the room, a high-backed domed porter's chair, over to the chandelier, and stand on the seat to pry loose the melted wax remains with her fingernails, replacing them with long tapers.

Fenella was finishing this task, late in the winter semester of her freshman year, when the Professor entered the office.

"Ahh, Ms. Lundgren. Thank you for your valiant service," he boomed.

When the professor blinked, his grey eyebrows concealed his eyes almost completely. He smoothed his neatly parted hair with his hands and gave his sweater-vested stomach two satisfied thumps and tossed his leather satchel into a corner of the room where it leaned against a mounted bardiche.

"I say, Ms. Lundgren. Do you have any notions about what exactly it is that I do within the confines of this room when I ask you to hold my calls?" he asked.

"Well, I've had some theories, but I'd like to imagine that you're writing or reading about medieval history or literature."

"Some theories. Yes! Ha ha!" said the professor, his caterpillar brows cocked. "Ms. Lundgren, would you like to know what it is that I do?" Fenella's face betrayed her hesitation.

"Oh no my dear, nothing sordid, upon my honor," said the Professor. Fenella laughed and shrugged her shoulders.

"Bring your office chair in here Ms. Lundgren and unplug the phone."

She did as she was told and reentered the Professor's office dragging her chair. Its casters rattled across the flagstones. The Professor walked to the far wall. Underneath a pair of manacles and a chastity belt, he retrieved two hanging keys. Then he opened a trunk placed at the foot of a suit of gothic plate armor, and brought a china tea saucer. He placed the saucer on the floor beside Fenella's chair. The professor extended his hand and put one of the keys into Fenella's palm and then curled her fingers around the warded iron and patted the top of her hand.

"Now," said the Professor as he twitched his nostrils, "Your studies here have included something of the artist Salvador Dalí, have they not?"

"Of course."

"What you may not have been exposed to, my dear, is Mr. Dalí's unique form of rest. The man slept very little. He could work prolifically for several days with not much more than a catnap. Dalí believed that if we could merely remove the crutches of consciousness, sleep, even in short segments could solve problems, unleash creativity."

Fenella nodded slowly.

"This brings us to the Dalí key nap. Sit down in your chair my dear. Yes, that's it, get comfortable. Now, hold the key loosely in between your thumb and forefinger, above the saucer down there. The technique is to relax completely while maintaining a hold on the key. You may want to focus on one specific thought before you let yourself go. When you have completely relaxed, the key will drop from your hand and clink onto the plate, waking you out of your reverie. And voila! You emerge refreshed and renewed. Obviously, this is a technique meant to be performed alone. You can't very well relax with my person next to you, agonizing about whether the key should suddenly drop. No, this is a solitary exercise, so relax my dear. Meanwhile I shall amble about the courtyard below, breathing deeply."

Professor Charles left Fenella then, closing the paneled office door with vigor. She attempted to comply with the Professor's wishes, closed her eyes and took several deep breaths. She thought about relaxing but she was too cognizant of the heavy chandelier above her head and the Pear of Anguish displayed to her right, and the countless broadswords and dirks and bludgeons surrounding her. She spent what she approximated to be twenty minutes sitting in her chair quietly, arms folded in front of her, and then she dropped the key onto the plate and audibly sighed.

"Marvelous," she said when she opened the door to the Professor's arched eyebrows.

৯৵৯৵

—Found, Video Diary –

Thurl is seated on divan with handheld VHS camera shooting up into his nose hairs. He begins speaking.

"It was in the Blatchington Hills mansion that I first noticed the change. Morning, at breakfast, with Nina ashing her cigarette onto the coffee saucer and Lexi feeding bits of her polenta and chorizo to Ashur under the table…" he pauses for a moment. "I couldn't stop drooling." The camera pans down to a linen napkin on his on Thurl's lap, soaked through. The camera pans back to Thurl's mouth and nose. "Nina and Lexi seemed not to have noticed. I placed the napkin to the side of my plate and initiated excusing myself and rising from the table, however my body stayed behind. I looked at myself, over and over. It was if I could see myself from the breakfast room door. I mumbled, "excuse me" and then I tried hefting myself up. My mind replayed the action, again and again, while my actual body remained still at the dining table. I had difficulty determining the exact amount of time I remained there, but at some point, from the viewpoint of the doorway I noticed that Nina had left. Then, sometime later, Lexi and Ashur flashed away as well."

Over the right of Thurl's ear, a man empties a container of fish into the expanse of the open tank of the Aquarium. The fish scatter like chemtrails.

"I remember jump cuts of chorizo on the parquet, Catalina clearing Nina's saucer full of butts and ashes, and repeating "excuse me" while rising, only to return to the beginning of the loop, forced to begin again. Finally, when I returned to looking from behind my own eyes and I regained control of my body, the sun in the breakfast room had travelled across the frescoes on the wall from the hillside cypress all the way down to the three-masted barque in the ocean. I noticed that the front of my pants and shirt front and a portion of the tablecloth and plate were all damp and that I was sucking on my tongue because it was so dry," Thurl points to his tongue for emphasis. "My body finally compelled itself from the breakfast room and into the kitchen. I filled a crystal highball glass with filtered water and drank it down. I refilled the glass for a second, then a third time. My stomach cramped. I could not quench this thirst." Thurl reaches for a glass of water on a side table next to the divan. He holds up one finger signaling to the viewer to "wait". Thurl empties the glass.

"See. Nothing." He sticks out his tongue. Waves it from side to side up close to the lens. "Let's continue…" Thurl wipes his glasses on his shirt, then places them back on his nose. "I was cognizant of how weary I was and how the light in the kitchen hurt my eyes. I walked across the house to my library and pulled the curtains across the windows then laid on my Chesterfield in the dark underneath the glass-encased model of a cargo ship, though sleep did not come. At some point, exhausted, I tried to heft my girth from the sofa only to find myself caught once again in an unbreakable loop. My eyes remained partially opened and the light behind the curtain rings rose and fell and rose and fell."

The clip ends. The next shot is a medium one, from a tripod, of Thurl seated in his office with the coelacanth behind him. He begins speaking once again.

"When I became aware once more, I was unsure of the amount of time that had passed. Lexi entered the library and she appeared not to have grown, so I supposed that I had been immobile for a few days at most. I was exhausted and brittle. I was certain that I hadn't eaten since before drooling in the breakfast room, though I felt no hunger." Thurl pauses to light a cigar.

"I made a call to the endowment office in the Rostunger wing of Perdita Memorial Hospital," says Thurl bitterly.

"Dr. Fong was jovial. Of course, he asked me why I hadn't been at the Benefactor's Dinner. He checked my pupils, reflexes, ears, and blood pressure. He made calls to a neuro specialist and sent me directly over to the center.

For several weeks, I underwent tests. They told me that there were abnormalities in my brain function, however no specific condition could be identified. Several drugs were prescribed with no improvement. I reported to doctors at the neuro clinic that I didn't recall eating since before the irregularities had begun." Thurl stands up from his desk, walks in front of the elephant's foot trash can. Places his hands on his hips. Looks into the camera. Sighs.

"It's funny. I've been trying to lose about 100 lbs. of fat for years. If I'd known that quitting food altogether wouldn't make the scale budge, I would have been a lot easier on myself," says Thurl. The shot cuts to a wider angle, with Thurl seated once again.

"The reports showed that I was neither malnourished nor dehydrated. I was sent for further testing on the Far Coast. Memories of my days became more tenuous. I have snapshots of boarding my private jet over and over, of drooling on white business shirts, of shielding my eyes constantly from the sun." Thurl returns back to his seat behind the desk. He takes his cigar from the ashtray, and takes two quick puffs.

"Then, in the waiting room of a sleep clinic on the Far Coast, I had a breakthrough. The windowless room contained a single aquarium. The filtered black light, the swaying movement of the plastic plants, and the constant stream of bubbles rising upwards through the air tube gave me a restfulness that I hadn't felt in months. I noticed I had more control over my mouth and tongue than I'd had in a long time." The coelacanth behind Thurl moves behind his shoulder in the tank. Its jaw hinges open on its intracranial joint.

"The medications and treatments and physical therapy were unhelpful. I didn't want to be hospitalized. I was desiccated and wary of company." Lucretia swoops into frame and lands on Thurl's shoulder. He fishes something out of his pocket and feeds it to her.

"When I arrived back in Perdita, I immediately put the Blatchington Hills house on the market and bought the abandoned Sugar Factory in cash. I told Nina about the move. She threw lit cigarettes and ashtrays at me. She slammed the desk drawer in my library repeatedly. She took off one of her heels and tried to smash the glass case around my model ship.

"Now look! The Sugar Factory has been transformed into a great estate. I always told my little ultracrepidarian she'd be featured in design magazines for her strong, unconventional, artistic living style." Thurl waves his hand around the smoky air. "She only calmed down when I described the events that we'd be able to hold in this riverfront compound." The video cuts to Thurl standing in front of the large fireplace.

"Undeterred by the need to eat or the ability to sleep, I pushed this ungainly body through the flurry of preparations needed to make the East Wing into the Aquarium. Meetings with engineers and designers in the library filled the daylight, leaving only thirsty nights. Permits such as these normally take years to issue but the Rostungers have connections!" He taps the handset on his black desktop phone.

Another cut. Thurl is back to a handheld camera. He walks through the Aquarium. Water and fish flash at odd angles in the extreme boundaries of the frame.

"Specialists from the Islands came to help me build it. Eight months later the pumps are switched on. I have now decamped from the Blatchington Hills House."

Cut to shot of Aquarium specialists releasing fish into tanks. Voice over. "Marine biologists bring specimen after specimen down into the water and with each release of life my body seems to gain a greater ability to move in accordance with my will."

Cut to shots of tv footage of boats on the ocean. "The specialists have asked to discuss the long-term placement here of an unusually large octopus that a fishing boat off the Islands have caught. They have been unable to place the animal in any public institution due to lack of funds, but the catch has made news in the Islands. Before relocating the specimen, legislators want to review my facility, so I am recording it for them."

Cut to pan of pump room. Cut to marine specialists feeding fish. Cut to close-up of a marine specialist holding a beaker of water and examining it. Cut to main Aquarium room. Catalina enters.

"I need to know where you want him," says Catalina, bringing a small boy down the staircase. He's getting lost up there and it's dangerous with the workers."

"I did not understand that we had a guest," says Thurl.

The boy smiles back at Thurl. Catalina turns her hands palms up and pats the boy between his shoulders, urging him in Thurl's direction.

"He doesn't really speak English," she says.

"Well, there's an entire education in this wing. I need to show the construction guys in. There will be new fish this afternoon. You can help me make sure they're fed."

Cut.

❧❧❧❧

DURING HER SECOND YEAR AT NEW CONCEPCIÓN College, Fenella moved off campus into a warehouse in the Harbor District with some other students. As well as being a house for seven, the warehouse doubled as an active film stage for the majority of the residents who were art majors.

The warehouse, though perpetually under construction, was built out to resemble something of a moody fishing village. A main street was created with several weather-hued buildings. The warehouse inhabitants scavenged the streets and the City dumps to furnish and decorate their town.

Silas lived in the Mercantile, among shovels and rakes and tins of oats. A hat and dress shop had been constructed by Camille, a theater arts major with a talent for costuming. Ramya inhabited the pet store along with an assortment of betas, a box turtle, a lemon Parisian frilled canary, a zebra finch, two mottled tortoiseshell cats and a shepherd-mix mutt named Goldberg.

Fenella built her room as the town's barber shop, complete with a rotating candy cane pole outside. She studied while seated on an antique barber's chair facing a wall of mirrors and a pharmacy cabinet displaying a collection of straight razors and glass cylinders full of combs in blue Barbicide. Black and white photos of boxers hung on the oiled walnut walls, and a Murphy bed pulled out when Fenella yanked on a coat rack featuring a fedora super-glued to the top.

A larger structure down the street with "Gymnasium" signage had a heavy bag and a ballet barre inside, and further in, a series of lockers, showers and toilets. It functioned as the town's communal restroom. An Astroturfed park with a covered bandstand, silk flowers, and a swing set was laid out near the entrance to the warehouse, and it was the site of the town's parties.

Timed theatrical lighting hung from the rafters. Red gels glowed at ten a.m. and yellow gels at one. Blue and purple key lights appeared at five, which was the signal to the town's inhabitants that cocktail hour had begun at the town's kitchen, "The Barnacle Tavern"; an appealingly working-class seafood restaurant dressed in fishing nets and hanging buoys, with café tables set with candles in red jars. Marvin, who lived in the bait-and-tackle shack, served Sidecars and Aviations to the town's inhabitants who drank them over debates on Althusser or Slavoj Žižek. Meanwhile, Jasper from the bank, and Bill from the candy store and bakery, usually cooked a communal dinner in the Barnacle's kitchen.

The citizens, when greeting visitors to their town, exuded a self-satisfied air of contentment and unity, though the dynamics of the warehouse more closely resembled the agonies of life in an actual town. There was a social hierarchy that came to govern resources and capital. Beer and toilet paper and blocks of cheese were owned and shared and coveted and stolen.

Problems arose concerning law and order and distribution of work. Cleaning up after dinner, sweeping Main Street, the purchasing of fish food, and the responsibility for collecting funds for rent and water and power were sources of heated debate. Spats arose over noise. Silences, whispers and posturing ensued when no one admitted to breaking the air-nailer. Frustration grew as new construction on the warehouse continued to mean extra time and work for Marvin who was the only one proficient in using the table saw.

The last few weeks before finals always saw an eruption of accusations about who was and who was not reciprocating when it came to assisting with other's video projects. Ramya and Jasper liked to scavenge articles from the outside streets—like lamps, chairs and metal municipal sidewalk garbage cans—but failed to repair or position them anywhere for months. This had the effect of creating a dump-like space within the warehouse that became a distorted version of the lots where the articles had been scavenged from in the first place.

Despite all the challenges that were involved in keeping such a living situation together, the warehouse townspeople possessed a reputation for "living one's art" throughout the college. And they had some of the best parties. Prestige kept Fenella's housing arrangement intact.

After Winter Break in her senior year, Fenella began working on her thesis, "*Conflicting Assemblage: The Marxist Dialectic in Postmodern Film and the Development of Chaos Theory*". During that period, a series of events led to a change in the atmosphere of the warehouse.

Bill had graduated the year before and a swarthy, hirsute politics major named Gerard moved into the candy shop. He kept to himself for the first semester, though by spring he had begun lobbying the warehouse town residents into building a saloon that could support larger bands and spectacles during house parties. Then Silas dropped out of school to go hitchhiking, and the Mercantile was taken over by a ceramics and women's studies double major named Pauline, who immediately supported Gerard in the saloon proposal.

While there had been differences of opinion about what should and should not be built within the town, a system of voting or rule by majority had never been put into place. Ramya suggested that because the saloon project was proving so divisive, that a decision-making structure should be implemented. Gerard called Ramya a "fascist" and Pauline referred to her as a "petty bourgeois". Despite objections from Jasper and Ramya, and non-committal uneasiness expressed by Fenella, Marvin, and Camille, Pauline and Gerard moved forward with construction, starting with a surprise decimation of the city park one Tuesday afternoon.

The warehouse split into factions. Fenella eventually sided with the "preservationists" as they began calling themselves. The preservationists steered clear of the site of the former park, congregating in the Barnacle at night for cocktails, and recounting the icy silences they'd received from the "saloon people" in the gymnasium that morning.

Construction of the new saloon wore on for months. Gerard had developed some table saw skills by watching Marvin, although he seemed only capable of operating it during the later blue and purple hours. Then, Camille, who had been talking for months about needing a larger work and living space than the dress shop provided, sided with Pauline on a new proposal to build a residential side street. This caused fresh outrage from Ramya, who argued that the site for the proposed residences would displace the bike parking area and where, now that there was no longer a park, could they possibly put them?

Marvin, who had tried to remain on semi-friendly terms with the preservationists attempted to mediate the situation. He promised that should the residential project be allowed to go forward, the saloon builders would finish their project in one month's time. Additionally, the saloon and residential contingent would agree to a simple majority rule system to approve all new projects in the future, and Pauline volunteered to build a garage to house Jasper's 1926 35C Bugatti restoration project, which had been an eyesore to the entire town, and to steal a bike rack from the City and position it on the residential street. Ramya, outnumbered, acquiesced, and the saloon construction dragged on while residential buildings were framed.

In late March, Marvin's heroin use became extremely evident, and saloon building came to a halt as the town's residents debated about whether Marvin had been stealing the Aviation gin and creme de Violette from the Barnacle's kitchen. Gerard became surprisingly vocal about the need to "do the responsible, adult thing" and get "our pal Marvin the help we all know he needs", and by mid-April, Marvin's parents arrived to collect his things from the bait-and-tackle shop. That same day, Gerard introduced a girl named Sunny to the town, who was not a student, but worked at a record store downtown. She carried stuff in a plastic garbage bag, and repeatedly stated that she was "cool about helping out with like, the whole roommate sitch". As Marvin had not paid his share of the rent in months, the town populace once again acquiesced.

Finally, in May, the saloon was finished off with a red velvet curtain backdrop taken from an old movie palace in the City that had recently been converted into a Chinese Methodist Church. Without holding a town vote, Gerard booked five bands, the Strasbourg Scandals, Rashers Rolling, Das Weeping Willow, Spelunking in Grenoble, and Flichor, none of who were known to any of the other warehouse members.

"Who the fuck are all these people?" asked Ramya when the crowds had gathered along Main Street and stuffed themselves into the saloon for the first band. "I've never fucking seen these people anywhere. It's like an alternate universe of art scenesters. Look Jasper, there's your dumbfuck doppelganger."

By the time Spelunking in Grenoble began their set, things were getting unruly in the town, and Fenella helped Camille to secure the private buildings, lock Goldberg in the pet shop with the rest of the animals, and kick a few people out of the gymnasium who had barricaded themselves inside to do coke, leaving the rest of the bladder-heavy party goers to piss on Main St.

Meanwhile, Gerard, who had been drinking heavily all night, spied Pauline and Sunny together in bed inside one of the Victorians on the residential street and reacted by climbing into the warehouse rafters where he removed the gels from a couple Kino-Flo par lights and directed them through the window of the bedroom where the two girls were amorously cavorting. Pauline and Sunny simply moved into the interior of the Bugatti parked in the windowless garage, while Gerard left the rafters to look for coke in the gymnasium, leaving the stage lights directed through the window of the room and onto the empty glass bowl of Pauline's bong, which magnified and redirected a beam onto a stack of papers near Pauline's bed. The fire quickly spread throughout the residential district, though Pauline and Sunny managed to escape with their lives, if not their clothes.

While the warehouse town wasn't fortunate enough to have a firehouse, it did have a large rolling loading door that Fenella pulled open before the party's attendees trampled one another in a panic to escape the flames. In the end, the human inhabitants of the town clustered together outside, and watched the warehouse town completely burn, unable to rescue Goldberg and the other animals who had been locked inside the pet shop. Professor Charles allowed Fenella to move into his office until she graduated.

"Hang your things on the iron maiden's spikes my dear," he said. "I'll bring you a blanket and a tatami mat from home."

Fenella took her showers at the NCC gym, and as it felt so much like being in the warehouse, it was the only within the hot steam and tiles that she was able to forget the loss of the warehouse. She continued working for the Professor and living in his office until she turned in her thesis in late May and submitted her candidacy for graduation. The economy in the City was experiencing a slowdown at the time, and Fenella's prospects for finding a permanent job that could pay the inflated rent of a room in the City were few. She missed the insulated and contained quality of the warehouse, even as she had despised living there for the last few months of its existence.

She signed up with a temp agency and went to a few appointments for rooms offering sublets, but the people she met with all seemed wrong, and the spaces were depressingly small and dark and pricey.

"Come back down our way," said Lucinda on the phone. "It's so much cheaper in Perdita. Dad and I can help you until you find something."

Fenella skipped graduation ceremonies. She said goodbye to no one in the City, although she left a large pitcher plant and a thank you letter on Professor Charles' desk on the afternoon that Daen came to get her in the pickup. She rented the studio apartment at the Andromeda the next week.

ఞఞ

The Amusements Expand

By Branca Agnelli

Quentin Rokeby, prior his death by railcar, acid, and ax heads in the Perdita Amusements pool, had plunged his businesses into a morass of debt. When no next of kin for Rokeby could be located, Mayor Horseley took the Pier and Amusements into town receivership for close to six months until Gustave du Jardin could purchase the business back from Perdita with a loan from 1st Concepción Bank.

That year, du Jardin extended the Amusement lands across Seahorse Road, turning the terminus railroad station there into a trolley park in an effort to attract more church-going folks. A picnic area surrounding the station was built, along with a series of giant swings hung between redwood trees. Additionally, du Jardin outfitted the saltwater pool with spectator stands, and began offering a thrice-daily show featuring diving horses and trained seals.

The City had recently finished a conversion from horse-drawn trolley to electric car, and when du Jardin noticed an advertisement in *The City Times* offering the horse cars for twenty dollars, or ten dollars without seats, he promptly purchased thirty of them and positioned them outside the picnic area on the dunes. Visitors from the City were now afforded distinctive overnight accommodations on the beach within the converted trolley cars, which proved to be quite popular.

The Amusements had once again become profitable, and du Jardin continued his expansion over the next decade. Further attractions included a balloon ascension, a Ferris wheel, a penny arcade and a carousel. Du Jardin studied industry advancements on the Far Coast and Continent and was prompt to keep his attractions up with the times. He outfitted the Drumlin Railway with a chain lift and extended the track to complete a full circuit, renaming the ride "The FUN-nicular".

WHEN THURL REVIEWED THE FOOTAGE HE HAD SHOT OF the Aquarium before sending it to the Island legislators for approval of his new aquisition, his bodily reaction to the video was immediate. Voids in his memory from the previous months of illness came to him. He felt glimpses of clarity and certainty. He felt quenched and revived.

With a renewed vigor, Thurl made more calls from the divan, ordering a video production suite and stage lighting to be installed on the other end of the wing, while the room under the Aquarium was decorated and equipped and his gap-year hunting trophies were installed in his new study. Thurl began to experiment with the video equipment. He had vague instincts of images that might help his body and mind.

He used photographs from his earlier years of traveling and had Raúl come down to build simple backdrops. He found, however, that the camera and editing equipment confused him. He tried to read user manuals but he felt his time was wasted when his technical acumen bumped against the sort of material that he felt his condition would benefit from. And his communication with Raúl was useless. His tongue became rigid overtime as he tried to explain the artistic direction the sets should take.

Thurl could not explain to himself why his reaction to the video of the Aquarium would be any different than the experience of watching the tank without the intermediary lens. Perhaps the remove of the camera made the subconscious abstraction operate more effectively in his mind. It was a workaround that allowed his brain to inhabit the liminal once again. It was freedom to have a recurring dream-state that was playable on demand.

The Madeira Murders
By Branca Agnelli

On July 6th, in the summer that launched the FUN-nicular, Perdita was filled with the regular sounds of screeching gulls and day trippers. The coaster cars rumbled over their sea-sodden supports. The orchestra at Adelaide's Quay lulled out Antillean waltzes across the wind-whispered dunes and the tule grass in the marsh. Seaweed bulbs popped and spit beneath bare feet and train cars grunted and sighed as they pulled into Seahorse Road. The band shell gleamed in the afternoon sun, causing those disembarking at the train station across the street to shield their eyes. The Andromeda Apartments tower leaned slightly more to the left, knocking the bell into an afternoon yawn.

A miasma of sorts formed over the lagoon at the mouth of the Picaroon, causing residents near the area to pull out incense sticks and uchiwa fans. At Calpurnia's Shoes, women noticed pinching in their heels, wobbling in their ankles. All of the flowers in front of 1st Concepción Bank; including the newly sprung corpse flowers, failed to open their blooms in the morning. Beneath the roof overhang of the summer-shuttered University Library, cliff swallows escaped the daytime heat in their nests. They flitted about the Knickerbocker Theater until they encountered a flock of murrelets down from the Teonchee Pillar, who cooed and roosted in the eaves of the Ferula Coffee House. Whiskey lemonade was set down between piles of chips at the Palais Royale while the rinky tink piano poured through the open windows onto Saceda Avenue. In City Hall, Mayor Horseley snored rhythmically on a chaise lounge. The Perdita First Christian Church choir, walking to practice, tipped their hats to the afternoon print crew who were arriving at *The Village Bugle*.

In the mountains, loggers took naps at lunchtime among the ferns while the mill echoed like far away cicadas down in the valley. Miners soaked their hands and handkerchiefs in sluice boxes and mopped weary eyes that had seen too many afternoons scanning for blues and purples. The staff at the Picaroon Lodge prepared the evening's bombe glacée and placed it in a copper box cooled by the stream, and the dyers at the Loffer compound sipped chilled leek soup after stirring the mauveine and roving in the cauldrons.

And on Ice Cream Hill, the screams of the FUN-nicular riders could be heard all the way from the beach. The screams sent the gulls bursting off towards the bare shoulders of Perdita's White Cliffs. Those screams, it was later said of that afternoon in July, combined almost seamlessly with shrieks from behind the gem-encrusted walls of Madeira House.

Mr. Michael Hartnell, a workman at Madeira, began pounding on the front door of the Geldoffs sometime near to 3:15 p.m. The Geldoff's housekeeper later described her alarm at seeing the man with blood seeping through his coveralls. He had been stabbed multiple times, but would recover.

The Geldoffs sent for the police, who arrived in force at Madeira about forty-five minutes later, and found the séance room and the south and west wings of the house on fire. When the fire captain declared the site all clear close to three hours later, police began investigating the gruesome scene inside. Harriet Smimes Carlyle lay dead in the kitchen, her head severed from her body. Gunnison Carlyle's badly burned remains were found upstairs in his study, in several pieces. Two mutilated laborers were discovered in the séance room, their bodies also charred by the fire. Another workman's corpse displaying multiple stab wounds lay at the end of a drag trail, amidst patch of pink ladies in the garden.

One of Madeira's former architects was called down from the City by authorities to assist them in locating the house's secret passages and rooms. In the early morning hours of the next day, within a hidden library, the trembling six-year-old Emmet Floyd was discovered unharmed, hiding inside a fireplace. Then, within the far reaches of the port wine cellar, behind a concealed door, a man covered in blood and smelling of kerosene was found. He was identified by Mr. Hartnell as the man who had attacked him with a pick ax.

The murders at Madeira caused a due sensation throughout Perdita and the City. Headlines in *The Village Bugle* and *The City Times* speculated about the identity and motive of the murderer as the police remained tight-lipped for days. Was he a fanatic Loffer, determined to make the pronouncement of his prophet Ewerloff come to fruition? Could he be a relative of Pickett Snellgrove, come to exact revenge? The papers theorized about disgruntled former laborers, angry creditors, and a former lover of Mrs. Smimes. Then official charges were brought against Bronislaw Dudek, who *The Village Bugle* revealed, was a fervent and misguided naturalist, enraged by the destruction of the Pobre Clarita Mountains by Carlyle Lumber.

Dudek's cabin, an odd hut crafted from Benitoite tailings, was searched. Several screeds were uncovered detailing his encounters with the devastation of the giant trees, the destruction of the watershed and the elimination of avian habitat. Within these writings, Dudek proposed a theory of sabotage against the technological society. Dudek was well known to the authorities in Barnby Dun. A few years earlier, he had been brought to trial when the Loffers accused him of slaughtering several sheep on their compound.

"Wooly locusts," Dudek had called them in court.

The Madeira Murders trial against Dudek moved rapidly, fueled by the sensationalism that surrounded it. Mayor Horsley, as acting executor of Gunnison's estate, hired William Durant, a famous prosecuting attorney from the City known as "The Varmint Caller". At the end of two weeks, Bronislaw Dudek was sentenced to death by hanging in the Perdita Prison yard.

In lieu of a clear will, Mayor Horsley was appointed as legal guardian to Emmet Floyd and head trustee of the Carlyle Lumber and Holding Company. Emmet Floyd was sent to a boarding school in the City. The Madeira House's burnt sections were torn down. The property was boarded up and the series of gleaming gates surrounding it were firmly locked.

BENNY FRESNEL'S FAMILY HAD A LONG SERIES OF WHITE greenhouses along the coastal highway close to ten miles outside the Perdita town limits. They were the major floral suppliers in San Califia for topiaries. Benny, as a young child, was taken by his grandfather as he tended the irrigation lines among rows of green flocked rabbits.

When Benny's father left at the age of five, he spent more time at Fresnel Nurseries, running up and down the misty damp fields of Valentine's hearts and mossy spheres. He liked to watch his grandmother work in her private greenhouse where she kept her orchids.

At thirteen, Benny was diagnosed with throat cancer. He was driven to the City once a week to be seen by the doctors and specialists at the San Califia Medical Center. Afterwards, as a treat, his mother would take him to the Academy. He found the hung whale skeleton, a relic from the Great Fire, to be calming in some way, as if the weight on his small shoulders were suddenly alleviated and he too could fly into the rafters, devoid of all problematic tissue.

Afterwards, he'd spend the night at his grandparent's house, which was to the rear of the greenhouses, nestled into pampas and mustard grasses. He'd smoke his weed in the dunes by the ocean, then he'd put on a headlamp and walk carefully into the labyrinthine darkness of the greenhouses at night. The misting from the irrigation lines was heavy after seven and in the chilly temperature he could see the fog of his own breath.

He'd be high and he'd wander through the rows as his beam of light peered into the damp hallways. Eventually, he'd sit on a bench in the middle of a field of velvety cats and hens and a feeling of earthy, close peace would settle over him.

The specialists at the San Califia Medical Center were able to remove the tumor successfully from Benny's throat. Sometimes, when he worked at Mystery Manor, children would ask about the scar on his neck. He would lean in closely and whisper,

"Bronislaw Dudek."

FENELLA SAT IN NINA'S OFFICE WITH A STACK OF UNPAID bills on the desk. She had sewn the hems into her own pants, and one was falling out. She stapled it back together. She hadn't seen Nina in days. Lokum took a shit on the carpet. Fenella pulled her blouse over her nose, grabbed the stack of bills and went down the hall to Nina's room.

"Come in!!!" yelled Nina. "Omg, where have you been? Get the dentist on the phone. I have the worst toothache." Blood oozed from her lip and was spattered across the bedspread. In her hands she held a pair of pliers. Next to the bed was a Percocet bottle with Candy Thorson's name on it. "And I have a gift for you, honey."

"Those pliers? Thanks," said Fenella reaching for them. "I really need a set of pliers, actually." Nina looked confused. She scratched her scalp and her arms.

"No, wait. No. Oh, here it is." She took another bottle from the nightstand. "If you're like me, you love your salt. And we all want to look our best for Lexi's party." She handed Fenella a bottle of diuretics.

"Thanks, Nina. I'm sure this will really come in handy. I'll call the dentist now."

On her way home, Fenella threw the diuretics into the dumpster behind the Addled Egg Diner.

꧁꧂

Mystery House
By Branca Agnelli

When Emmet Floyd Carlyle, the orphan of the Madeira House murders, turned eighteen and graduated from high school, he returned to Perdita. He enrolled as an undergraduate at the University of Perdita, and resumed control of Carlyle Lumber. He found Madeira House in a shocking state of disrepair. The remaining main port cellars had been cleaned out and vagrants had been inhabiting portions of the house for some time. The elements and the vandals had turned the structure into a tangled and worn carcass. The furniture that had been stored in the attic had been ravaged by mice, and the gems in the surrounding walls had mostly been pried loose.

The Carlyle Lumber and Holding Company had fared little better over the years since the murders. The firm had never fully recovered from the negligent leadership of Gunnison during his period of construction obsession, and under the inexperienced hand of Mayor Horsley, who had afforded himself a handsome yearly salary as interim C.E.O., Carlyle Lumber merely eked by, deposits rolling in as slowly as the logs around a turn in the Picaroon.

Emmet Floyd reviewed his situation in dismay at first. Friends counseled him to sell both Madeira and the Company. They told him to travel for a few years, perhaps he might pursue painting on the Lido? It was surely thought that Emmet would have no qualms about parting with the property that had been the site of so much misery for himself and his family. Emmet Floyd did indeed opt to sell much of Carlyle Lumber's forest properties and processing facilities to the Geldoffs.

However, upon a review of the Company's assets, he discovered and retained a small area of land adjacent to the Seahorse Road train station in Perdita, which had not been sold in Gunnison's earlier sale of Carlyle railroad land. Additionally, using his memories from childhood, Emmet Floyd located and opened several hidden port wine cellars. The bottles he found had reached a considerable maturity, and Emmet Floyd was able to auction the vintages at a profit.

Emmet Floyd then used the lumber company and wine sales cash to invest in oil exploration in the south. He also began construction of a resort hotel on the Seahorse Road property in Perdita that overlooked the ocean and the Amusements. The Azimuth Hotel's octagonal ballroom with blue conical roof, became the new landmark of Perdita, replacing the much smaller Palais Royale.

The Azimuth proved a success as the Amusements continued to draw larger crowds to the Perdita seaside every year. Gustave du Jardin was pleased about the development. The new hotel drew more affluent clientele, and further expanded Perdita's reputation as a destination.

In the following years, Emmet Floyd finished a degree in business management from The University of Perdita, and saw heavy returns on his oil investments. He built a comfortable house in the Beaux Arts style in the newly forming neighborhood of Blatchington Hills, and then turned his attentions towards a rehabilitation of Madeira House. He brought several craftsmen back to the property to restore the moldings and frescoes and stained glass. The gardens regained order and bloomed to life once again.

Gustav du Jardin, who was something of an elder statesman in Emmet Floyd's eyes, remarked to Emmet one afternoon after a meeting of the Perdita Chamber of Commerce, that the walls surrounding Madeira House were perfectly suited for crowd control and ticketing. A few months later, Emmet contacted du Jardin to obtain the information for a wax figurine artist in the City. By Emmet Floyd's twenty-fifth birthday, he had opened Perdita's newest attraction, the Madeira House Waxworks. He ran a streetcar between the Azimuth, Seahorse Road station and the Madeira House on Ice Cream Hill.

Emmet Floyd arranged his figures within a series of the largest revamped halls, banquet rooms, and libraries within the house. The grand foyer featured an assemblage of characters that Emmet presented as "Characters of the Coast". Benitoite miners, loggers, a sea diver outfitted in a Mark V diving helmet surrounded by wax kelp, and firemen from the Great Fire in the City had been cast in heroic still life, and the room was filled with music from a player piano that solely repeated the National Anthem. Madeira's main dining room housed an exhibition called "Lost to Time." Extinct species such as the dodo and the Pasquotank Parakeet were rendered here, as well as a "Liwa Chief in Ceremonial Headdress."

Mounted inside the room's china cabinets were death masks of executed aristocrats that Emmet had acquired from the Continent. Visitors to the waxworks were then led into the central gardens, where Emmet had the séance room reconstructed. Within was "The Sporting Green" exhibit, featuring local legend Cyril Legume, the recent national épée champion Laurent Frances, and the mighty racehorse Notus. The tour continued back inside the Grand Ballroom with a large display entitled "The Hall of Infamy". The enormous wax cast bow of a ship rose from the parquet floor, surrounded by the struggling half-torsos of sailors in a depiction of "The Sinking of the Nuestra Senora de Las Robles." The perimeter of the ballroom featured the sweat drenched outlaw Pio Bigote with drawn pistols, a woman of ill repute ravaged by syphilis, and Loffer founder Olaf Ewerloff with his successor Horace Almond, displayed with outstretched wooden wings fitted onto their arms.

The final exhibit room in the waxworks caused an uproar when it was announced, but undoubtedly drew the bulk of the visitors to Madeira

House. Down the stone staircase, and inside the main wine cellar was the shocking and macabre "Chamber of Horrors." The stabbing murder of Quentin Rokeby by Coarse Edgar was the least surprising of the displays within the chamber. The main tableaux featured the shaggy, ax-wielding personage of Bronislaw Dudek with raised ax over the severed head of Harriet Smimes Carlyle, Emmet Floyd's own mother. A huddled rendition of Emmet Floyd himself, as a child, peeked from a fireplace grate beyond.

The final tableaux in the chamber was of Emmet's father Gunnison, engaged in his infamous duel with Pickett Snellgrove in front of the obelisk of the City's Rosicrucian Society Hall. Waxworks patrons were then led back out of the cellar and into the garden library. Located in the rear of the house, the library had been remodeled with a vaulted ceiling and a series of stained-glass windows featuring sunbursts. There, waxworks guests were bid farewell by a wax cast Jesus, sponsored by the Perdita First Christian Church.

FENELLA WOKE UP TO A HUM FROM BEYOND THE PIPES in the Aquarium. This was a rumble lower in pitch, disturbing though also familiar. She felt it within her calf muscles as she lay in bed early in the morning before starting production. There was something about this vibration that terrified her, that worried her molars, yet it also prompted her out of bed.

She went searching for the hum in the main room of the Aquarium, walking around the asparagus beds as the chandeliers tinkled and shuddered from the girders. Finding nothing, she moved into the pump room. She'd watched Thurl set the pressure on the tanks a few times as he gave instructions to her for projects. She inspected the dials and levers and switches. She checked the hydrostatic pressure and the salinity gauges, the Ph, and the ammonia levels. Steam escaped from the valves as they regularly did but the sound emanated from elsewhere. Fenella could feel it in the tips of her fingers and her toes.

She climbed the back stairs to the steel platform above the large Aquarium tank. The hum rose in pitch. She looked across the top of blue-black lit water. For the first time she noticed that acrylic divided the tank in the back. Schools of damsel fish swayed in the front of the tank. Through the murky depths, she could see all the way through to a distorted image of the main Aquarium room with the asparagus beds underneath. Below and to the right were darkened tunnels in which the fish could swim to additional tanks within with bowels of the East Wing.

The school of damsel fish turned like the flip of a coin, then darted away out of sight. The kelp shuddered. A shadow appeared in the water in the divided tank, close to her on the platform like a cloud moving in front of the sun. The hum grew louder. The feeling in Fenella's fingers and toes and teeth became almost painful.

And then she saw it. A large tentacle reached and stretched out of the water. It had suckers the size of dinner plates on each arm. The tip of the tentacle curled like the great reddish fiddle fern that grew deep in the woods in Barnby Dun. The arm dripped water onto Fenella's head as it arced across the room. Its suckers fumbled with the lock at the side door. Fenella, while holding her breath, peered back into the water. The sound came from it. She fought the urge to retreat back into the stairwell from whence she came.

Fenella moved slightly, delicately, towards the door with the massive tentacle. It was as thick around as the supporting columns of the Periwinkle Palace. Next to the door was a tray of Dungeness crabs. Fenella grabbed a crab and touched it to the tip of the tentacle. The tentacle wrapped around the crab and retracted back into the murky black of the water.

More rumbling. The metal platform Fenella was standing on began to shake. Then came a voice.

"If I wanted a crab, I could have easily gotten one myself." Fenella's shoes echoed on the metal platform as she started, then stopped.

"Excuse me, is that you?" Fenella asked. Four massive tentacles slipped out of the water onto the platform towards Fenella's feet and two eyes the size of car tires rose above the surface of the water. One of the dripping tentacles, with the grace of an elephant's trunk, formed a polite gesture, similar to proffering a handshake. Fenella tentatively touched the hand, and memories from Misri Bay and her little red swimsuit flashed.

"My name is Hera," said the octopus.

"I think we've met," said Fenella.

"I'm glad you remember," said Hera.

The Perdita Sanitarium for the Enfeebled

By Branca Agnelli

When Emmet Floyd had Madeira House remodeled, he sought to heal the rift between the Carlyles and The University of Perdita Archaeology Department, whose head was still Prof. David Geldoff. Emmet made a sizable contribution to the department, and allowed a small team headed by Geldoff to dig underneath certain sections of the port wine cellar. The team unearthed a number of new Liwa artifacts, mostly pottery, and to show his gratitude, Prof. Geldoff invited Emmet to a mummy unwrapping party at his family home on Ice Cream Hill, where he undressed a figure unearthed by Geldoff himself in Thebes for the amusement of the department and several friends. At the party, while examining an amulet, Emmet Floyd was introduced to Dr. Vernice Blenheim, a speleologist at the University who was studying the cave systems that lay between the Pobre Claritas and the seaside. They were married later that year, and soon had twin boys, Douglas and Arthur, followed by the birth of a girl, Marie, two years after them.

Vernice involved Emmet and her children in her caving explorations through the system that opened at the Saceda limestone quarry. When the boys were twelve, and Marie ten, the family successfully navigated the cave system from the foothills of the Pobre Claritas all the way to an outlet on the seashore, for the first recorded time. Emmet became particularly interested and adept at collecting cave specimens and was present when Vernice identified a new cave spider species, which they named "Meta Vernicious", or commonly, the Vernicious Cave Spider.

As Emmet's boys entered high school, the national economy took a severe hit. Emmet's longtime friend and mentor Gustave du Jardin, frustrated with declining attendance and the Amusements and suffering from gout, sold his company and retired. Attendance at the wax museum suffered further after the sale. Bookings were down at the Azimuth as well. Emmet made adjustments to rein in costs, as his investments suffered. The wax figures at Madeira, that had brought so many crowds in the early years, had become relics in twenty years' time. He closed the museum and sold the characters to several disparate collectors. Emmet had Madeira remodeled once again, and through his relationship with Prof. Geldoff, he secured a contract with the University to house visiting academics there.

Madeira House then entered into a leisurely phase of its life, cloaked in pipe smoke and woolen sweaters, hardbound books, and good-natured debates. The house's inhabitants hid good scotch in Madeira's secret cellars, set up experiments in the ballroom, played cribbage in the library in the winter, and Hoover ball in the central grounds in the springtime. They provided a steady if meager income for the Carlyles.

Douglas, the oldest of Emmet's boys, suffered a fall into the water during a day of boating, the summer before his sophomore year. He complained of lumbago and chills that night, and by morning was running a fever. Two days later, Douglas could no longer move his legs. He was diagnosed with polio. Emmet spared no expense in Douglas's rehabilitation. He brought expensive doctors to Perdita from the Far Coast and had a hydrotherapy chamber built at their house.

That summer, a fire broke out at the Azimuth Hotel. The sparse crowds at the Pier and Amusements watched from below as the flames swept through all forty rooms and gasped as the great dome collapsed into the scrub and sand. The cause of the fire was undetermined. Emmet Floyd collected on his insurance and announced to *The Perdita Village Bugle* that he had no intention to rebuild.

Douglas, through hydrotherapy, was able to regain some ability to walk through the use of braces and canes. He became studious while his brother Arthur maintained the reputation as a gad-about, spending his weekends in the City at the racetrack. Emmet Floyd brought Douglas inside the workings of the family business, and they managed the family's incomes between Madeira House, oil developments, lime quarry leases, and the Turbinado Sugar investments throughout the national downturn.

After Marie graduated from high school and married, Vernice began to weary of life in Perdita. Emmet Floyd ceded management of the family businesses to Douglas, and the couple relocated to Grenoble where they planned to continue their passion for caving in retirement.

Arthur was happy to be bought out of the Carlyle Holding Company. He took his funds and built "Seahorse Ranch", south of Perdita where he planned to breed and train racehorses. Douglas was relieved to have

Arthur removed to the country as rumors had begun to surface about Arthur's indiscretions with stable boys at the City racetrack.

Douglas was involved in an indelicate conversation where he was attempting to quash the gossip about Arthur during a debutante ball at the Collis Mansion, when he was approached by a young lady in white satin with a gardenia in her auburn hair.

"I find it very rude that such a handsome looking gentlemen should be so absorbed in conversation when there are young ladies about with empty dance card slots," she said.

Douglas's companion blushed and introduced Mr. Carlyle to Miss Dolores Pearson.

"You must excuse Mr. Carlyle, but he is enfeebled," offered the man across from Douglas.

"Nonsense. I'm quite sturdy you know, and I can tell that Mr. Carlyle won't need to be talked into leaning on me a bit," said Dolores.

As Douglas stood on his leg braces and cane and put a heavy hand on Dolores' warm shoulder, he became enchanted with her.

The next year, Turbinado Sugar obtained an exclusive contract with Rock Candy Shandy Soda Pop, and Douglas and Dolores were afforded a high society wedding at the Benitoite Club in the City.

By this time the accommodations at Madeira House had become too outmoded for the University to continue their lease, so shortly after their wedding, Douglas, with Dolores' help, remodeled Madeira House, and repurposed it for used as a sanitarium and hydrotherapy rehabilitation home for children with polio. The seaside location of Perdita made Madeira House an ideal location, and Douglas and Dolores both found running the center rewarding as an avocation, and they enjoyed a working partnership together.

❧❧❧❧

The JDLDC
By Branca Agnelli

The Judgement Day Libation Deliverance Commission was a group of nearly twenty communitarian anarchists who resided in the Balchraggan Lake area of the Pobre Claritas for a period of close to forty years. Comprised of disaffected members of the Perdita University faculty and Continental intelligentsia, the group was mostly known as nudists until the famed "Andromeda Maneuver". The JDLDC targeted the Andromeda apartment building because of its visibility to the hordes of visitors across the street at the Pier and Amusements. It was planned as propaganda against the bourgeois capitalist frivolities of the park, in the hopes that it would ignite a worker's revolt.

On the appointed day of the bombing, however, the bomb's charges failed to detonate properly, resulting in no damages besides the belltower's northeast corner. The left hand of the igniter however, JDLDC member Jimmy Chapman, who would be known later in life as "Sinister Jim", was blown off cleanly.

❧❧❧❧

ONE EVENING, WITH THE CREW ENSCONCED IN THEIR peasant beds, Fenella tiptoed up the stairs to the rear of the aquarium and made her way to the metal platform. She sat down and hearing or seeing nothing in the dim expanse, began to trace figure 8's in the water for a while before tapping the surface with her forefinger, creating small ripples across the surface. Presently, a column of bubbles appeared below and rose up to meet her finger, and not long after, the specter of a great hulking shadow appeared from the depths of the tank. The tip of a tentacle breached the surface and patted Fenella's arm like a doting aunt, while the mantle surfaced, causing great amounts of water to slosh up and over the platform. The backside of Fenella's dress and her shoes were now wet.

"Yes, my darling?" said Hera.

"I've been wondering," said Fenella.

"I'm sure you have," said Hera.

"How did you know I was drowning?"

"I could taste your loneness and the zinc oxide from miles away."

"But thousands of people drown every day. Why me?"

"Have you seen the size of the ocean? You were nearby. Easy pickin's."

"Did you let them catch you? Did you know they'd bring you here?"

"Funny little gull I know. He was out by the harbor entrance buoy last season when I was on my way back to the Islands. Told me a few of the gulls got into an old sugar factory. Ambushed a shrimp bucket in a loading dock he said. But it was what the gull saw near the back of the loading bay that intrigued me. He said he saw a little boy, barely clothed, standing next to two cat-sized deer. Said something was off about this kid. Well. I trust this gull, and I've been around a very long time, so this intrigued me."

"So you let the boat...scoop you up?" asked Fenella.

"Oh yes, darling. Yes. And much so business these men got up to. These men have no time to sway. But then of course in addition to the boy, you're here too. This is how it works much of the time."

"What's 'it'?" asked Fenella.

"Coincidence, or magic, it's hard to discern. And you've done well, found your people after all that wish-wash. You found him too." Hera points through the water with one of her tentacles. Beyond the water, below, was a distorted light; the flames of Vaclav's fire. "You understand where he comes from, right?" Hera let the tips of her arms go limp while she spun around creating an effect like the Sky Swings at the Amusements, then her arms drop. "And then he ends up here? Into this wealth? By accident? I argue for magic, Honey."

❧❧❧❧

<u>The Perdita Pier, The Sokoll Years</u>
By Branca Agnelli

Jazz and racoon fur coats at the Perdita Pier and Amusements were proving too much for Gustave Du Jardin's aging sensibilities. With David Geldoff acting as an intermediary, he was able to locate a buyer for the Amusements in the newly arrived Iulian immigrant Rahab Sokoll. Du Jardin retired to Ice Cream Hill where he devoted himself to the hybridization of tulips for the rest of his days.

Sokoll added a Wurlitzer organ into the Periwinkle Palace and opened its dance floor to roller skating. He filled in part of the lagoon to make room for the new coaster, The Whip, as well as two dark rides, The Tunnel of Love and The Old Sawmill. The "FUN-icular" was renamed "The Kraken" for its new circuitous tracks that looked like tangled armatures and the commercial appeal the name would have for sailors.

A boxing ring was added near the updated Shoot-the-Chutes ride and steamboats came down from the City along with the regularly scheduled trains to bring visitors in for matches. For the Flyweight championship between Jack Columbia and Mickey Leonard, Sokoll brought in twelve flagpole sitters as a spectacle to pole sit in a circle around the boxing ring for a week before the match. Long-distance swimming races were held between the City and Perdita to further promote the event. The day of the fight, weightlifters performed feats of strength, including the soon-to-be-famous Toots Kachinsky, a strong woman who could deadlift a seal.

When Mickey Leonard won the title in a fifteen-round decision, a ticker tape parade was held in his honor on Seahorse Road. Bird's nests made from ticker tape in the years following the parade became especially popular collector's items around town and were referred to as "Champ's Nests".

Sokoll rebuilt the Azimuth Hotel on Seahorse Road. His incarnation was streamlined. It featured the newest anti-earthquake steel construction. The new Azimuth became the tallest structure in town at ten stories, and featured a bank of elevators trimmed in chrome with doors inlaid with sunbursts of obsidian and jade, rock crystal chandeliers, and two Egyptian cats flanking the entrance's two-story golden doors.

—Statement for Internal Investigation—

While the original forms and certificates concerning Vaclav's adoption by the Rostungers were lost in Nina's office, they had been duplicated. The Iulian Orphanage sent Vaclav's paperwork to Muffin Laidley (me), who made a copy for the PHDS's files, and then sent the originals along with Vaclav when I dropped him off at the Sugar Factory. I would have come into the Factory with Vaclav myself, but I was running late for a facial and I really felt I'd done due diligence when I left Nina no less than five messages on her answering machine reminding her that the child was coming.

The documents given to Nina and the set kept in the Perdita Hurt Diminishment Society files within my home office consisted of an Intergovernmental Agreement of Alien Transference, which had been officially processed through the City's customs office, as well as several forms showing various immunizations and medical checks performed in both countries. Additionally, a brief letter was sent along, addressed to me, expressing gratitude from the Iulian government to the ladies of the Perdita Hurt Diminishment Society for "most grateful assistance with products of People's Government". The Iulian Government had also sent along a form listing Vaclav's basic particulars.

Given: Vaclav
Surname: ?
Sex: Man
Mother's Origin: Moravian, looks from there
Age: Four, Maybe Five, Could be Six

I was ever ready to be an officious and exuberant friend, especially to someone from the Carlyle clan of Blatchington Hills. Knowing of Nina's reputation for misplacing items, however—I kept Vaclav's paperwork neatly placed in my home office in a folder labeled "Iulian Orphan Campaign, PHDS Adoption Drive and Fundraiser, TRANSMITTED!". The paperwork remained very readily available for two months until my daughter Dabney, who was going through a brief period of rebelliousness immediately following her deb ball, directed her druggie boyfriend Ricky Ray towards my files when asked by him where we kept "bills and shit."

During her entanglement with Ricky Ray, Dabney was overheard talking to Peyton Norberg at the Blachington Woods Country Club over a Chinese chicken salad, with dressing on the side.

"Yeah, he was convicted of identity theft, and yes he's been to jail. Okay. So what, Peyton? It's not like everyone's from B.W. you know. It's not like his addiction defines him."

A few months later, during a review of her annual credit card spending, I discovered a number of unsavory charges on her triple diamond rewards card. Suspicious merchant listings ranged from "Terminal Drugs and Bait" to "The Longshoreman's Motor Lodge", and "Frida's Alpenhaus", an infamous strip club near the harbor where women reportedly wear lederhosen and little else. A subsequent search through my files revealed that the Iulian Orphan Campaign paperwork as well as several credit card statements had gone missing.

Fearing that a confession to losing the Iulian Orphanage paperwork would only add to the rumors surrounding Dabney, as well as the possibility that such an announcement would cause disparaging remarks to be made about my organizing abilities, which could possibly put my undersecretary status at the PHDS in jeopardy, I kept mum on the subject. I would have been mortified to reveal to Nina that I had forgotten the name of that darling new Iulian son of hers . . . Vaseline something? That is the name I could recall at the time. I consoled myself about losing the paperwork with the thought that there was actually no way to even bring up the subject, as I could not even refer to the child in a remotely elegant way. I resolved to put the entire affair out of my mind by going to the La Oasis Spa for a double session of cuticle oiling and detoxification. La Oasis Spa featured the Wellspring line of products, which utilized only the finest of sheep's placentas, hand-mixed by marginalized women in Moravia.

Dabney's boyfriend Ricky Ray never realized he had in his possession information regarding an Iulian orphan. He had simply done a quick glance over of the paperwork then handed the whole lot over to his roommate and partner, Tweaker Steve. Tweaker Steve was an expert at finding the good info, or so I have been told by the sergeant.

Since Tweaker Steve could find no connecting accounts under Vaclav's name, his paperwork was tossed aside, where it remained for some time in a precarious pile near the empty iguana tank in Tweaker

Steve's bedroom. Eventually the entirety of Ricky Ray and Tweaker Steve's apartment was cleaned out by a crew who had been hired by their landlord after Ricky Ray and Steve abandoned the apartment that they had failed to pay rent on for the previous six months. The crew entered, scooped up the empty iguana tank, all the nasty bits of bloody Kleenex, crusty socks, roach filled ashtrays, cd's with cross hatches on them and piles and piles of scattered papers. Everything was hauled to the Perdita Municipal Dump, according to what Dabney and I could ascertain from the cleaning crew and the landlord, anyway.

The only other information in existence, in regards to the identity of Vaclav, is briefly mentioned in the letter of transmission filed with the City. Apparently, it was stored in the central vaults of the Iulian Government. The information contained in these files was considerably more illuminating than that transmitted to me, as it contained a dossier on Vaclav's mother. This all came out in the court proceedings later.

Agnes Irshava's earliest mention within the Iulian Government files was when she was pregnant and picked up near the Haustrian Border during a raid on a known dissident's apartment. Agnes was listed as telling authorities she was originally from Transcarpathian Ruthenia, but failed to give information on how she became associated with the Haustrian Border activists. She was detained until she gave birth. The child, listed as Vaclav, is noted as being transferred to the Petrescu Orphanage shortly after.

Agnes was declared "ideologically objectionable" by the Iulian Government and sent to work at the Zvolen People's Farm, which was, in reality a factory run by the Iulian underworld who submitted bogus documents to the Iulian government declaring units of steel production in exchange for government funds. No farming or steel work was ever done at the People's Farm. It was a processing operation for the re-labelling of stolen and smuggled good for foreign resale. Agnes spent most of her time at the farm picking off sticky labels, which might read

"Grade C Sheep Sperm", printed in Slavic Cyrillic. And then she would affix new labels in English that might read "Wellspring Rejuvenation Mask—Containing Purified Placental Extract, hand-mixed by the Moravian Woman's Micro Investment Collective." Can you believe it? When La Oasis Spa went down, you better believe it went down in a big way, Buster.

The copy of the report I read says, "No information was added to Agnes' file after the date of the Gossamer Revolution, although it is known that several workers from the Zvolen People's Farm were shot in the marches that proceeded it. In the chaos that followed the Revolution, women from that area were known to have been exported through the underworld's international connections for use in prostitution. Coincidentally, the City, north of Perdita, became a primary destination for these women; though Agnes' fate was left undocumented.

"The wing of the Iulian Central Vaults where Vaclav's information was most likely stored was spared in the bombing of that building during the Gossamer Revolution, though it was not to exist for long. As part of the National Reforms, the Revolutionary Government completed a massive multi-year campaign to digitize all the records originally kept in the Central Vaults, with a promise to make them public once the process was finished. Before any of the files could be released to the public for Truth and Reconciliation, the information was completely obliterated during a botched electronic espionage attempt by a foreign Superpower, which erased all the information stored on the Government mainframes and their attending back-up supercomputers."

So anyway, that's the full story. As you can see, there was nothing more I could have done, and no way I could have known.

Signed, Muffin Laidley

❧❧❧❧

DOUGLAS JR. AND HIS SISTER JUDY WERE RAISED SPENding their summer playing checkers with the polio children in the Madeira gardens, accompanying them to picnic outings at the beach, and going on bird watching treks through the Pobre Claritas in the sanitariums' open-air Jeep. In the winter, the Carlyle children attended dances where the other children moved stiffly in braces and twirled rhythmically in their wheelchairs in the great parqueted expanse of Madeira's largest ballroom while big band albums turned on the hi-fi. Douglas Jr. learned to play the piano on the baby grand in the library and conducted a weekly sing-along for the children. Uncle Arthur donated the funds to transform the west field outside Madeira's gates into a clay polo field, and Judy managed wheelchair polo games there.

When she was eighteen, Judy moved to the Far Coast to study ballet. She had a torrid affair with a modern dance choreographer and then left school and found a job with a Scandinavian industrial designer. Later she used investment funds from Douglas Sr. to found a contemporary textiles firm.

Douglas Jr. attended New Concepción College, studying piano, with the goal of completing an avant-garde symphony by the time he graduated. He also ran the disparate enterprises of the Carlyle family, attended board meetings for the sanitarium, and held a yearly gala at Madeira House to raise money for the Crippled Children's Fund. When he graduated, he moved back into the Carlyle's Blatchington Hills house and finished his symphony, which was performed once by the Perdita Symphony following a large donation sent by Douglas Sr. from Grenoble. The following year, Douglas Jr. married Phoebe Remillard, the daughter of the Symphony Guild's chairman. Phoebe began working in a managerial position within the Madeira Sanitarium, while Douglas Jr. worked on his next modernist symphony about an orderly addicted to morphine, tentatively entitled "Ack, Ack, Cotton Shooter Tracks".

Over the next six years the Carlyles welcomed three children; Jonah, Philip, and Nina. During this time, the polio vaccine had been approved, and criticisms of the sanitarium surfaced, citing the stigmatization and cultural isolation that institutions such as Madeira promulgated. Douglas Jr. shut Madeira House once again, and hired a full-time security guard who took up residence in the gate house cottage by the far wall. The family moved to Blatchington Woods and resumed a more traditional, private life. Phoebe retired and filled her time with benefits for the Symphony Guild, flower arranging, bridge, and dressage lessons at Uncle Arthur's ranch.

When Nina was four, the coastal area from the City to Perdita began to gain a reputation for tolerance of a new kind of hedonistic freedom. The Left Coast began attracting youths and revolutionaries from the Far Coast and everywhere in between, and they settled on the wharves and beaches and parks in heaps of old silks and lace, determined to experience sunny days with an intense and dogmatic devotion. Douglas Jr. had been working on his second symphony full time for close to eight years by this point, and unlike Phoebe he greeted the raucous influx of bohemian thinkers and beautiful vagrants to Perdita enthusiastically.

One afternoon after visiting Uncle Arthur regarding after a staffing incident on the ranch, Douglas Jr. picked up a young woman hitchhiking towards Barnby Dun. She told him that she lived at the newly reconstituted Judgement Day Libation Commission farm on the grounds of the old Loffer Ranch at Balchraggan Lake. Soon Douglas Jr. was contributing funds to the Commission, helping them to edit their newsletter, and regularly making the drive to Barnby Dun in his gold Fleetwood Brougham to skinny dip in their pond, take LSD and to "smoke the red eagle" as the Commissioners called it.

As long as Douglas Jr. restricted these particular activities to a few acres in the Pobre Claritas and the confines of his music studio, Phoebe turned a blind eye. She discreetly took over management of the Carlyle businesses and investments, made polite excuses for Douglas Jr.'s absence from social gatherings at the Blatchington Hills Country Club and set up extra bridge games. It was when Douglas Jr. announced his intention to invest a considerable sum to establish an Institute on the Perdita Coast for the express purpose of studying dolphin-to-human telepathy that Phoebe intervened more forcefully.

She wrote Douglas Sr. and Dolores in Grenoble, and with their help, succeeded in securing a fiscal conservatorship over her husband. The elder Carlyles made several telephone calls to their son threatening to write him out of the will completely if he did not curb his habits. Douglas Jr. responded by selling his Steinway. He left a note for Phoebe informing her that he had gone to the Islands and that he might return when he had "cleansed his chakras properly".

Philip had left for college by this time, so Phoebe, Jonah, and Nina relocated to Bankers Hill in the City, where Phoebe said there was still "some semblance of propriety and good breeding left intact." The remaining years of Nina's childhood were filled with the tinkling of coffee cups and teaspoons and lemonade glasses from Phoebe's bridge room, examinations of photographs of her father softly shrouded in cigarette smoke, and views of paisley and feathers and flowers and bare skin and tambourines amassing in the green expanse of the park below their apartment.

When Nina was fourteen, she and Jonah were sent to different boarding schools on the Far Coast. She spent Christmas and Easter vacations at her mother's apartment in the City, and summers at an equestrian camp in the mountains near her school. Her first return to Perdita was during her senior year in high school, when her grandfather Douglas Sr. passed away, and her grandmother Dolores held a memorial service for her husband in town. Douglas Jr. returned to Perdita for his father's service as well, looking greatly aged and behaving markedly reformed.

Douglas Jr. moved into the Blatchington Hills house with a convalescing Dolores while Phoebe maintained her apartment in the City. When Nina graduated from high school, she accepted a spot in the freshman class of a tony private college on the Far Coast. She declared herself a sociology major and spent her college years passing with C's and D's and making fun of the townies who sold her pills and coke and pot. In her senior year, she met a young investment banker from the Metropolis on skiing holiday at the local pub. He bought Nina an imported beer, and then brought her into the bathroom for a few bumps. She spent the balance of her time in college driving to the Metropolis on weekends to do coke in Christian's loft.

Meanwhile, Douglas Jr. spent four years receiving outpatient therapy and rehabilitation for his habits, and after methadone, transfusion, and electroshock treatments, he pronounced himself cured, and took Phoebe, Jonah, Nina, and Philip on a celebratory trip to the arctic hot springs of Deildartunguhver. While there, he completed the "Glacier Sonata", which would be performed later during a program at the City's Opera House.

The summer after Nina's graduation, Dolores passed away, leaving complete control of the Carlyle Companies to Douglas Jr., after a generous sum had been paid to Judy. Shortly thereafter, Douglas Jr. finished his second symphony, with the final title of "Niels Bohr on the Sand". Phoebe gave up her lease on the apartment in the City and resumed cohabitating with Douglas Jr. after a period of fourteen years.

Nina married Christian at the Blatchington Hills Club four months after her grandmother's funeral, and Douglas Jr. found him a management position within the newly incorporated Carlyle Industries. Nina's parents bought the couple a four-bedroom house Blatchington Hills, and Nina began to reacquaint herself with life in Perdita.

❧❧❧❧

THURL'S NEPHEW, RUDY ROSTUNGER, WAS KIDNAPPED at thirteen by the radical group the Fog Operational. Communicating through cryptic letters sent to *The City Times*, the Fog Operational demanded five million dollars as well as free food to be distributed in the Salinan Creek neighborhood of the City. The Rostungers refused. A toe was sent to the family. Then another. Then a finger. Rudy was finally released nine months later onto a street in the City. He was able to say very little about his captors. He had been kept blindfolded in a closet.

The F.B.I. eventually located the Fog Operational house near Lake Balchraggan in the Pobre Claritas. A massive shootout ensued. All the members of the Fog Operational were killed. In retaliation, prisoners at San Califia State Prison rioted and killed three guards.

In college at New Concepción, Rudy joined the Democratic Student's Association or DSA. In his junior year, the DSA split into factions over the "Serendipity Hill Statement", a manifesto adopted at a convention held at the University's campus. The manifesto decried capitalism's chokehold on natural resources and the dismal state of civil rights. After anti-Marxist members left to form the Democratic League of Students, the remaining members of the DSA reformed to create the Committee for Nonviolence. Rudy dropped out.

One night, at a bar in the Canopy, Rudy went to wash his hands in the men's restroom. A man with a long beard, a string of beads, and long flowing white robes and sandals walked in. He offered Rudy a hand towel.

"Thanks," said Rudy. But the man held onto Rudy's hand. He turned it over and looked at his palm. He examined the stub of the missing digit. Then the man kissed the stub. He told Rudy that he would be healed by LSD. The man gave Rudy a tab of acid. The artwork on the blotter paper looked like a bear.

Rudy began following the man, who called himself Guru Baba Raam. The Guru's other followers called themselves the Root Temple. The Root Temple ran a free store in the Canopy that gave away weed, zucchini, naturally dyed hemp garments, and a newspaper written by the Temple called, "The Crest". To fund the Temple and the free store, members grew vegetables in the back of their shared Victorian in the Canopy District and sold heroin in the Salinan Creek District. Soon, Rudy was signing over his trust fund checks to the Guru. The Temple was provided with extra wheat flour and martial arts lessons. The Guru got a Cadillac.

One day, Rudy grew tired of growing zucchini, selling heroin, and signing over his trust fund checks. He left the Temple with five of the commune's guns. He bought Lou Reed wraparound shades. He bought a derelict Victorian in the Shallow Pay District. He painted it black.

FENELLA SAT IN THE MASTER CONTROL ROOM. BENNY walked in with Lucretia on his shoulder, and took a seat next to the board.

"Ever wonder why the kid wears a loincloth?" asked Fenella.

"Only every minute," replied Benny. Fenella slipped a tape into the VCR labeled "Tarzan".

The action begins abruptly as Vaclav, on a small promontory, covered by Astroturf pounds his tiny chest with his fists, then grabs a rope and swings off camera. The mic picks up a squealing, a bellyaching giggle.

"Again!" yells Vaclav off camera. He appears from the back of the small Astroturf promontory, framed by silk vines. He is smiling. He swings once again on the rope and Fenella stops the video at the height of the swing. The boy's face reveals fantastic joy, a departure from the calm, reserved, and mature child they have been spending their days with. Fenella starts the video once more.

"Again! Again!" yells Vaclav. The tape ends.

"So pretty much best time ever," said Benny.

"Ever," Lucretia screamed for emphasis.

THE SWEENEYS WERE THE WORST KIND OF MOUNTAIN folk. Most children at Fenella and Ina's school in Barnby Dun feared the tiny green-eyed slits of Gary and his younger brother, Franklin Delano Sweeney as they bore down upon them, throwing their sneers and fists around. Nonna Agnelli regularly referred to the entire clan as "Spam sucking trash". The Sweeneys lived in a ramshackle cottage on a wooded lot with rusted cars and ATVs and general refuse that seemed to be flipping the bird at the majesty of the tree canopy overhead. Most nights growing up, Fenella could hear Shirley Sweeney shouting, and the sporadic "tink-whiz" from the Sweeney's rifles when they shot beer cans.

When Fenella was eight, she brought a friend home from school one afternoon. They were busy building a fairy village with sticks and rocks and swallows' feathers in the front yard as Daen dug up a patch of the lawn to fix a broken sprinkler. Out of the corner of his eye, Daen saw a dark, bounding form leap silently from the ferns, and then he heard a low rumble. White gums above bared teeth flashed in an arc towards Fenella's freckled face.

Daen took his shovel and hit the dog square in the head. The black mutt whirled around and caught Daen on his back side. Daen hit the dog again twice with the shovel; two heavy thuds and sent the dog backwards across the lawn. Then the dog turned and went towards Daen again, this time slowly, with a bloodied eye. Daen emptied a burlap sack he used to keep his spare sprinkler heads, and caught the dog's head inside as it lunged again, twisting the sack's opening with a stick around its neck, tourniquet style, and with torn pants, Daen dragged the dog to the Sweeney's property.

A young kid with small green eyes on a dirt bike snorted and spit when he saw Daen, then ran towards the Sweeney's front porch.

"Mom, Pork Pie's bit someone again," the kid yelled.

That night, Daen heard the sound of a shotgun from the Sweeney's propety. He never saw the dog again.

FENELLA SAT IN HER PEASANT BED GOING OVER NOTES. The German Expressionist film was in post-production, and she and Benny had been discussing a Murnau-inspired movie. Walter seemed to be in better spirits and Benny's hacking cough had dissipated to where it was a mere punctuation to the pump noises at night in the Aquarium wing.

When Fenella had asked Vaclav what he knew about Hera he had closed his eyes and folded his small shoulders into themselves.

"She sees," is all he would say before retreating to his little apartment behind the fireplace. She hadn't yet said anything to Walter or Benny or Pierce.

"Did you know that only five percent of the world's oceans have been fully explored?" said Fenella one evening at dinner.

"Apropos of?" said Benny as the rest of the table picked at their Greek salads sent down by Peter.

"Did you know that octopi, or octopuses, or octopodes or whatever don't really have tentacles, technically they have six arms and two legs?" countered Fenella. Walter wiped his mouth.

"Is this about a new film, Fen?" he asked.

After dinner Fenella left the table and went down to the main Aquarium room. Tucked away in the corner of the tank she spied Hera, heavy lids closed. As her mantle swayed, it turned from mottled yellow and white to all white. Perhaps she dreamed that she was in pursuit of a crab. Then she turned very dark. Maybe she was thinking of something larger, like the planet or escaping from her confines. A moment later her body became spiny like she had subdued something and was preparing to eat. In a fluid motion her body relaxed and she displayed the colors of wine, plums, and bruises.

The next day Fenella gathered the group on the steel platform above the large tank. Fenella knocked on the metal panel of the wall, unsure of what to do next.

"Hello? Excuse me?" she called. Vaclav hid behind her legs. Pierce, Benny, Walter, and Raúl all looked at each other as a hum began to rise out of the pool. Benny showed Walter the raised hairs on his forearm. Beneath them, eels slinked into the kelp at a rise in the hum's pitch.

Quite suddenly an arm flashed blue, then purple, and rose from the water before pulsing a mottled-moss color. The tentacle undulated and it stroked Walter's neck. He backed towards the far wall. The tentacle then moved towards Benny's chest. Benny screamed.

Then more tentacles boiled and slipped from the water along with Hera's eyes and hood. The additional arms cocked themselves at the tips.

The hum stopped. The mantle broke the surface of the water. The beak opened and water came splashing back into the pool. Two watery eyes took them all in on the platform. The dik-diks' eyes watered in return.

"How do you do?" said Hera, shaking hands with a trembling Benny and Walter and Pierce and Raúl. They looked at Fenella as the color drained from their lips. Lucretia shrieked and cawed, and flew up to the ceiling and began making figure eights.

Pierce sat down on the steel platform. He pinched the flesh of his right hand with the thumb and forefinger of his left hand. Benny began laughing. Walter pushed his glasses over his nose until they rested on his head. Raúl was high-fiving Hera, silver teeth shining in a smile.

"How is it that you can speak?" asked Pierce.

"How is it that you can?" asked Hera. "I'm so glad you're here everyone," said Hera. Steam escaped from a valve. Hera shot water from her funnel. The stream arced over Vaclav's head like a rainbow. He squealed with delight.

"It's so nice to be around kindness. And I can tell you're all kind," said Hera. "That lobster on the other side of the acrylic is a bitch. I've known T. Rexes with better temperaments. And they've only given me a set of blank keys, a chessboard, and some sea pens to keep me company. They're afraid I'll impale the sharks on the coral like that aquarium octopus on the Far Coast. And don't get me started on Thurl. Every time he dips so much as a pinky in this thimble of mine, I can taste the nicotine for the rest of the day. Not even enough rocks down there to make a decent lair." She gesticulated with four twirly tentacles while two others worked around the room giving friendly hugs.

She moved closer to Fenella. With trepidation, Fenella slid her hand down Hera's gently pinching suckers, which acted almost as a thumb and forefinger, tasting and smelling Fenella. Fenella carefully reached toward the massive mantel.

"Yes, you may touch me," assented Hera. Hera's mantel was softer than cotton. It reminded Fenella of Ina's pulsing baby head, or the top layer of Lucinda's butterscotch pudding. Then, Hera's tentacles began to fluff. She withdrew them from the party on the platform, flipped her mantle upside down and plunged to a lower depth so that she appeared to be an umbrella. She bellowed and her sonorous hum created sonic waves on top of the water. When she reemerged, she said, "My aching seventy-five brain lobes. I can see panoramically, you know, but I can also see through time, and I do wish that we could chat more. Because you see, we're all in danger." Fenella's brow wrinkled. She and Benny exchanged glances.

"Vaclav, come here," she said.

"Yes, about now . . . I'll have to ask you all to hold onto something."

And then, as if on command, the water in the tank slopped over to one side, and up over the steel platform. It washed over Fenella and Benny's shoes. Vaclav squealed. In that same moment, Hera began to howl and vibrate and flush a mottled brown, changing her papillae to stalagmites and stalactites every fraction of a second. The Aquarium's girders ached and complained. Fenella lost her footing and fell onto the platform as water sloshed around her elbows and ears.

The water moved back the other way as if it were tipped inside of a cup. There was another feeling beneath them as if the platform was made of crackers being crumbled into a soup below. And suddenly, the motion and the feeling stopped, along with Hera's call.

Benny and Hera's arm lifted Fenella to her feet. She wrung out her hair.

"Was that an earthquake?"

"Yes," said Hera. "And despite what they've said about this tank, it's not strong enough. Take a look for yourself below."

Fenella and the others climbed down the stairwells until they entered the Aquarium's main room. Water came from the seams of the six-inch thick acrylic. It formed into rivulets and dripped down below onto the asparagus plants.

ꕥ

ONE MORNING, DAEN FOUND A MEMBER OF THE SWEENEY clan passed out on the Lundgren's front lawn.

"Buddy. Hey buddy. It's time to wake up," said Daen as he shook the man's flannel shoulder.

The man was surprisingly apologetic and polite when roused.

"Aw Jeez, man. I didn't mean to cause no trouble," said the man. He extended his hand. "Gary Sweeney. Sorry to have to introduce myself this way."

Daen nodded.

"Look man," said Gary. "I'll be honest with ya. I just got out of jail. Stole a truck right after I turned eighteen. It was stupid. But I've been looking around for work, and I'm not finding anything, you know, it gets me down sometimes."

Daen rubbed the scruff on his chin.

"Yeah, I had a few beers last night. Guess I'm not used to the stuff anymore, I haven't had it in so long. Probably wandered over here to get away from my mom yelling at everybody. Listen, Daen, right? Say, I've got nothing to do today, you got anything you need doing over here that I might be able to do as a way of apologizing? "

Daen was taken by the Gary's manners and the softness of his voice. He felt that perhaps he could approach the whole situation about the night noise at the Sweeney's a little better if he showed some good Loffer-style neighborly love.

"Well, we're in pretty good shape over here," said Daen. "But listen, I got a customer over at the shop the other day who's leaving his security job at the Madeira House, you know the place?" Gary nodded.

"Well, if you can get your parole officer to vouch for you, maybe I can talk to the guy. I hear the job comes with housing, okay pay. No promises, you understand, but I can introduce you to the guy, see what comes of it. You know my shop in town? Barnby Dun Automotive? Come by tomorrow, say three o'clock and I'll see what I can do. Don't forget to bring something from your parole guy."

Daen followed through and introduced Gary to his customer at the auto shop. Gary's parole officer showed up to Gary's interview with one of the Carlyle Industries' property management representatives at the Madeira House gate cottage.

"He was charged with grand theft auto at eighteen. It's a shame, with a better lawyer he might not have served time at all," said the parole officer. "He was no trouble while he was in. He got a certificate in the handyman's education course that we offer."

Gary got the job and moved from Barnby Dun down to the gate house cottage.

Two years later, early on an August morning, a car was flagged down by a girl crawling on the side of the road near Ice Cream Hill. The girl had dragged herself from of a ditch below the road. She been stabbed several times. At the hospital, she told police that she and three friends had gone to Madeira House for fun, because it was haunted. She said that all of high school kids in Perdita knew that if you brought Gary the security guard beer, he would let you in through the gate.

She and her friend, along with their boyfriends had been drinking and wandering around the house with flashlights looking for the house's secret rooms when Gary surprised them and threatened them with a knife. He tied up the boys and raped each of the girls repeatedly throughout the night. Then he stabbed both girls and dumped their bodies in the ditch by the road.

Police found the second girl, dead in the ravine off Ice Cream Hill, and the two boys still tied up, and stabbed to death in the ballroom of Madeira House. They found Gary Sweeney four days later at a makeshift campsite deep in the Pobre Claritas.

Ten years passed. Then *The Perdita Village Bugle* ran an article about Carlyle Industries' intentions to reopen Madeira House to the public for tours. There were some calls of outrage to criticize the profiteering from the infamy of three teenage deaths. Douglas Carlyle Jr. was interviewed in a follow up piece by the *Village Bugle.*

"Madeira House is a unique and historic architectural gem that deserves to be shared and appreciated by the surrounding public. I refuse to let that murderer ruin the legacy of the house for the Perdita community. Madeira House will serve as a monument so that those poor kids' deaths will not be forgotten. Let's not forget that the Carlyles have been victims of murderers as well, but we refuse to stop our lives because of the deeds of evil men. Reopening Madeira House is not just an important symbolic gesture. It will provide badly needed employment to Perdita's student population, many of who are suffering in the current economy."

Anticipation and excitement at viewing the "Madeira Mystery House" as it was to be called won over public sentiment. Carlyle Industries was granted all necessary construction and operating permits in a timely manner from the township. The day before opening, frozen lemonade and pretzel carts were rolled out from inside the old gatehouse cottage and placed underneath a giant purple question mark that lit a series of marquee lights, starting from the edge of the curly cue and progressing all the way to the punctuating dot.

Ticket holders to the Madeira Mystery House were given a tour of the house and gardens. They were told of the many tragedies and myths surrounding the house, from Gunnison Carlyle's discovery of Liwa artifacts, to Adelaide's untimely death, about the Loffer Curse, and the furious periods of building. Sometimes they were treated to apparitions in the sweat of the window panes by the coffee machine in the gift shop and a tinkling of bottles in the cellars. Blood from the knife of Bronislaw Dudek it was whispered. A desperate plea it was said. Patrons were allowed to light a candle in the ballroom in remembrance of Mrs. Delby Smimes Carlyle and the teenage victims of Gary Sweeney with a candle purchase of $1.50. The ending statement in the Madeira Mystery House guide script to be read in the ballroom was written as follows:

"It is said that the victims of Madeira House contact persons who choose to remember them, often times through the mirrors in this very ballroom."

NINA ROSTUNGER INVENTED THE APPELLATION, "THE Confectionery" in time for the "Evening of Compassion" in an effort to distract her guest's attention from the brutal exteriors of The Sugar Factory. Despite printing social stationery and cards with a home address listed under "The Confectionery" title, everyone still referred to the building as The Sugar Factory, as they had always done, though Candy Thorson took to using "The Confectionary" as a mocking reference to Nina's missteps when speaking in private.

While the name and the exterior of the Factory remained largely unchanged when Thurl Rostunger purchased the building for his primary residence, the interiors did not. Thurl hired scores of contractors to alter the cavernous industrial spaces to suit his needs before moving in. He had an enormous portion of the fifth floor domed in glass and made into a Conservatory. A section of the first floor was converted into a French country-style kitchen. He built a wood-paneled library, dominated by two marble obelisks—which invited a nostalgia for the tombs in Alexandria—and had the steel-framed windows there replaced with arched rondel glass that cast aureoles of yellows over the long tables.

Thurl gave over the entire north wing of the Factory to Nina and Lexi. An indoor pool was built in the style of the Diocletian Baths. A rare suite from a palace in Haustria was deconstructed, shipped to Perdita, and rebuilt inside the Factory as a receiving room for Nina. Thurl had always had a fondness for the Alhambra, and so he built a formal dining room and ballroom in the Moorish style for Nina's events. And for Lexi, a petite hameau where she could play village in a pastoral, albeit indoor setting. Rubber sheep grazed around a faux daub and wattle farmhouse inside the former loading dock.

Despite these vast improvements and alterations to the Factory, the building was of such an enormous size that large sections of the structure were left untouched. They remained cold and industrial. The echoing voids of these spaces created a chasm between the delights of the North Wing and Thurl's appointed rooms in the East Wing, where he maintained a largely solitary, cloistered life.

The desire to live near the Picaroon River, and perhaps in the Factory, was rooted possibly within Thurl's family history. His great-grandfather, Ormand Rostunger, made the family fortune when he founded the eponymous shipping company, "Rostunger Shipping Inc.", which had originally served as the transport link between the early sugar plantations on the Islands and the refinement and processing plant where Thurl now resided. The rapid expansion of the City and its economy allowed Ormand to increase his fleet, meeting the need for passenger and mail transport. Later, after the discovery of the valuable gemstone Benitoite in the Pobre Claritas, Rostunger Shipping became the primary carrier of the valuable cargo to foreign and domestic capital markets. By the time of Ormand's death, the Rostungers were referred to as magnates.

As the river inlet and the sea were the foundation for the family's wealth, the Rostungers always had something of an affinity for the aquatic. As a boy, Thurl was an avid angler, and loved fishing in the quiet streams near Barnby Dun. When he was twelve, he was presented with his own dinghy. He often sailed out of the Perdita Harbor and around the Picaroon River inlet. Thurl was a championship diver in high school, regularly practicing at the Perdita Amusements indoor pool, and at University, Thurl obtained his undergraduate degree in Oceanography with an emphasis in Ichthyology.

Coincidentally, Nina's family also had a connection to the Sugar Factory. Her great-great grandfather, Gunnison Carlyle, the timber baron, was an early investor and majority shareholder in the Turbinado Sugar Factory. Much of the enduring family wealth stemmed from the sale of the sugar facilities during Nina's childhood to a foreign investment firm. After several decades of declining manufacturing in the Perdita area, the investment firm decided to liquidate its holdings in Turbinado Sugar, and the stockholders were quite relieved to find a willing buyer in Thurl Rostunger, who happened to be Nina Carlyle's third husband.

Despite all the fantastic improvements to the Factory, and its uninterrupted views of both the river and seashore, the majority of Perdita viewed the Rostungers and their new home with a mixture of confusion and disdain. The Carlyles and Rostungers were not the sort of people that embarked on adventures in urban pioneerism. Because his intentions were unknown, Thurl Rostunger's plans could easily be construed as sinister.

To inhabit such a monstrous structure was to inflict damage on cozy notions of hearth and home. The requisition of such vast amounts of space was regarded as gauche and voracious, to be sure, but it was the silencing of the refinery and its operations that mostly swayed opinion. Workers who had toiled so many days and years inside the smoking carapace of steel and brick now stewed in their beds and couches when they thought of the people inhabiting their former place of employment. The Factory was a silent, haughty embodiment of loss and greed and of the vast differences in the circumstances of men.

THE 31ST HAD COME. FENELLA WORE A CLEAN, BLACK A-line dress and smoothed her fly away hairs. She straightened the D2 tape on the control room desk. Lucretia announced Thurl's arrival with a shriek. Thurl used both hands on the industrial handrails to heft his girth up the stairs into the control room trailer. In the corner he eased himself into a club chair with an audible release. He laced his fingers together on top of his leg.

"German Expressionist Dinner Party. How did you fare?"

"I think you'll pleased," said Fenella.

The film opened after black with no credits in a village of peasants dancing a folk dance on a black and white striped rotating disk in front of a village. A close-up of Vaclav revealed his joy. It was followed by an exterior shot of a village building, then a closer view of a candle lit window. Inside, a dinner table was set with black gelatinous food. Around the table, kohl rimmed diners ate the gelatin with spoons while Benny the somnambulist walked counterclockwise around them. The sound of a humpback whale played over the action. The shadow from a gramophone was shown on the wall of the peasant house along with the eaters. The eaters finished their food and began to yawn. They climbed into small beds. The film ended on one long whale cry.

"Again! Again!" cried Thurl.

"If I may," began Fenella. "Part of the purpose of the film is relaxation is it not? May I show you a technique I learned in college for sleep and relaxation? It may help. It's called the Dalí Key Nap." Fenella cued the tape up and brought a saucer from Vaclav's apartment. "Now, should I leave you alone to relax?"

"Yes, please," said Thurl, sinking back in his chair. Fenella made a turkey sandwich in Vaclav's diminutive kitchen then returned to the control room. She tiptoed up the stairs and peeked through the door's window. The German Expressionist film played on a loop. The keys had dropped onto the saucer. He was in a state of reverie.

MURNAU/HERA FILM
by Benny Fresnel and Fenella Lundgren

FADE IN:

EXT. LOCATION #1—EVENING

A dark and heavy fog surrounds the Factory and the Picaroon. The full moon shines brightly over the Turbinado sign.

P.O.V. camera slowly tracks down the hallways of the Factory. The shots are superimposed onto one another until they become a dizzying array of corridors.

CUT TO:

Black. A hum begins very low, but begins to rise. Pan everything in audio mix left to right.

CUT TO:

INT. LOCATION #2—Aquarium MAIN ROOM

Establishing shot of Aquarium glass ceiling. Hum of pipes becomes bellows of Hera.

CUT TO:

Montage of Close Up fish in Aquarium. Sculpins, Starfish, Leafy Sea-dragons, superimposed onto one another in blacks and whites and greys.

The roar of Hera begins to get louder.

CUT TO:

Seagrass swaying.

CUT TO:

P.O.V. shot, tentacles moving slowly through the water. The roar is at full volume now, and should cause the speakers in the theater to distort, if possible.

CUT TO:

Lucretia'a beak, open graphic match to Hera's beak. Zoom out to Hera's eye. Leave steady shot for ten minutes, then graphic match—

CUT TO:

EXT. LOCATION #1

Medium Close Up of moon of above the Factory. Pan down into the depths of the Picaroon.

❧❧❧❧

WHEN FENELLA DESCRIBED THURL'S DIRECTIVE TO HERA, she laughed so that the tips of her tentacles shook in emphasis.

"Oh, he'll never be healed, but let's do it for art's sake."

Fenella put on a diving suit and jumped into the large tank to shoot footage of Hera. Pierce and Vaclav worked on the P.O.V. shots in the corridors while Benny and Walter grabbed the B-roll of sea plants and other fish. Lucretia liked to hang out in the editing suite, sitting on Benny's shoulder as he edited the material together, shrieking at the loops and fades. Every once in a while, to appease her, Benny let Lucretia peck "Return" on the keyboard so she felt like she was helping.

When they had a final cut, the group gathered on the steel platform above the large tank for a wrap party. Fenella and Vaclav baked a vanilla cake in his little apartment. An extra tray of crabs was sent down for Hera. They filled a table with beer, punch, and popcorn. Fenella wheeled a monitor in on a cart and played the fifteen-minute film in the dark. Afterwards, Fenella brought the lights up and everyone clapped.

"I've never had popcorn before," said Hera. "It's delicious." She passed each kernel from sucker to sucker to beak.

Afterwards, they had a dance party. Hera's arms were partners to all. They played Smokey Robinson's "Going to a Go-Go", "Hi-Lo" by the Quick, "Strychnine" by the Sonics, "Cry, Baby" by Garnet Mimms, "After the Goldrush" by Neil Young, and "Oh Bondage! Up Yours!" by X-Ray Spex. Walter, who hated to dance, taught Vaclav and Lucretia how to play jacks. Lucretia was especially adept at the game, but Vaclav was uniquely delighted.

❧

THE CONSERVATORY INSIDE "THE CONFECTIONERY" HAD been decorated with pagodas, strung with paper lanterns, and had arched bridges over temporary ponds filled with actual koi fish. The faux-Chinatown had three different food stations; a dim sum table next to the acrobats, a sushi station next to the fishing village vignette, and a dessert station under one of the grander bridges strung with silk wisteria. A man on a guzheng played a plaintive song underneath the ferns. The acrobats stretched in their shiny yellows. Outside the windows the Turbinado sign flashed red.

Candy Thorson, in a dress so small it seemed as if she were wearing a single sequin, approached Fenella. All of her fingers were covered in band-aids.

"What happened? Are you ok?" asked Fenella.

"I'm fine," Candy replied. Her elven face betrayed her. "Would you give this package to Nina? I need to find my gloves." Candy handed Fenella a manila envelope.

"Of course."

Fenella left the domed room, went through the series of hallways and entered Nina's Hall of Mirrors. She was still in a slip on her bed eating chocolate ice cream. Lokum was licking the lid. When Fenella entered, Nina dispensed with hello.

"Is that from Candy? Great, give it to me." She ripped open the bag. Inside was a prescription bottle, with Candy Thorson's name clearly on the side. Another read "Xylazine—For Equine Use Only." "What a lamb. Hand me that glass of water, would you?" said Nina.

Fenella took a room temperature glass of water from the nightstand and passed it over. Nina twisted the top of the bottle, poured a large handful of pills and gulped them down with the water.

"There's a bag in my desk I need you to flush before the security with the Senator gets here. I tried to make heroin. Also, if you could find Lexi? Her party is starting for chrissakes."

Fenella found the dark, balled ziplock inside Nina's pencil drawer. She flushed it down the toilet, then made her way to the petite hameau warehouse—Lexi's room. She navigated through the statues of sheep encased in real wool coats, surrounded by meadows of hydroponically fed violets and daisies. At the rear of the warehouse was the faux daub and wattle farmhouse. Fenella pushed through the composite door made to look like weathered timbers.

Inside, the rooms were completely dark, lit only by a bank of monitors on Lexi's desk. There was a thick, acrid smell.

"Hey, you there? Your party is starting," said Fenella. She could make out a silhouette in a robe in front of one of the screens.

"I'm tracking satellites," said Lexi.

"Why satellites?" asked Fenella.

"To see where I can be hidden. I'm going to set up a fortress where satellites can't see and I will have a robot army."

"A robot army. Isn't it easier to just have a family?" asked Fenella.

Lexi pulled the robe around herself closer.

"Don't you know anything? Children kill their parents."

"Well, your party is starting. I know you don't want to miss the acrobats."

Fenella left the petite hameau and returned to the Conservatory where she was shocked to encounter Thurl, whom she had never seen outside of his wing. He looked agitated.

"Fenella, just the young woman I wanted to see. Is it too late to do an installation in here? I'm thinking of doing a little something with a seafaring theme right here by the fishing dock." He pointed to a set piece with fishing nets by the dim sum food station. His eyes were stiff. His tongue lolled from his mouth a bit. "Find Raúl. He'll help you sort something out."

"We've just finished a Murnau-inspired piece using some of the animals in your Aquarium. Should fit right in with the scenery."

"Excellent," said Thurl. He took out a pocket square from his tuxedo and mopped his forehead. The guzheng reached a poignant silence before continuing.

After gathering the projector in the Aquarium wing, Fenella and Raúl struggled to get it installed just right as the guests began filing in.

"Hide it in these ferns Raúl. The power cord can tuck behind here, like that."

Benny and Walter entered through the side door.

"What are you guys doing up here?" asked Fenella.

"Like we'd miss this fête, Fen. What the fuck? Sushi AND pagodas. Omigod. Crazy."

"Can you at least try to find some pants without holes guys? Really, it's like…"

"No one's gonna notice Fen. I'll be the toast of the party because I won't talk about school or stocks." Fenella threw up her hands.

The party wheeled along. Children, newly introduced, watched contortionists. The guzheng woozed and the Turbinado sign flashed on and off outside creating a throbbing illusion among the lychee martinis of the guests, as if they were so many beating hearts around the room. The notes fixed themselves into the blurry excesses of the dome. The party lights mimicked the mango gelato on the tables. The older men shuffled about in tuxedos, looking like their asses had been shot off by rifles, the backs of their pants drooping like flags in the summer heat.

Lexi ensconced herself next to the dessert bar and began on the matcha tea éclairs. Nina laughed and tossed back her auburn hair in conversation with the Senator and Muffin Laidley. They were breaking open fortune cookies and reading the fortunes for fun. Uneaten cookie halves spilled off the draped banquet table at the dessert station. The server behind the station looked agitated.

"'The earth will open up and swallow you whole'…what kind of? You open one."

"'The Great One will have a reckoning and nothing will be saved from the wreckage.' What kind of dumbass cookies did you get, Muffin?" snarled Nina.

"The ones at the party supply store! The regular ones, I swear!" squeaked Muffin.

"You just don't get it Muffin," said Candy Thorson who slid up to the bar then and inspected the matcha green éclairs without taking one. "The is the Confectionery. What will people say?"

Thurl dabbed at the corner of his mouth with a napkin. He seemed out of sorts with his hands crammed stiffly into his pockets in a room full of people eating and drinking. He made his way over towards the fishing dock set piece. Fenella pressed "play" on the projector and Hera's tentacles began to explore in light beyond the har gow on the dim sum table.

Thurl was immediately on the ground. His eyes rolled to the back of his head and he began to shake. Spittle flew from his open mouth. Muffin Laidley screamed.

"The Confectionery. How sweet it is," said Candy Thorson.

Just then a loud, high-pitched crash soared above the guzheng. Many of the guests thought at first that one of the acrobats had fallen into the sushi station. A shower of glass and feathers fell from the roof onto a screaming crowd. Cormorants writhed in the matcha éclairs. Blood appeared across the acrobats' yellow silks.

"Live in a SUGAR FACTORY!!!!" Nina screamed. "Make it into a Fucking PALACE!!!" he said. "All for those goddamn fish!"

Down and slivers of glass flew from her tresses as she whirled her head around the room for emphasis. She had a dead look in her eyes, like cooled lead solder. Suddenly she pivoted in the direction of the East Wing and Fenella had a stinging sensation in her fingers and toes, and the chaotic cries of the glass-covered crowd began to sound like the static of being in between two radio stations. She pulled Benny towards her.

CHORUS:

Some among us mortal
men find uneasy shelter
Strange and cloudy harbors
Bury beast and wanderer

The castaway fawn-boy
Iulia across the sea
to Underworld of Sleep
Frigid waste to king feast

Prevail wise Perseus
against the tangles of
Gorgons, look to Hera
wild Goddess with no womb
Young Fenella sweetened
by the World of Mirrors
drops the beggar's dented cup
Is prospering more dear?

BOOK THREE

❧❧❧❧

WINNIE STOOD IN FRONT OF THE ALGERINE. IN A BUNdled sheet she carried the entirety of her trousseau; an ambrotype of her mother, her Sunday dress and a silver pendant of the Paschal Lamb. She gingerly entered the hotel lobby; a first for her, as she customarily came and left the laundry through the back entrance. Today, the back entrance was locked shut, and no one had answered her pounding fist.

The lobby of the Algerine was deserted. This surprised her, as the front door was unsecured. The walls of the building encased the foyer in a stark silence apart from the clamor in the streets. Winnie made her way around a table inlaid with Japanese marquetry depicting a series of cranes. An oversized arrangement of calla lilies on top stretched their white spathes up to the frescoed ceiling, indifferent to Winnie's thick arms and ankles.

She clutched her red hands tightly around her bundle. Her hands were always dry and cracked from the laundry. She often called them her "manglers".

She felt intimidated in the lobby, too lowly to call out Paolo's name. A beam of light hit a medallion in the Persian carpeting at her feet, and she noticed how the smoke had managed to infiltrate the air with a gauze.

She exited the lobby and stepped back onto the Algerine's front courtyard. The wind swept over the top of Shallow Pay Hill, and she hugged her bundle closer to her chest, and felt the aching chill on the backs of her shoulders. She walked to the corner of the courtyard, where she could stare southward towards the Celestial District and onwards to harbor. There were shouts of men below, and she strained to single out a familiar note in the staccato rhythm of the tones. Turning opposite, she raised her hand to her brow and found it odd to be able to look directly at the rising sun. She found the sooty-earth smell of smoke and gunpowder almost preferable to the coal and sweat of the Algerine's laundry.

A barrage of gunfire sounded down the hill, to the south, followed by the tin clip of hooves on pavers. A wagon, drawn by a pair of snorting horses, pulled into view outside the courtyard. The wagon came to a sudden stop then, as the horses bolted and shied. The wagon rocked back and forth across the steep grade for a few seconds before one mare stumbled and bucked and the wagon tipped, spilling its load down Shallow Pay.

Through the dingy linen that hung in the air, Winnie recognized a familiar flutter of skirting as the body of the wagon driver was thrown into the street. Lifting her petticoats Winnie rushed down the hill. She felt her knee joints bristle and twinge with the impact of the first few steps down the precipitous grade. The wagon scraped transversely across the hill as the hitched mare attempted to right herself.

"Damnit! DAAAMit! Damn!" yelled a woman.

Jars that had managed not to break upon impact gained enough momentum to bounce and smash in a tinkling syncopation that collided with the bellows of the woman. Winnie eased her way to the pair of black and bay Morgans, who brayed and shuddered and threatened to send the cart behind them trundling further. She placed her red hand to the hot neck of one them and cooed and hummed from her navel.

Once the horses calmed, Winnie turned her attention to the woman, who struggled to free her dress from the woody tangle of a newly-planted Liwican buckeye in the front garden of a terraced row house.

"Spoil the Spoon!" said the woman as she dusted her rear, and examined her hands, bloodied from the reins.

"Miss Easter! Oh Miss Easter, it's you!" said Winnie, and then cupped her mouth, afraid of startling the horses again.

The woman looked back in surprise.

"Winnie! Thank God . . . Oh Winnie, look at this. My specimens! Look, Cephalanthera austiniae!" She kicked a piece of broken glass towards the horses. "Rotten shavetails!"

Winnie carefully unhitched the mares from their traces, collars, and breeching and tied them up around a wrought iron gate. At Miss Easter's feet a hash of display jars mingled with mountings and vasculum. The wing of a stuffed cormorant lay separated from its body, and the hulking form of a taxidermied grizzly lay supine in the gutter, arms outstretched, blank-eyed and grasping, hapless and defeated.

Miss Easter examined a torn pressed mounting of a white orchid. She inspected it closely, then skillfully picked something from within the paper and glass with her thumb and forefinger. It was a dislodged canine tooth from the bear. She sighed and then tossed the tooth and orchid pressing back into the ruined pile on the cobbles.

"That, Winnie, was Cephalanthera austiniae. They call it the "Phantom". Can't make its own food, you know."

"You hurt Miss Easter?"

"No, no, only bruised."

"Shall I try to round up some folks to upright the wagon?" asked Winnie. Miss Easter straightened.

"No. Winnie leave the wagon, the wheels are broke...But I do need your help. Untie those horses, if you would. Now that all my specimens have met their end on Shallow Pay, I've got to see if anything's left at the Academy."

Winnie again spoke soothing words to the mares. They were without stirrups, so the women used the stiffened body of the bear as a stepladder to mount them.

Winnie's first job after arriving in the City had been with Miss Easter. She'd worked as a cook and washerwoman and kept house. She'd kept Miss Easter company too, tapping her shoes in the kitchen when

Miss Easter played piano, or joining her in games of Conquian over tumblers of whiskey and tea. She'd had a nice room at Miss Easter's, with a window that overlooked the bay.

Miss Easter's discipline was botany, and she displayed many specimens of the natural world around her home library. She had a human skeleton in the corner near her parlor fire, surrounded by fossilized whelks, pinned blue butterflies, and a number of iron meteorites. Stuffed dark-eyed juncos, cedar wax-wings, and a Bornean fruit bat were stilled in flight above the chaise, and the arms of the mighty silenced grizzly made a canopy over Miss Easter's work chair. Bundles of preserved linen were framed and mounted above the window dressings, a souvenir from a mummy unwrapping party that Miss Easter had attended in Perdita.

While she worked for Miss Easter, Winnie would often find the woman asleep at her desk, and before touching Miss Easter's honey-touched hair gently and urging her to go to bed, Winnie would take a few moments to look around the library, studying the oily sheen of purple finch feathers and the whorls of conches, and moving her finger lightly over the bookshelf's linen spines.

When she dusted the specimen cases in the library, she was always careful to avoid disturbing any paperwork she found. Winnie saw in Miss Easter's scrawl the encoding of a murky and mysterious mass that lurked over her when she passed the steps of libraries and universities. Winnie viewed Miss Easter's looping cursive as something sacred and unknowable; the spells and secrets held only by the gloved elite.

A year-and-a-half later, a melittologist from the Academy studying the Vespula wasp proposed that Miss Easter accompany him on a study trip to the Islands as the expedition's botanist. Miss Easter agreed, and shut her house for a year, at which point Winnie found a new position at the Algerine Palace. She had not seen Miss Easter since.

Winnie's mother had once told her that she had a "plain but pleasant face." Winnie had always felt comfortable around Miss Easter because perhaps, it was something she thought they shared. The intervening time had not been unkind to Miss Easter; her mouth turned down at the edges a bit more perhaps, and her face seemed fuller, the dimple on her chin more pronounced, but her hair had retained its gold-touched luster, and it appeared as though she had taken to wearing a hat to protect her skin while in the field.

The women rode the mares to the top of Serendipity Hill, and Miss Easter stopped to survey the City.

"Looks to me as though the fire's heading down Salinan Creek. We'll cut through Norton Park and the Canopy," said Miss Easter.

Winnie nodded. They galloped until they reached the southern end of Norton Street which led to the Park, and then the street became alive again with disordered populace. Men piled chairs, pots, paintings, and children into handcarts, buckboards, and drays. A family of five hefted a grandfather clock into an ice wagon. Infants wailed and dogs yelped, and then, in the distance, behind Shallow Pay, a large explosion echoed through the valleys and a shaft of smoke rose from the hill. A distinct beat of silence followed, and then a greater panic radiated through the streets. Winnie and Miss Easter struggled as they rode to avoid the scurrying ruck about them.

When they reached the quarter of the City known as the Canopy, they dismounted, as the entire neighborhood was built on a steep grade, preventing any streets from being built through it. Stepped boardwalks were the thoroughfares there, and they led to successions of declivitously perched houses largely hidden from one another by the dense plantings that formed baldaquins of lush vegetation over the walkways. Flowering banana trees and ghost ferns were interspersed with the Andalusian ruffles of datura blooms that glowed with the feverish morning. The horses traipsed clumsily on the stairs, and Winnie was relieved to find that the narrow walkways were largely empty of the Canopy's inhabitants.

She heard a rough sea brogue then and looked past the foliage to see a group of men and women passing jugs of wine in a brigade fashion, up a ladder and onto the roof. A man shouted saltily, and then the entire contents of the wine jug was released onto the shingles. A rivulet made its way onto a network of branches, then crisscrossed down the bell of a datura blossom and dripped onto the purple plume of a hearty looking cultivar. A fat droplet fell from the tannin-tinted leaves and splashed across Miss Easter's brown freckles.

"Cordyline australis," said Miss Easter, as she wiped the wine from her face and pointed to the plant. "You might know it Winnie, as giant dracaena. And here's a bronze loquat. Non-natives these. Savor them my dear, you may not espy them for some time."

Leading the horses up the narrow stairs took precious minutes. Winnie tugged at her Morgan horse to keep her from grabbing a quick mouthful of lupins. Her own breath became short with the ascent, and her small bundle grew heavier, as she had nothing with which to tie it to the horse. Reaching the top of the Canopy, they looked back only to see both Shallow Pay and the Salinan Creek ravine crinkled in flame. Miss Easter's eyes met Winnie's, and then she used the handrail at the top of the steps to remount the mare. Winnie followed suit.

Winnie and Miss Easter quickened their speed towards the Academy. The sizes of the houses grew as they turned down Lazarus Street, which was empty except for a few packs of dogs. The Georgian revival building housing the Academy's collection eventually appeared from behind a row of cypresses. Miss Easter dismounted her horse deftly and handed the reins to Winnie.

"There's a cart out back," she said. "Hitch it, and I'll meet you in the rear courtyard after I load up the Herbarium."

Winnie led the mares across the Academy lawn and through the side yard, which opened to a graveled back lot where a number of greenhouses had been constructed only that year. She looked in a rear shed and found the cart and pushed it out. She was working to get the tracings attached to it when she heard crunching gravel. Miss Easter pushed a wheeled bookcase from the rear door of the Academy, loaded with mountings and assorted specimens.

"Gilias and Ptelea," she explained. "Load these and then come inside and help me fetch the fungi and phanerogams." Winnie did as she was told, and when she'd emptied the cart, she pushed it through the back door of the Academy.

"Miss Easter, Miss Easter!" she called.

"Here! Here!"

Winnie followed the voice until she came to a large hall, lined with tight rows of shelves and great glass cases. A bleached whale's skeleton overarched the room's expanse. The skeletal fin revealed boundless articulated phalanges that looked as if they could delicately pluck a particular domed jar from the collection below. Miss Easter's eyes followed Winnie's up to the bones, suspended in flight over them both.

"From water to air to conflagration," said Miss Easter. "Fare thee well, old girl."

DAEN LUNDGREN WALKED TO THE BACK OF THE LEAN-to. The tread in the soles of his work boots were filled with woodchips. He didn't notice the slivers in his callouses. He ran through a verse in his head about the Great Hormazd, about how the sheep on the land should not be permitted to lay waste. Orange light from his wife's hand-blown and hand-cut stained glass rainbow catchers reflected the afternoon light and highlighted a small mole to the right of his eyes. He was a man of few words in the Norse tradition, stolid, much like the redwood sculptures he carved out back with his chainsaw.

The light from the rainbow catchers flitted on the leaf litter in the copse to the right of Daen's work. The sea shimmer of the ocean, down the mountain, at the toes of Perdita, showed up like a home movie, red-shifted, saturated. The mirrors of cars passing from the road across the way were white lightning on the toes of Daen's work boots.

Daen began to cut a new form. It was late summer and the rush to make Santa or reindeer was still months away. He walked to the clearing beside the lean-to and pulled his plastic goggles down over his eyes then the cord of the saw. Blue smoke rose to the blue needles of the pines. His other totems eyed the blades of the saw warily. It was a departure from the "Gone Fishin'" bears he usually carved. The imperfections in the glass turned the reflections on the noses of the bears and the black beaks of the totems into rock candy. Daen brought his blade into the log at an angle. A rounded hood appeared from the log's top. It was unrecognizable at first. The redwood curls piled around his feet like ginger locks in a barber shop. He began to carve something from the back of his mind, something perhaps from a dream, something faintly embedded into the sound of the chainsaw engine. An appendage appeared, then another and another. Until there were an even eight.

⁂

BIRDS HAD CRASHED THROUGH THE DOME AGAIN. LEXI'S party guests cried in collective horror as blood rose to meet cuts on arms, foreheads, ankles. They streamed in panic on either side of the pagodas. Shared memories were brought back to the tremblor of '71, when a chasm opened at Tex Cunnington's used car lot near the Alpenhaus.

It was large enough that it swallowed an El Dorado whole. They also recalled the collapse of the train trestle between the Amusements and The Ducale. After the Quake, it was remembered, the Picaroon turned silty and murky for a few days afterwards as loose dirt and rocks shaken from the mountains filtered down the river.

Fenella had seen early silent footage of the Great Quake and Fire in the City in college, and again in Thurl's library. It was a silent montage of Downtown with boarded up windows, soup lines in front of the Norton District, and the train car beach rentals turned into temporary shelters.

Candy Thorson held her high heels in her index and middle finger despite the piles of broken glass everywhere. She carried an empty martini glass in the other hand. Her dimples were showing and she was smiling. Muffin Laidley's eye makeup was smudged and her hair was worked into a general frizz as she directed everyone towards the exit.

"The valets will have our cars waiting in the main entrance everyone! Follow me! Thank you for coming!" EMTs pushed the other way, towards Thurl.

"There's nothing they can do for him," Pierce said to Fenella. Fenella saw Nina who was still by the buffet. The open dome had let in the night fog and her hair had turned curly. Nina's eyes narrowed, like Lokum's. She turned her head towards the corridor that led to the East Wing.

They could hear Hera's howl. Fenella sensed the vibrations of it in the back of her tongue. It felt like riding the rails of a wooden roller coaster.

Nina pushed Muffin out of her way. She hiked up her evening gown and started towards the corridor that led to the East Wing.

"I hate the way this is going," said Fenella who struggled through the wailing crowd after her. Benny, Walter, and Raúl followed. They were blocked at one exit by the EMTs who stood over Thurl and the acrobats, and at the other by Muffin Laidley.

"Fenella! If you could deal with the caterers…"

Finally, via the loading dock, they reached the top of the stairs under the main Aquarium tank. They could hear sounds like the air being let out of an inflatable mattress, more hissing noises, a feeling of decompression. As they descended the stairs, they could see the asparagus bed filling up with liquid. The plants began to uproot themselves. Water began to run down the walls of the Aquarium, behind the golden frames of the tanks set into the wall. It filled Vaclav's apartment and oozed beneath the fireplace. It rained down on Lucretia's iron cage. The sand in the Polynesian set dampened and small tidepools formed. The papier mâché used to build the Méliès and Aztec sets turned to mush. Still Hera's howls continued in the knocking quiet as the pumps in the Aquarium silenced.

Fenella and Raúl waded into the pump room. On an upper catwalk stood Pierce. Below him, lay Nina, unconscious.

"What did you do?" asked Fenella with wet hands to forehead when they had climbed the metal stairs.

"Nothing," said Pierce. "She did it to herself. I was yelling at her to stop. She had a big wrench and was swinging away at pipes. She hit this one loose and it fell and hit her in the face. I think her nose is broken." Blood ran across Nina's cheeks and chin. It had already thickened in the strands of her auburn hair and made thick serpents of sinew around her face.

"Raúl! Get the EMTs down here, too!" said Fenella. "Pierce, start trying to get this pipe put back!" She ran down the catwalk and plunged herself back into the waist-high cold water. She found Vaclav, Dusan, Kasimir, and Lucretia on top of Thurl's desk in his office. Behind them, the ancient coelacanth floated belly-up in its tank.

"Benny!" she screamed. "Where's that back-up generator? Re-prime the pumps! Help me find the list of the default settings . . . " Fenella waded into the main Aquarium room. She could see through the main tank into the back one. It looked like a gathering storm cloud. She plunged into the fifty-degree water and alligator-crawled her way to the stairs, then slogged to the top of the platform. Hera had inked in her tank. She matched the water like a calligraphy brush.

"Involuntary, yet toxic, even to me in these close confines," said Hera. "The dopamine in the ink almost made me forget to unscrew the drain cap. Would you please turn the water on down there?"

"Certainly," said Fenella in shock, "but who's wearing perfume?"

"The smell of geraniums?" said Hera. "Inking and a floral smelling chemical. Signs of stress. Jellyfish do the geranium thing too, you know."

In five hours' time, the East Wing was draining. The tanks were back to stable levels. The pumps were functioning and the temperatures were back to normal. Vaclav and the animals sat in front of the fire while Vaclav's clothes dried. But the losses had been heavy. Fenella scooped a lifeless leafy seadragon out of a gold-framed tank. She looked at its small pectoral fin that resembled kelp and wished she could breathe back life into the fluttering little paddle. She carried it over to a rolling cart lined in plastic and dumped the body in with the hundreds of others.

At the top of the large tank, Hera flushed a grey-green color.

"We will have to make sure Nina never gets in here again," said Benny.

"No," said Hera. "We will have to do much better than that."

"I have a plan," said Fenella. "I can get the keys to everything; hoist, cargo door, aquarium truck. We just need to wait for Thurl."

"TESTING! TESTING! 1, 2, 3! ALRIGHT! ALRIGHT! YES, IN-deedy! Before we get started with our sacrament here at the epicly satanic Periwinkle Palace, before we convene with the elemental powers that will make us divine, can I announce that a Chevy Camaro with the license plate STNSLRD has left its light on in the parking lot? The horned one hates dead batteries children."

The great pipe organ behind the band shell groaned. The red stage lights roamed around an altar and a topless woman with feathered hair. Two shirtless men in leather pants with bass guitars and studded grieves on their forearms appeared in the wings. They started playing a metal double-lead on their twin Ibanez Icemans.

"Ladies and Gentlemen, some of you many know that I like my father and his father before him was born in the caul. My mother had to pop the amniotic sac after I was born. This is a sign of great favor by the horned one. It symbolizes man's destiny to find his own way in the universe—to serve himself and himself alone. The amniotic sac is its own world, just like you here have your own moral universe. Take what you want children! It's yours!"

The crowd cheered. Zippo lighters flicked on. Girls raised their ringer tees to show their tits. Dudes made the sign of the beast with their hands.

"Now, some of you have asked, 'What about Linda? Wasn't Linda doing what she wanted when she jumped onto that hydraulic organ at our City event to go-go dance when she got crushed to death?' She sure was. See, that's the way to go out. Doing exactly what you WANT to do. Not pushing papers around for someone else. See, that's the message of the Great Horned One. Okay, Reggie and Marty here are gonna give us some righteous bass licks while we do a little animal sacrifice with our definitely-not-a-virgin Kimberly over here. Come here sweetheart. Here she is folks. Everybody say hi to your Mistress of the Night for the evening, Kimberly! Kimberly's going to rub my shoulders while the guys are bringing the piglet around for the sacri—oh—are we ready for it now, Chuck? Okay, okay, lay off Honey, later, later! Kim, it's time for a little pig blood!

"At this time, I'd like to thank our friends at Rostunger, Carlyle, and Finkelstein for taking our case pro bono. There are many anti-religious freedom forces at work in this country these days and without their help, there would be no sacrifice tonight."

At this point, Rudy Studebaker Rostunger set the mic in the stand, opened his robes wide and let the long sleeves fall. He turned his back to the audience. Three number sixes were stitched onto his back in red sequins. The audience chanted, "Six, six, six! Six, six, six!"

In the parking lot, Gary Sweeney turned off the lights to his Camaro. He would never get back inside the gates of the Palace before the sacrifice now. It was just his luck.

❧

D2 SECURITY CAMERA TAPE TRT 10:45:24

WEST WING CAMERA 00:01:24

Thurl is taken by EMTs, unconscious, out of the Sugar Factory grounds on a stretcher. He does not reappear for four more days.

EAST WING CAMERA 00:02:36

The sounds of alarms. Six hours later, eight white vans arrive in the courtyard of the Sugar Factory. Catalina lets them inside. They are in white lab coats. They wear plastic gloves, eye protection, and badges. They check the calibration of the pumps. D2 tapes are seen floating outside the master control room. The men haul away fish carcasses in opaque plastic tubs. They pump the remaining standing water into the Picaroon. Sand from the Polynesian set is visible throughout the East Wing as the water drains. Papier-mâché pulp clings to peasant quilts.

"The Alhambra set is strewn with decapsulated brine shrimp," Benny is recorded as saying.

"I found the elephant's foot trash can in the Méliès room," says Fenella.

PLATFORM CAMERA 06:36:10

The men in coats begin to gather on the platform. Fenella and Benny follow them up to the lip of Hera's tank. A large silicon net swings into place with spotlights and hydraulic screams.

"Excuse me," says Fenella, "what is it that you exactly plan to do here? Do you have Thurl's permission to be here? I'm going to have to ask you to stop until I see some written documentation…" The men do not respond. An eye like Ganymede surfaces. Then a mottled mantle with cratered papillae crests above the rim of the tank.

Hera funnels water towards the men, knocking them down onto the platform with a focused blast. The men regroup, wringing out their lab coats. They retreat down the stairs away from the tank.

COURTYARD CAMERA 07:15:46

A harpoon-like device is being removed from the rear doors of one of the white vans by a team of white-coated men.

EAST WING, PLATFORM CAMERA 07:56:15

A man is seen loading the harpoon device outfitted with a large syringe of an unidentifiable liquid. A liquid arm with the girth of a power pole shoots out of the water, and grabs the harpoon from the men. The harpoon vanishes into the depths of the tank. A deep howl emanates and bubbles rise to the top of the surface. Two minutes later, the harpoon is thrown, bifurcated into beak-sized chunks, and lobbed onto the platform with a clatter that reverberates around the entirety of the East Wing.

Hera camouflages one of her arms white. It confuses a man in a lab coat. He thinks it is one of his labmates until the arm reaches into his pocket and grabs his keys. Hera then picks up each lab man by the waist and throws them out the door, locking them out daintily with the key afterwards.

COURTYARD CAMERA 08:46:47

The men in the white vans drive off the property.

TRT 09:04.25 EAST WING PLATFORM CAMERA

Hera rises from the tank to face a soaking and shaking Fenella and Benny. She climbs out completely, shrinking her mass to fit on the platform. She uses two of her arms as undulating legs to propel herself forward and walk on the metal towards them.

"There, there," says Hera, patting their shoulders lightly.

"But you could have escaped any time," says Fenella. "Why did you stay?"

"Oh, let's call it nostalgia," says Hera with moon eyes, "but your days are numbered."

WINNIE AND MISS EASTER SPENT THE NIGHT ON THE dunes outside the City in the back of the cart among the specimens. Surrounding them were the makeshift tents of hundreds of City inhabitants. Miss Easter kept her pistol cocked and ready in case someone should try to make off with the horse. They slept under Winnie's bundled sheet, using her Sunday dress as a pillow. In the morning, the fog and dew had crept into their bones, and the bass rumbles of dynamite in the City proper became like a noise internal, a guttural release from the pits of their stomachs. When they awoke, they sat at the edge of the cart with their feet dangling and surveyed the smoke, the men in nightshirts, and the children who played in the sand without shoes.

"I aim to go south," said Miss Easter. "Reconstitute in Perdita. You'll join me, Winnie?"

"I'm sorry Ma'am but no. You see, I've been married since I last worked in your house."

"I see. I expect you'll try to find him then, in there."

"Yes," said Winnie.

"Should you run into trouble Winnie, which I expect is likely considering the situation we now find ourselves in, send word to Perdita. You can reach me at the Palais Royale Hotel. I believe I'll put up there for a while until I can find something more permanent. "

"Yes Ma'am, thank you."

"I'll take you back towards the City on my way out, if you wish, dear. And thank you for your kind efforts yesterday. Years of study in here," said Miss Easter as she patted the bed of the cart.

"Yes Ma'am."

FENELLA KNEW SHE NEEDED TO STALL NINA WHILE SHE worked on a plan. She toiled late in Nina's office sorting paperwork, paying bills, and filing so that she could spend more time in Thurl's wing figuring out her next step. She collected the piles of cups made into ashtrays and set them near the door for Catalina. She sat at Nina's computer, refurbished with new keyboard keys, and entered appointments. The mail application that was opened advertised line after line:

"Xanax Now No Prescription Online Pharmacy!" and "Oxycontin—Online RX!" and "Meds RX shipped FAST!

Fenella moved the postal mail addressed to Nina onto her walnut desk after blowing the cigarette ashes off onto the floor. A package from Muffin Laidley with a return address from the Yeguada shook like a maraca. On her desk was a pledge to the Hurt Diminishment Society for $100,000. On her desk was a statement from 1st Concepción Bank showing a draw on the margin account of $2.5 million and an overdraft on the checking account. There was a note on the desk asking Fenella to look to see when her trust checks were due.

Fenella had always been able to spot the Sugar Factory from her bedroom window in Barnby Dun by the Turbinado sign at night. It was the small red dot bleeding through the waves of her octagonal stained-glass window. It was a cherry, a puppy nose, an evening ember, Nonna's raspberry panna cotta. There was a smeary brightness to it in the fog and pine drip that was like a holiday marked off months away in a calendar, too far away to parse to be real.

Now, as Fenella gathered her things to return to the East Wing, and as she looked through Nina's windows framed in swagged silks, something caught her eye beyond the bulbs with "The Sugar On Top!" It was farther on up, beyond, in the mountains. An orange glow in the direction of Barnby Dun. The peaks appeared almost backlit, as if they were on a backlot on a wild west set.

She realized she hadn't called home in days. She had been so engrossed with the films, Lexi's party, and the Aquarium cleanup that she hadn't picked up a newspaper in weeks. There was no television in the East wing, only monitors. Radio signals didn't penetrate. She tried to remember the last time she had been outside.

Fenella made her way down the stairwells in her flannel pajamas and bare feet. She opened the rolling door and the smell of smoke confirmed what she already knew. Back inside, she called Daen and Lucinda from the Aquarium phone in Thurl's office. There was no answer. She then called Raúl as he was the only person she knew with a car. He pulled the truck around to the courtyard. His hair shone yellow-black under the sodium lights.

"You want me to drive you into a fire? In the middle of the night? Anything else?"

"If it were your parents…" said Fenella, scrunching her face in apology.

His teeth flashed. Then they were up Ice Cream Grade and with each turn a new layer of film dropped in front of their eyes and the smell in their nostrils became heavier. The road bent darker and the orange glow advanced.

They made it as far as Daen's mechanic shop on Barnby Dun's main road which was part of the Highway. There, near the Barnby Dun Super, the Post Office, and the ice cream shop, the sheriff and volunteer fire fighters had staged their vehicles and were stopping cars.

Raúl and Fenella parked in the mechanic's shop lot and got out of the truck. Fenella watched the firetruck lights flash and rotate on Raúl's cheeks. She coughed and it reminded her of Benny. She stepped on a small pine cone in the parking lot. It turned to dust beneath her foot with a distinct crunch.

Just then she saw something at the window of the shop. It was a hand waving. It was Nonna Agnelli.

"Damn forest is a dry as an old throat," she said.

"Where is everyone?" asked Fenella.

"Off to save their shit," said Nonna Agnelli. "Let it burn, I say. It's all crap, I say. Beats disposal fees, I say."

"They left you here?" Fenella asked incredulously.

"I'm taking vinegar for my legs, so I can walk around better now. Besides, Branca should be back soon."

"Raúl. would you take Nonna back down to my apartment at the Andromeda? Do you mind? Here are my keys. We'll leave a note on the door, Nonna."

"Where are you off to?" asked Raúl.

"It's only a mile or so to my house," said Fenella. Raúl nodded. He kicked at the parking curb with the toe of his shoe.

"Well, don't get burned dude."

"I won't, dude," said Fenella.

ঌঌঌঌ

Miss Cecilia Easter
c/o the Palais Royale Hotel
Seahorse Rd., Perdita

Mrs. Winnifred Dell'Orso
c/o "Little Oyster Shoes" Kitchen Camp
The Dunes, City Commune

Dearest Winnie,

I am tremendously saddened to hear of the tragic news of your husband's poor fate resulting from his heroic decision to bravely intervene on behalf of the citizenry as they sought to battle that most unwieldy of elements. He undoubtedly saved other personages and a great deal of property, and in so doing, incurred the gratitude of the populace as well as a hallowed place at the knee of the Lord in the afterlife.

It was sound of you to write to me, poor dear! While greatly disheartened at the news of your husband as well as the catastrophes visited upon your home and place of employment at the Algerine Palace (Ah, the City has lost such an exquisite gem!), I was buoyed and honored by your confidence in me, your good friend, during this hour of great need.

In response to your inquiry as to whether I might have an opportunity for employment for such a period of time as to enable your restoration to some semblance of security, the answer is most assuredly, yes! Since arriving in Perdita, I have resided here at the Palais Royale, and have endured the most unrefined of company, such as those that frequent that insufferable card room, but as the Academy and Herbarium are utterly destroyed and as the City is in such a great state of disaster, I have decided to remain in Perdita for an indefinite period, and have made arrangements with the University to continue my studies.

The region has a vast number of uncategorized and unknown species, and I have already been fortunate to discover and name one, a spineflower varietal now called "Chorizanthe cetea". As I am quite involved once again with the taxonomy of the surrounding flora, and subsequently I am in need of a washerwoman, cook, and maid of all work, as I intend to set up my own household here in Perdita, and foresee many hours of work in the University library and in the field. Additionally, I have been mulling over the possibility of a new business endeavor, which I believe would also benefit from your assistance and I would like to discuss it with you, in person, at greater length.

Enclosed is a first-class rail ticket to Perdita for next Sunday. I will meet you at the Seahorse Road station in my rig. Please use the rest of the enclosed funds to buy some provisions until then, as we have received news here of the dearth of comestibles available in the City at this time of great upheaval.

Ever your faithful bosom friend,

Miss Cecilia Easter

—Handheld sign on Seahorse Rd—

EL TERASQUE
LEXIGRAPHICAL CORDYCEPS
CELESTIAL PHENOTYPES
KULKISMENHYPRLAXIATALBOT
BARPORFILLIONS of POPULATIONS
STONE COLD FOX

~on reverse~
La Oasis Spa
~Featuring~
Products by
Wellspring

ঌঌঌ

ON HER WAY THROUGH THE SHERIFF'S BARRICADE, Officer Pearson, whom Fenella had known since kindergarten, informed Fenella that residents had an hour before the evacuation order was set to take effect.

Fenella worked against the traffic, up the grade. RVs and trailers hauled by F150's headed down the mountain with sheep, horses, ATVS, blanketed mounds. Headlights like the eyes of bucks rolled by slowly past Fenella's red-cast ankles. She walked past the schoolhouse, the tarot card reader's A-frame, the roller rink in the Quonset hut. She took mental pictures. At Sentinel and Main she took a left to continue onto the highway, towards the turnout, the lean-to, and the shingled house.

The smoke was bad enough that her eyes stung. She used the headlights from passing cars to see her way. The night was muggy even though there was a strong wind. She took off her sweatshirt and tied it around her nose and mouth. Then, around a tree-choked bend, by the pine-needled turnout, a likeness of Hera, silhouetted by beams of car light. As Fenella approached, she realized the octopus was one of her father's carvings. Still when she touched the cephalopod's wooden tentacle, it was as if she expected it to flush and register her presence.

She heard car doors slam and through the tree boughs she could make out Daen and Lucinda carrying boxes from the shingled house to the truck. Fenella removed the sweatshirt from her face as she made her way down the agapanthus-lined path.

Daen saw her and held up what he was carrying; the octagonal stained-glass window from Fenella's room with the blue waves.

❧❧❧❧

Peony Woodward Mecklenberg: A Conversion
By Branca Agnelli

Thurl's great-grandfather Ormand Rostunger met his wife Peony Woodward Mecklenberg while she was a barmaid at the Alpenhaus near the Harbor. In the early days of San Califia, with society in its infancy and the City merely a windblown outpost on the Left Coast without so much as an opera house to its name, the marriage was smiled upon. There were few women in those days, after all.

Peony had seen much bad behavior at the Alpenhaus. Quentin Rokeby had been a regular. Sailors were the main clientele. She was a ripe candidate for the Temperance Movement. She began going to meetings. It was there that she encountered a contingent of Loffer women. They took turned holding each other's babies. They had intricately braided hair. They looked hale with strong, straight teeth. After the meetings, she'd watch them walk back up Saceda Avenue singing "Gather Round the Herd", while their braids swung in unison.

She began asking them questions. Was it true that they had horns hidden in their hair? Were they required to have relations with the Head Butter? Were they forced to weave all day? The women laughed and handed her a copy of *The Celestial Mandate* and a cornflower blue shawl spun from their wool.

Peony converted in the fall. Ormand indulged her as it was something to keep her occupied. He had daily business correspondence with the City, the Far Coast, Gran Columbiana, the Islands, the Continent.

Religion was for women, he had always believed. When Peony gave birth to her son Lyman, he was born in the caul. The Loffer women told her that being born in an intact amniotic sac was a sign of God's favor. Peony decided to give thanks by donating a large sum to the church for a proselytizing mission to the Islands. She left Lyman with a nursemaid and embarked with Olaf Ewerloff as captain on the S.S. Fee Jee.

The ship docked in Misri Bay after a week's sail. The Loffers waited another three weeks on board to get clearance to disembark because of a recent cholera outbreak. Finally, as the Loffers rowed ashore, their voices rose above the waves as they sang joyous rounds of "Sing Ye Praise of Pasture". On shore, they pitched tidy white tents inside the jungle.

Several members of the party noted in their diaries the presence of very large wasps near the campsite. The wasps endemic to the Island would later be classified by Dr. Cecilia Easter as *Vespula glassinae*. Peony's swollen body was buried above Misri Bay, on Lord Monboddo Peak.

❧❧❧❧

THE SHINGLED HOUSE IN BARNBY DUN WAS LIT WITH Lucinda's glass, oranges and pink against the wood-clad walls. They had finished packing up the truck.

"Thirty minutes!" The bullhorn boomed from the passing truck. "Thirty minutes to evacuation!" In the kitchen, Dad began reading from *The Celestial Mandate*. It had gold-leafed pages and looked like a layer cake bound in white leather.

"For the Heavenly Creator will redeem us, and will not grind his believers into ashes so long as they remain faithful . . . "

"Well, this thing has finally cracked," Fenella thought. "Sometimes it's like that. It all builds up like an ocean swell."

"Great Hormazd, we take this consecrated oil and place it upon Fenella's head and ask ye, Dear Father . . . "

"I'm not actually sure," she said. Then he started talking again about the power that he held as a Loffer layman and the health and safety benefits that the blessed oil would bestow upon her, how it would protect her in the fire and she felt a little cramp in both of her calves and she realized that she had been bouncing the tips of her bare feet on the orange linoleum for the good part of ten minutes. "Why mess up perfectly good hair? Besides, it may not be for me."

"You shouldn't play with your salvation, Fenella."

"Oh, salvation. Do I really deserve to be punished? Some things in that book," she said.

"This book is the only thing."

"I thought it was our family?"

"That too," he said. He put his hand on the counter, put the consecrated oil back into the fridge next to the butter. He removed the carton of orange juice. Poured a glass. Held it up to Lucinda's stained-glass swag light to examine the pulp. "There's a place for those that are given the truth and choose to deny it," he said. Tears began to land on Fenella's bare feet. She felt hot on the back of her neck. The cramps rose to her stomach. She wondered if her period was about to start. He reached for *The Celestial Mandate* again. "We open to Chapter Twelve, Verse Five."

"I must go," she thought. "The lean-to, if I could just get to the lean-to." There were places to hide in the lean-to. He began reading again in a grave voice.

"The bearers of this truth shall go forth and bear witness to the full truth of Hormazd and *The Mandate* and woe unto them that knoweth this word and bare false witness against it, for they shall be cast upon the rocks and . . . " Fenella realized her calves were bouncing up and down again. She could feel cramping forming inside them like the gears in her bike locking up. She took a deep breath and forced her legs to be still.

"Stop," she wanted to say. "I will not be joining this crusade."

But Daen's fingers simply turned the onion skin pages of the book. He placed his hands on her shoulders.

"Fenella, let the patriarchy protect you." She was so tired of crying. Her eyes wanted to pull blankets over the rest of her body. "There is a veil, a veil between this world and the other, and this oil will simply dissolve that veil, you'll see so clearly. The power of Hormazd will come into focus." The weight of his hands felt warm on her neck. She could feel his great worn callouses from his tools, from holding the chainsaw just so.

"Could I have some orange juice too?" she asked. He opened the refrigerator, took out the orange juice, removed the consecrated oil by the butter, placed the vial of oil next to the microwave. He poured her a glass of juice into an orange and pink tumbler that had been blown by Lucinda. She took a gulp. He brought her a tissue. She blew her nose. He gave her a hug.

"Ready?" he asked. Fenella took another sip of orange juice and looked at the vial. It looked very small. Much smaller than the glass of orange juice.

"Ok?" she said. She began to sweat. He took the vial from the countertop, and removed the cork stopper.

"It's a little cold now from being in the fridge. I usually like to have it out for a while. We'll wait, it feels better that way. You'll be fine." He put both of his hands on the top of her head. The warmth of them calmed her. She felt absolved. She stopped sniffling.

Somewhere south of the Teonchee Pillar, where Ewerloff received *The Celestial Mandate*, a Liwa fisherman stopped to cool his shoulders beneath the shadow of the petroglyph of the great fish. Lars Lungren, great-grandfather to Fenella also arrived at the petroglyph of the Pillar, fueled by rumors of buried gold from the Saceda shipwreck. Whisker pulling on one side. A sip of water on the other. Teetering on this ledge, on this outcropping, on the edge of a continent, on the knife's back of a tectonic plate.

The mens' hands can tell from the way the tall grass has broken if a lonely sheep has wandered through that way. Their fingertips know the tie of sinew, the boil of bones, the saw between the rings of ancient redwoods. The ginger curlicues that look up to the blade in sorrow. Fenella imagines herself there. In between them in her clean denim. She harangues Lars about the origin of the Fish petroglyph. She argues that instead of it being holy might it not just be Liwa? The Liwa fisherman does not understand the Lundgren's English. He is amused with their bickering. He sees them gesticulating to the fish petroglyph. He draws in the sand. He draws something that looks like an octopus. Look at us, Fenella thought. Dusty in this wild forest with the sea trying to beat down the front door. Sheep eating to the hardpan, soot on hemlines, hymnals and fevers giving way to wagon loads, flumes, miner's pick axes. Someday, the San Califia Railway will carry everything back to the City, the washing machine taking the Teonchee dirt with it, the crumpled Dodge Dart. School shootings. The Sugar Factory on the Liwa shellmounds.

"Okay! Oil Should be warm now." Daen removed one of his hands from Fenella's head, grabbed the open bottle of oil with the other and poured a few room-temperature drops onto her head. "Dear Hormazd and Heavenly Father! We ask ye to protect and hold Fenella so that she may witness your power, dear Lord!" Fenella closed her eyes. She thought about the color of the bougainvillea in the Andromeda's courtyard. "We ask ye to keep her safe from temptation, to make her a valiant servant of your flock, to bear her up as one of your chosen." Fenella knew she would be told that she was be clean again but that she should not shower until the next day because of the oil's potency. Fenella removed her father's hand from her head. She stood solidly on the linoleum. She put the vial back in the fridge herself.

"No," she said. "I do not need your protection. I am not a Loffer. It's time to get into the truck, Dad." Daen let his hands fall by his sides. He looked into the rafters and touched the rim of Lucinda's hanging orange and pink stained-glass light.

"Okay, let's go," he said. "Need to pick up Nonna. She hates your place. Besides, she's always wanted to stay at the Azimuth." Daen moved his hand on a beam in the kitchen. "Well, kiddo, say goodbye to the old hacienda."

WHEN WINNIE JOINED MISS EASTER AT THE PALAIS Royale Hotel in Perdita off Seahorse Road, she was not to wait long for news. Miss Easter had just purchased a plot of land to the south of the Amusement from Gustave du Jardin, over the train trestle; a bargain piece of property, a marshy tract south of the FUN-icular.

"This town needs a proper place to reside," said Miss Easter. "I aim to make that a reality.

"Paolo would have liked to see his family live somewhere picturesque," said Winnie patting her belly. Miss Easter removed her gloves. She smoothed the lace collar across Winnie's shoulders.

"Let's build in the name of Paolo," said Miss Easter.

Taking inspiration from a daguerreotype of Paolo's hometown from Winnie's salvaged bundle, Miss Easter had the Palazzo Ducale built in the course of eight months over the inlet of the Picaroon. In the spring, Winnie gave birth to twin girls, Sophronia and Zylphia Dell'Orso. Winnie oversaw the laundry and cleaning at the Ducale. The girls were handed from laundress to laundress, and slept in wicker baskets of fresh linen. To bring in extra income, Winnie built pigeon lofts into the side of the beach cliffs, and trained the birds as her father had taught her. With one telegraph office in town, Winnie kept a steady business sending messages to the City; an old laundress friend on the other end received the pigeons and messages in the Canopy and sent them on their return missions. The skies above the Palazzo were filled with coos, feathered missives, and the cries of twin babes.

NONNA'S WISH OF CRAP BEING BURNED WAS FULFILLED in some way. Franklin Delano Sweeney, hearing of the incipient evacuation order, was anxious to use up the rest of his meth-making chemicals before any of the authorities or nosy looters could come by their sheds to find it. The hasty cook caused an explosion.

Dwayne and Shirley Sweeney were found dead inside the debris after the Ice Cream Grade Complex Fire had been finally put out. Franklin Delano was booked after a four-month stint in the burn ward at San Califia Medical Center. The county did an environmental remediation of the property. It was repossessed by 1st Concepción Bank. The rusted cars rusted further. The Spanish moss grew thicker around the breaks in the pines. The poison oak choked off the dog run. Leaf litter covered the rusted bullets on the forest floor.

The Lundgren's house, as well as downtown Barnby Dun, was saved by an influx of firefighters sent down from the City—perhaps the last-minute change of winds also played a part. Farms and wineries on the Eastern slopes of Pobre Claritas didn't fare as well. Dead sheep, charred vines, miles of blackened forest and log homes were the pockmarks left behind. *The Barnby Dun Soothsayer* reported the heavy winds as sounding something like a howl.

~

RECOVERED SECURITY FOOTAGE REVEALED THAT QUIET once again settled onto the Sugar Factory. With Daen, Lucinda, Nonna, and Branca safely ensconced at the Azimuth Hotel and away from the smoking embers in Barnby Dun, Fenella turned her attentions towards Hera and Vaclav. Thurl returned from Perdita Memorial Hospital. Fenella and Raúl saw him from the upper windows of the Factory, arriving in a black sedan, and entering the building with a cane, his large shoes leaving shuffle marks in the gravel. Catalina said that he was recuperating in the Haustrian Palace suite. Nina was equally as reclusive, hiding her broken nose within the depths of the Diocletian Baths. Lexi's whereabouts were easier to pinpoint. Gunshots rang out through the corridors of the Factory at all hours.

"Oh, the salinity in here is awful. I know it's not your fault dear," said Hera to Fenella who stood on the top of the tank's platform. "But it will all be over soon. Gather everyone together again. I'm getting a terrible notion."

Dusan and Kasimir's clinking hooves broke through the sound of the pump's hums. Lucretia rode up the stairs on Benny's shoulder as he bickered with Walter.

"I'm telling you, we can save the film, the damaged parts can be cut," said Benny.

Pierce pinched the fleshy part of his left hand then grabbed a fist full of his thick hair and pulled for a moment, grimacing. He raised his shoulders then lowered them with a deep breath. Raúl's keys rattled with each step. When they reached the top of the staircase, Fenella buttoned the top of Vaclav's corduroy jacket and smoothed down his hair.

"So," Fenella began, "I think we've all come to realize in the last few days that this situation has become really untenable."

"No, duh," said Benny.

"So I've been formulating some plans about how we can safely relocate," she said.

"Where could we possibly go?" asked Pierce. "If we leave with him it could be . . . bad," he said directing his eyes at Vaclav.

"Fen! You said it would be safe here and it's all full of psychos," said Benny.

"We gave up our lease," said Walter.

"You guys should calm down," said Raúl. "You'll all learn this is typical. They fuck shit up, we fix it, it's normal for a while, then they fuck shit up again. It's just a job."

"Excuse me," said Hera. "We have no time to argue." Pumps churned and hissed behind a wall. Lucretia flew off of Benny's shoulder and began to circle the tank. She squawked a panicked, greased keen that reverberated against the glass. She picked several sunflower seeds from Benny's front shirt pocket and began dropping them into the tank like she was marking coordinates. Then one of Hera's arms appeared out of the surface of the water, then another, and another. The first wrapped around Fenella's legs, the second, around Vaclav. The third plucked Lucretia from the air, until all of Hera's eight arms were full with Raúl, Pierce, Walter, Benny, Dusan and Kasimir. Hera lifted the entire party off of their collective feet, and then she let out a great howl that rose throughout the East Wing, and the entire Factory. The next moment, there was a thunderous crack, and the lights in the Aquarium went dark. The octopus brought everyone in towards her mantle and covered their bodies with masses of suckers. The wall of the room split to the sky. Concrete, rebar, water, and glass rushed towards them.

At first it was like a flash blindness. Patterns exploded behind Fenella's pink eyelids. Then there was cold. There were sounds of rushing water, and a knocking as if there were guests arriving in a dream. There was great turgidity in the water that surrounded them, and squeamish feelings in her stomach. There was the feeling of being cradled, of being bathed. She was in a fetal position, like an egg in a shell. She had the sensation that she was one of those little mussels clinging to the cliffs in the Islands, that she was impossibly sticking to the rafters like the gecko, woven precariously to the top of a plumeria tree like a wasp. After a time, she felt a tightness in her lungs that caused her to begin to panic. She thought of the koi sucking up greedily to the surface of the pond. She pictured wasps and jellyfish seizing her lungs.

Then Hera's tentacle unwrapped itself and Fenella lay wet and cold on the banks of the Picaroon, taking deep, greedy breaths near the others on a pile of smooth stones. The ringing sound of a buoy was an elegiac chime. Hera was partially submerged in the river nearby. There were deep gashes and cuts into her flesh. She pulled a piece of rebar embedded into her mantle and moaned. Black blood ran into the river. In the dusk light, Fenella could make out the electric blue of damsel fish from the aquarium swimming near her mantle.

The Sugar Factory smoked across the river. One of the Factory smokestacks had broken in half during the earthquake and had fallen into the Picaroon. A pile of granite bricks rose above the night tide. There were the sounds of sirens in the air. Wailing and shouts could be heard in the distance. Catalina? Peter? But the tangled razor wire around the Sugar Factory site seemed to mark the entire lot off like a tombstone. She saw then that the floors had collapsed. The Turbinado sign had finally gone dark.

Fenella shivered on the banks of the river as the aftershocks continued. It was like the feeling of stepping off The Kraken or one of the other colossal rides at the Amusements, like being on a boat while on land, like fainting while being perfectly conscious.

Fenella wondered if Nina been numb to the pain of it all. Did she merely reach for her tranquilizers in the rattling packages? She thought about Lexi. Had she been afraid like a child in the end? And what of Thurl? Where was he when the Quake struck? Did the crushing of his body finally bring him to reverie, she wondered?

They looked into twilight realizing that Peter and Catalina and the other house staff were in the wreckage.

"Marcos, he did all kinds of things around the place. Why couldn't we have saved them too?" asked Raúl.

"No time for them to get from the West Wing honey. An octopus only has eight legs." Benny looked at Dusan and Kasimir. "And excuse me I know you are not getting anthropocentric with me," said Hera, waving a tentacle in reprimand. The party made their way onto the banks, dripping water from their hair, emptying out the odd number of shoes that had remained on their feet.

"Goodbye now," said Hera. Her eyes reflected the dusk. "This fresh water is no good."

"But where will you go?" asked Fenella.

"I don't know. You people have ruined just about everywhere. Somewhere in the deep sea. All three of my hearts will miss you."

Hera waved goodbye, and then she propelled herself further into the Picaroon. She swam through the live and dead bodies of leaping blennies, fluffy sculpins, and chocolate chip stars. She navigated around shopping carts and scraped against the shallows of the Picaroon's drought-ravaged channels. The moon was rising along with smoke over Perdita as Hera slipped underneath the footbridge near the Palazzo

Ducale, and into the lagoon's brackish waters. With the first salty wave she flushed a resplendent magenta.

WHEN THE EARTHQUAKE STRUCK, THE PERIWINKLE Palace smashed like glass candy crushed underfoot in the parking lot on opening day. The Boardwalk rippled and cracked like hardening peanut brittle. The flume ride sent its logs shooting into the lagoon before twisting in on itself. The hand-carved and painted carousel, imported from the Continent, was reduced to splinters. Its golden top, punctured by the ride's poles, crumpled like an aluminum can. The Tunnel of Love was compacted in an accordion-type fashion; a few of the fiberglass swan cars ended up in the parking lot. The ceiling collapsed into the saltwater pool. Imported by Gustav du Jardin himself, the Ferris Wheel flashed its spindle of lights one last time before going dark and coming to a stop.

The Kraken coaster undulated wildly. She flashed her wild eyes and her speakers broke mid-bellow, the mechanical arms up top reached and faltered, crashing down on top of the funnel cake rotunda, before toppling into The Whip next to it. Sparks from the video arcade caught the Pier on fire. The wind whipped through the pipes of the Wurlitzer and made mournful bellows as the band shell around it burned. It melted the bumpers off all of the bumper cars and incinerated the stuffed toy prizes as well as the barkers' stalls. By evening the sea wind whipped the flames into the bones of The Kraken. She lay devoid of voice and appendages, but with every new spark of fire that ate at one of her ingeniously crafted trusses, her red eyes beat and pulsed the collective shame, injury, pain, grief, and loss felt by the town. By evening the Perdita Pier and Amusements were gone.

The Andromeda had also seen its final days. The tower had fallen onto Seahorse Road at the first tremor. The rest of the building was shortly transformed into a leaning, condemned carcass that surrounded spired artichoke plants and a perfectly preserved pond, with a koi fish that gasped and choked at the flecks of ash that landed on the surface of his home. Sand blew in from the beach and collected in the crevices of the broken Hiberian tile and white stucco of the crumbled walls before nightfall.

Fires also ignited in the Madeira Mystery House, burning it down once again. Incredibly, no tourists were harmed. The Knickerbocker Theater sustained some damage to its historic plaster murals but was found to be structurally sound. Frida's Alpenhaus and Sancho's were only closed for a week. Giuseppe's Apennine restaurant had to relocate as a beam in their leased space had cracked along with all of Lucinda's custom glasswork.

The Azimuth's anti-earthquake technology proved to be before its time. Daen, Lucinda, Branca, and Nonna rode through safely with only the white powder of fallen plaster on their hair and clothes. The Ferula Coffee House was destroyed, along with La Oasis Spa, though Calpurnia's Shoes and the Bargain Trough only had minor damage.

The University closed down for a semester. Barnby Dun had a lot of downed trees and power lines, and several acres of blackened forest. A bolt in the tarot card reader's A-Frame failed, causing the collapse of her home. It is believed that she was killed instantly when a beam crushed her skull.

Up in the City, fires and deaths occurred mainly in the lower lying areas outside of the core downtown neighborhoods of Shallow Pay Hill, Serendipity Hill, Norton Park, and Salinan Creek. Thirty-eight students were killed at the New Concepción College dormitory Beardsley Tower when it collapsed. Damage to the Academy of Sciences included the whale skeleton, which fell from the ceiling. The whale had been lovingly restored after the Great Fire. Carved wooden bears appeared on the streets after owners' apartments were damaged and people suddenly had to move. The bears rolled at odd angles on the steep streets, noses to the gutters. Many cool record shops and small restaurants never returned.

The earthquake caused a tsunami warning in the Islands. Puele, now with tall daughters of her own, untied the curtains and watched television. Mrs. Onishi swept and put on a sweater. The red-haired boy with freckles, now a man, got into his truck and headed for the mountains.

In ten years, the former site of the Perdita Pier and Amusements became a supermarket and condominium complex. The name given to the condominium complex was "Jardin Shores", as a tribute.

IT TOOK EIGHTEEN MONTHS OF COURT HEARINGS AND document processing as well as the sworn testimony of Muffin Laidley, Fabiola and Larry Guelphe-Finkelstein, but Fenella was granted custody of Vaclav by the State of San Califia. Vaclav expressed a strong desire to be homeschooled and to continue making films and to live with Fenella. As sole surviving beneficiary of the Rostunger family, Vaclav inherited a substantial fortune, with Fenella named conservator.

Fenella secured a ten-year lease on the vacant Picaroon Lodge. She and Vaclav shot underwater scenes in the pool. They made a forest set in the old dining room over the river, where Lucretia nested in the timber rafters. Lucretia had recurring nightmares about the way Ashur the dog, and Lokum the cat at the Factory had died. Fenella and Vaclav slept while the sounds of the river played and swapped tales underneath their beds. Benny and Walter constructed a set of apartments in a converted block of rooms that overlooked the redwoods. Raúl took another set of rooms. He enrolled in The University of Perdita with plans to become a social worker. He began volunteering at the Perdita Free Clinic. Dusan and Kasimir began to frolic in the glen next to the Lodge, occasionally sleeping outside. They stopped eating asparagus and began to eat the wild miner's lettuce and nasturtium growing in the forest.

Vaclav began wearing clothes. His favorite became small, striped overalls in the style of a train conductor. Fenella built a school room in the old Presidential Suite for Vaclav. She papered it with maps of Iulia and San Califia. Pierce found a grad student in the Education Department to come in and tutor Vaclav, though he himself took over the Sciences. During recesses, Lucretia and Vaclav continued playing jacks together.

Pierce brought up the subject of moving in several times with Fenella. She always found an artful, yet kind way to deflect, though he spent the night regularly. She couldn't explain to herself or to him why she couldn't embrace a relationship with him fully. She told herself she wanted freedom to direct films without his influence but it was something more, something deeper. She felt as if the gecko in the Islands had sung the sad song of it so long ago, bits of pain coalescing into orange spots.

Pierce, having read the history of the Lodge when Fenella leased the property, discovered the tale of Quentin Rokeby. He loosened a bit of rock in the wall where it was said that Adelaide used to leave her keys and letters. Instead, he'd leave homework assignments for Vaclav, folded up and tucked into a hidden cranny behind a removeable rock. This excited Vaclav to no end.

Daen and Lucinda liked to come and visit on Sundays. Sometimes they'd bring Nonna and Branca Agnelli. Daen began to teach Vaclav how to whittle. Lucinda made a new glass suncatcher for Vaclav's window. It had two deer in a green meadow.

One day Pierce made an excuse, asking Fenella to check to see if Vaclav had fetched his work from the rock, and then he followed her as she went to look. Inside the cache was an engagement ring. A solitaire diamond surrounded with a ring of Benitoite. Fenella turned ashen when she found it and burst into tears.

Pierce and Fenella didn't speak for six months. At Christmas, he asked to visit. He brought salt licks for Dusan and Kasimir, and a new Arriflex 435 camera for Fenella. He spent the week between Christmas and New Year's building raised beds behind the Lodge for Vaclav's new garden. By New Year's Eve Fenella and Pierce were sleeping together again.

Still, Fenella insisted that Pierce continue to live at the Palazzo Ducale. At night he could hear the ocean's howl as the tides continued to rise and the waves began to splash over the Ducale's Pier with more insistence, each night.

BENNY AND WALTER DECORATED THEIR NEW APARTments inside the Picaroon Lodge in the Hollywood Regency style. They installed picture frame wall moldings, pinched pleat silk curtains, and a placed sleek mirrored tables that directed dramatic light around highbacked wing chairs and zebra print rugs. Both of their bedrooms featured a luxurious four poster black lacquer bed. In the sitting room was a white curved sofa that faced a geometric white block marble fireplace, over which they installed a retractable screen for projecting films.

Walter took his Fluoxetine, Bupropion and Citalopram. Benny took a long hit of weed until his tiny chest convulsed into coughing. Once he stopped, he gave a final pinch of salt to the asparagus and soba noodle salad. He put some on a plate for Walter. Outside, a breeze rustled the shrubby hazels at the base of the redwoods. Walter used the remote control to turn up the gas fire and pulled an alpaca blanket around his knees and shoulders. Benny grabbed the other remote. The velvet curtains swung closed on motorized rails. The projector flicked on. Walter ate the salad. Benny ran his finger across the scar on his neck.

"Well Sam Spade, I will say you do have a most violent temper," said the Fat Man in the film. Teeth and brill cream shine flared white. The bridge outside the window in the movie reached like a spider.

SOPHRONIA AND ZYLPHIA GREW UNDER THE LOVE OF Cecilia and Winnie. They could find a fossil by the taste of minerals in the soil and could feel the bones of a pigeon to tell if it would be a good messenger. They learned to fish over the pier of the Palazzo Ducale, and to swim like harbor seals. They learned how to make Pane di Pasqua, arancini and caponata from one of the washerwomen.

Sophronia grew thick-thighed and thick-hipped with proportionately large breasts. She was active and strong and deftly used the toe holds to climb the cliff faces to the pigeon lofts. She loved to hike in the Pobre Claritas or rent a bike and ride it along the boardwalk or Seahorse Road. She had beautiful forearms from canoeing the Picaroon. Her arms telegraphed confidence and power to all. She knew this and liked to keep her sleeves rolled up. Sophronia loved to sit on top of the white cliffs of Perdita and to watch the birds dive into the sea with the orange cloak of dusk and fog gathering around them.

Zylphia became an avid reader. She pored over Miss Easter's books as a child and developed an interest in archaeology in her teens. Zylphia remained in the cold corridors of the Ducale where the fog swirled endlessly. Despite living steps from the beach, she never shook sand off of her shoes. She was as pale as a dove. She had to lobby the Regents to enroll in the University. It was only through the pioneering examples of

Dr. Easter and Dr. Vernice Blenheim that she was able to make her case. In some of her biology courses, she was made to sit behind a curtain.

After graduating, she set off for Gran Columbiana on an expedition funded by Cecilia.

Sophronia married a washerwoman's son, little Giuseppe Agnelli. Together, they opened Giuseppe's Apennine restaurant. Sylvia Agnelli grew up playing jacks in the lot in back of the kitchen. When Slyvia grew, she took her daughter Branca to Barnby Dun to raise her on her own. When Branca had Lucinda, Slyvia Agnelli became Nonna.

Branca became a teacher. With Slyvia's help she opened a school in Barnby Dun. She borrowed techniques developed in schools constructed on mounds of rubble with tools scavenged from bombed-out factories in cities across the war-ravaged Continent. She combined that teaching style with the ecological and ethical values central to the Liwa tribes predating the Reinaldo landing. In addition to reading and arithmetic, she taught her students woodshop, bookbinding, and traditional Liwa grass weaving.

The classrooms were inside of geodesic domes and yurts and the lunchroom was inside of an old school bus with all the seats removed. The children were encouraged to wear whatever they felt like. They wore top hats, roller skates, pajamas, and bathing suits to school, shocking the new students who had immigrated from the Far Coast and the Continent. On rainy days the kids would push the wooden stools and lunch tables made in the wood shop down the bus' stairs and into the soggy mulch, where banana slugs would climb over them. Miss Agnelli would straighten the chairs a bit, then grab her guitar and sing "This Land is Your Land", "Take Me Home Country Roads", and "The Big Rock Candy Mountain" while the kids roller skated inside of the bus. Fenella was one of Branca's very last students before she changed careers to become an archivist for the library.

❧❧❧❧

ONE MORNING, WHEN THE TWINS WERE LONG GONE from home, Cecilia and Winnie took a quilt over the footbridge to Saceda Avenue, where they kept their carriage. They hitched up four Morgan horses and drove along Seahorse Avenue. The FUN-icular's peaks and valleys echoed the spires and crevices of the Pobre Claritas behind them and the monstrous crests and pits of the waves at the edge of the continent just beyond. Cecilia and Winnie's wagon clattered over the crushed oyster shells in the road until they reached the town's limits. They rumbled past the headstones of those long gone and those newly departed, until they reached the last of the artichoke fields. At the reservoir, they made a right onto the track that led to the mountains. They passed stands of manzanita and madrone and tiny tributaries to the Picaroon. Monarch butterflies, on their migration from Gran Columbiana, mottled the blue sky overhead with their masses.

When they reached the chalky outcropping of the Teonchee Pillar, Cecilia unhitched the horses while Winnie spread out the quilt. From their vantage point, they could see all the way down the coast, where the ocean met the shore in white ruffled petticoats. The sun began to crawl into the sea, towards the Islands. The fog moved into the upper reaches of the Coast Redwoods where it whispered tales of the waves and the wizened trees listened with closed eyes and open palms. The birds in the forest began to make their evening calls.

Cecilia moved a tendril of hair out of Winnie's face and patted her plump hand.

"Hello my dark-eyed junco," said Cecilia.

"Hello my cedar wax-wing," said Winnie.

CHORUS:

We rise once more, lowly
citizens of sea-soaked
Perdita, thin, grimy
We climb earth's crust, broken

Sleep Sugar Factory
Fenella, golden one
rises in victory
A muse is since reborn

Hera stands triumphant
Yet creeps ocean's monster
oil, garbage, rampant
Will the Left Coast prosper?

Hail O Fire-Feathered Ziz
The steady hoof of mountain ram
Branch above river's twists
We praise the Mother-City

ACKNOWLEDGEMENTS

I'd like to thank High Frequency Press and Scott Wolven and Shanna McNair for fostering this book through its many forms, as well as The Writer's Hotel for the push and insight. Thank you also to The Writers Studio for the years of instruction and camaraderie and the opportunity to hone my craft. Shout outs to Litquake, The Writer's Grotto, and LitCamp for keeping me connected to the San Francisco literary community. Special thanks to Abigail Ramsden, as well as the ladies of Positive Response; especially Kate Haug, Kris Malone Grossman, and Alex Di Sclafani who have been my sounding boards throughout the process. Finally, I'd like to thank my family who has given me the time and space to work.

ABOUT THE AUTHOR

Allison Muir is a San Franciscan born writer and artist. During her varied career she has written and designed projects for *ReadyMade* magazine, coordinated postproduction for clients such as Industrial Light and Magic, Dreamworks and Pixar, and has produced and written for Al Gore's Current TV. Her short fiction has appeared in numerous literary magazines and she has been a regular performer at the Litquake literary festival in San Francisco, as well as KGB Bar in New York City. She is the lead singer of the all-female punk band The Gum Tree Girls. *Sugar House* is her debut novel. Find out more at sugarhousebook.com.

www.ingramcontent.com/pod-product-compliance
Lightning Source LLC
Chambersburg PA
CBHW020500310726
48979CB00016B/2732/J

9781962931328